Enjoy!

Gracie xx

COLD NIPS & FROSTY BITS

FOLLOWS ON FROM LIMP DICKS & SAGGY TITS

TRACIE PODGER

"You bought a what?"

"A vintage caravan," I replied.

"Lizzie, you can just about drive a car. How are you going to tow a caravan?" Joe asked, his voice was laced with shock and I could picture his wide eyes.

I chuckled and shrugged my shoulders, not that he could see since we were talking via the telephone.

"Tell me about it," he said.

I'd seen an advert in a local magazine offering for sale a gorgeous, silver and ice blue, nineteen-fifties towing caravan. It would sleep two, which was just perfect, and had the most wonderful Formica countertops and a little stainless steel sink with a fold down tap. I could picture the small wooden table, which doubled up as the centre of the bed, covered with a floral tablecloth and dainty cups on saucers placed on top and waiting to be filled with tea from a matching pot.

My thoughts appeared to have gone completely over Joe's head; he couldn't get past the fact I had only recently taken up driving again.

"I'll have lessons. I'm sure Ronan has a trailer or something I can tow," I said, starting to feel indignant at his mocking.

"Yeah, with a Land Rover!"

"Maybe I might just use one of those Land Rovers to tow my caravan then. And since you appear to be mocking Christine, you won't want to come to the mountains for a skiing holiday in her, will you?" I snorted.

"*Christine?* Tell me you didn't call a caravan Christine? Do you know about the *car* called Christine? Do you?" Joe's voice was reaching fever pitch, the height of which was giving me a headache. "And you don't know how to ski."

"Is Danny with you?" I asked, wondering if he would calm Joe down.

"Yes, he's laughing at the thought of you towing a caravan," Joe lied; he'd already told me Danny had popped out to the shops.

"I'll just have to send you pictures of me in the snowy mountains with Christine. I'll be all snug, wrapped up with a gin and tonic and a book."

Joe laughed. "I'm coming with you, but not on its first outing. I have no idea how to tow a caravan either."

I raised my eyebrows and smiled as Ronan walked into the kitchen, he was dusting off snow from his dark hair, which left it standing on end, and caused a puddle on the floor. God, he looked sexy. I didn't need to speak before Maggie did.

"Get away with ya, I've just washed this blooming floor," she said, smashing Ronan none too lightly on the shins with her mop. He hopped from foot to foot to avoid her assault.

"What's going on?" Joe asked.

"Maggie's just beating Ronan, usual day up here," I replied with a laugh. "So, I'm going to pick up Christine tomorrow and I'll send you some pictures." We said our goodbyes and I placed the phone on the table.

"What did he say?" Maggie asked.

"He laughed at the thought of me towing a caravan, then told me he was going to join me on one of Christine's trips out. What's so funny about the name Christine, anyway?"

"Ah had a girl once, her name was Christine. She was a bonnie lass, but muckle as a coo." I turned to see Charlie walk into the kitchen, grab one of the ham rolls from the table, and walk back out without another word.

Charlie had a knack of completely diverting any conversation with random verbalised thoughts that often took a little time to either digest or translate. Not only had he never left Scotland, but he'd never left the Inner Hebrides. He had his own brand of localism and in all the time Ronan and I had been together, I still had no idea what he said. I was sure it was deliberate of course; I'd often see him give a sly wink to whoever was in the room at the same time.

"Coo...?" I asked, to nobody in particular.

"Cow," Ronan replied. "He said she was as big as a–"

"Yes, I understood that. Anyway, Christine?"

I didn't get to the bottom of why I couldn't call my caravan Christine; Maggie had simply shrugged and shook her head, and Ronan had muttered something under his breath before putting the kettle on to boil.

"When do we need to pick her up?" he asked. I admired his backside in the tight jeans he wore. "Lizzie?" he interrupted.

"Huh? Oh, sorry. Any time tomorrow the man said."

I had spoken to the owner, or rather the husband of the owner, who, he said, had "*sadly, left us.*" It was enough of a sob story for me to almost offer the full asking price, and for Ronan to wrestle the phone from my hand to explain we would inspect the vehicle before committing to buy it. I had, in my mind, already purchased it, of course.

"You have the address?" Ronan asked, pouring hot water into the teapot.

"Of course I have the address…somewhere."

He filled his travel mug with tea and left the kitchen with Max, the dog, in tow.

Maggie pushed a plate of home-made biscuits towards me. "A year nearly," she said, spitting crumbs everywhere, and referring to our upcoming anniversary.

"I know, who would've thought it?" I replied, equally spitting crumbs everywhere.

Ronan had said he wanted us all to visit the local pub for a meal to celebrate our anniversary. I hadn't thought it necessary; it wasn't as if we were married, and I wasn't aware dating couples celebrated anything. He had been insistent, though, and, secretly, I was pleased he wanted to. Ronan was an anti-romantic in most ways, but then totally over the top in others. He often bought me flowers; lilies made me sneeze and convulse with allergy, regardless of how many times I told him not to buy them. Then he would pen me a little note to leave on his pillow if he rose before me in the morning. Just a couple of sentences to tell me how much he loved me. It was clearly important to him we celebrated, so Maggie and I were off into town to get 'all fixed up' as she called it.

———

I held the door closed and wrapped the blanket around my knees while I waited in the passenger seat of the oldest of Ronan's Land Rovers for Maggie to climb in.

She huffed and mumbled about her knees as she did. "Ready?" she asked, it was a standard question that needed an answer; to be ready meant to be holding the bloody passenger door shut, or tie it with the piece of rope I'd found, to stop it bouncing open as we hit every pothole Maggie managed to find.

"It would be simpler if someone just fixed this door, you know," I answered. She chuckled and revved the engine until it sounded like an Airbus.

Before I managed to even shuffle back into a comfortable position, we were off. Maggie's breakneck speed of about twenty miles per hour meant it would take us twice the time to get into town. I checked my watch; we should just about make our appointment. She leaned over the steering wheel and I wasn't sure if that was because she needed glasses to see, or she thought she was motoring along. In fact, I realised it was because she couldn't quite reach the pedals, so needed to sit on the edge of the seat and hold on to stop slipping back. I guessed the seat was as far forward as it could be, although it wouldn't be past Maggie to realise she could move her chair closer.

There wasn't much opportunity for chat; Maggie had wound down her window slightly to help dry the condensation on the inside of the glass and she was concentrating on driving through the snowy lanes. I had my mouth clamped tightly shut in fear *because* she was driving through the snowy lanes. Still, as Ronan had informed me, she wasn't likely to kill us if she crashed at her top speed. It wasn't a comfort, but I needed to get my hair done and possible death wasn't going to stop me.

"Oh! That was a…" I hadn't the chance to tell Maggie there was a person wedged into the hedge as she cornered, not in her usual spot of the middle of the road, but over on the wrong side of the lane. I looked over my shoulder to see the gentleman in the middle of the lane waving his fist at us. Thankfully, the roar of an engine protesting at being driven in the wrong gear masked whatever expletives he was shouting our way.

She parked, as usual, on the yellow lines outside the baker's and turned off the engine. Also as usual, she sat back with a triumphant grin that we'd made it in one piece. I shook my head at her.

"What?" she asked.

"There's an optician's up there, go and book an appointment," I said, untying the rope from the door that had been attached to my wrist, before rubbing the chafing. "I'm also getting someone to fix this door."

She laughed as she opened hers and ignored the beep of a car that nearly took it out. There was no point in locking the vehicle, not a soul other than Maggie could get it to turn over, even if the key was left in it. It was her 'baby' she often told me, and therefore the only reason it wasn't on the scrap heap. I joined in her laughter as we crossed the road to the hairdresser's. We were still chuckling as we pushed open the door.

"Morning, ladies, how are you today?" Ali called out. She was busy putting rollers in the shortest grey hair I'd ever seen. The face belonging to the head was pulled so tight I wasn't sure if that was a smile or stretched skin.

"That looks painful, May," Maggie said, wincing as she spoke. All May could do was gently nod.

Carly, the young girl who would be washing my hair, beckoned to me. She was a sweetheart and, as much as I meant no disrespect, wasted in this *old lady salon*. Fortunate for me, unfortunate for her as blue rinses and perms weren't going to advance her style training. However, she was great at understanding exactly what I wanted, even if it did mean presenting a conker and asking for the same colour. She managed it, and although still a trainee, she was the only one I liked to colour my roots, wash, and dry my hair. Also, I thoroughly enjoyed the head massage she liked to practice on me.

"So, you bought Cassie Hargreaves' old caravan, then?" Ali said, looking over at me while washing Maggie's hair.

"I'm off to look at it tomorrow," I answered, not in the least concerned she knew. The whole town would know, it was just how things worked here.

"She treasured that caravan," Ali said, adding a dramatic sniff to her sentence.

"I'm sure she did," I replied and then lowered my voice so only Carly could hear. "What happened to her?"

"Ran off with the herdsman, so I heard."

"Ran off with the–"

"Herdsman, Eric his name was. They'd been having an affair for years." Carly spoke so nonchalantly that one might believe running off with a herdsman was normal.

"I thought she had died."

"So would anyone who talks to her husband. He's a bit of a *ceann cnag*, to be honest," she whispered, accentuating the Gaelic and as she painted on the beautiful conker-coloured hair dye she'd concocted to cover my grey roots.

I had long before learned the art of watching an expression as a means of translating a word I didn't know. I got the impression perhaps *ceann cnag* was derogatory. Maybe Mr. Hargreaves wasn't the grieving old man he wanted me to think he was. I settled back with a steely resolve to get my Christine for the best price and not be suckered by his sob story.

———

That evening we had a rather eventful meal at the pub. Everyone wanted to discuss Christine, and the stories of Mrs. Hargreaves and the herdsman became more exaggerated. It had gone from an affair, to Mrs. Hargreaves having a secret baby in that caravan. Maggie and I had scrunched our noses at the thought of what we'd come across. I had a mental image of dried placenta and the medium-rare steak sitting on my dinner plate all of a sudden had lost its appeal.

There was a small part of me that almost changed my mind. Perhaps Christine wasn't the best idea I'd had. Also, I'd begun to believe maybe Ronan could mind read, as when he finished his steak dinner he sat back with his arms folded and smiled at me in an 'I told you so' way that often irritated the fuck out of me.

"What?" I asked, frowning at him.

"Nothing."

"It's not *nothing*, so out with it," I demanded. Maggie, who was sitting next to me, peered at Ronan.

"I was just thinking how green you've gone after listening to all that old rubbish. I highly doubt she had a baby, she's as old as Maggie." Maggie raised her eyebrows, offended.

I decided to save her. "But still young enough to run off with a herdsman, have sex in Christine, and leave whatever nasties on the couch!" The thought appalled me, obviously, and it didn't help when Maggie gagged beside me. I was further put off of my bloody steak. "I think I'll just have dessert," I said.

2

Mr. Hargreaves dabbed at his eyes with a rotten old hankie. I shuddered at the bogie-encrusted scrap of material near something as sensitive as his eyes. I wanted to reach out and touch his arm but the threadbare green jumper—something I could have knitted and I'd never knitted in my life —seemed to move of it's own accord. I looked from the moving jumper covered in dog hair to the mangy mutt that sat on the floor and scratched continuously.

"Aye, ma missus, she upped and left me, she did," he said, between sniffs and eye dabs, and the occasional scratch to his arm.

I found myself scratching along with him. "I love Chris... the caravan—" I started before Ronan cut in.

"It needs work, Eric, and you know that you've overpriced it. Maybe hoping some daft Englishman...or woman...will pop up and pay the asking price for it, huh?" He side-eyed me.

I wished in that moment I could send messages telepathically. Instead, I slid my foot to one side and connected with Ronan's boot. He took no notice.

"I love..." I started but caught the glare from Ronan. I scrunched my eyes in the hope he'd translate that to displeasure at being interrupted.

Ronan walked around the caravan again. It did need some work; a lot of work in fact. It had been many years between those photographs posted in the advert and the vehicle we were looking at right then. For starters, it wasn't a gentle blue anymore but more orange with rust. The interior looked as if it had housed sheep, and I shuddered some more when I caught a whiff of wet dog. I imagined the interior to be riddled with fleas.

"Ma herdsman stayed in this when he was here," Mr. Hargreaves muttered and, knowing what I did about the herdsman and Mrs. Hargreaves, my eyes instantly went to the sofa and the idea that the whole thing would need to be gutted.

I had no desire to sit in a place that might have leftovers of the mysterious herdsman and Mrs. Hargreaves extramarital relations. I still wanted Christine, though. She would be the project I needed...well, I didn't *need* a project, we were busy sorting the estate and all it's newly formed activities, but it would be a wonderful accessory, I thought.

I saw Ronan and Mr. Hargreaves shake hands and Ronan smiled at me. "It looks like you now own Christine," he said, and I frowned in confusion.

"Yer man drives a hard bargain. I shall be oot of pocket but at least it's moved to a good home," Mr. Hargreaves added, still dabbing at his eyes. I began to wonder if he wasn't sad at the loss of the caravan but had conjunctivitis instead.

"Happy anniversary, babe," Ronan whispered. He held out a key to the caravan door and then leaned down to kiss me.

"I…oh, thank you," I replied totally flummoxed by his gesture. "I haven't got you anything."

"You have. You just don't understand exactly what you've given me. Assuming that was what you were going to say and I haven't just spoken a load of mushy crap."

"You just spoke a load of…" I laughed. "Of course I was about to say that, and thank you. I love her already, and you, of course."

Money was exchanged and Ronan reversed the Land Rover to Christine's tow bar. He hitched her up. "If this doesn't make it to my home, Eric, I want my money back," he shouted as he climbed back into the car. I was waiting in the passenger seat. "He's as crooked as they come, that one."

I heard a clank and winced, but then we were off. As we made our way home, and to the amusement of Ronan, I kept looking over my shoulder to be sure Christine was still attached.

"I want to be the first to have sex in her," he said, laughing some more.

I shuddered. "I think herdsman and Mrs... Eeww! Anyway, who else do you think would be having sex in her, other than us?"

"I think she'd make a great guest cabin," he replied.

It had been decided, in addition to the naked art group, we would offer an area for camping, glamping, holidays in lodges, and static caravans around the loch. It was a beautiful location and we didn't really need to do too much. An office had been built, hard standing for towing caravans created with little hedges separating each pitch, and we already had bookings for the coming spring. Maggie and I were excited about the prospect, she more than I when she discovered that we'd hire help during the season. She was still in a panic over the filming about to take place.

Ronan had argued that he hadn't wanted the castle to be leased as a location for a period mini-drama; that was until he saw the fee. After discussion with the production team and the locations manager, he agreed but only after Charlie had been allowed to be an extra.

For the past few days, Charlie had been walking around the estate with a cravat and a flat cap. He toted a rather *spiffing* cane, as he called the whittled branch he twirled. I held back that he looked more like someone out of *Peaky*

Blinders than landed gentry. However, he was happy with his newfound movie role and he was a great source of amusement to the rest of us with his awful English accent.

"I have been to the field. We need to repair some walls, forthwith, old chap," he'd declared one time. After staring at him for a little while, we all collapsed with laughter; he wasn't impressed.

"Ack, away with you, bawbags," he'd said before stomping off.

"What are you smiling at?" Ronan asked.

"I was just remembering something Charlie had said about repairing the wall. He was practicing his English."

"Does he know he won't have a speaking part?" Ronan asked.

I shrugged my shoulders. "It's entertaining us, so let's not tell him that," I replied.

————

Christine was safely deposited in the courtyard and Maggie stood with a tea towel in her hand admiring her.

"What a beauty," she said, using the tea towel to cover her hand while she opened the door. I guessed she'd also thought about how rotten it could be after it's previous activities.

"I need to completely gut it and I'm sure Ronan can make

me some new units. I thought you might be able to teach me to re-cover the sofa and make some nice curtains."

Maggie had single-handedly re-covered an antique sofa and made floor-to-ceiling curtains for the library. She smiled broadly. "I think that's a great idea and I know exactly the material we can use."

Maggie and I had spent some time clearing and cleaning all the unused rooms in the house. In the attic, now an organised storeroom, we had piles of beautiful material that seemed to have come from all over the world. No one could remember why it was there; unless it was down to Ronan's mum receiving it as gifts. Strange, but then, that was Ronan's mum all over.

"How are the paintings selling?" Maggie asked, as she retrieved a tape measure from her apron pocket.

"The ones we took to London all sold. We need to organise a sale here," I said, "In the spring we could set up a marquee on the lawn or something. We've got buyers screaming for more. I can't believe it, Mags, who would've thought they'd so popular?"

"We'll have to do some of our own," she added, with a chuckle.

Ronan's mum had been an artist, of sorts. She had poured paint on a large canvas and rolled in it and had splashed colour over others. I could actually see the attraction, there was something mesmerising about the images, a freedom of expression if one opened their mind to what they were seeing. Not that Ronan could…or would, of course.

"Yeah, I could just see pictures of us naked and covered in paint selling for thousands."

"Who's naked and covered in paint?" Charlie had popped his head through the doorframe. "Yer never gonnae get this cleaned up withoot a match and some petrol." He chortled as he spoke.

"Get away with ya," Maggie and I said in unison. We looked at each other wide-eyed and burst into laughter.

"Oh God, we're morphing into each other," I said, and then laughed some more.

———

Walking side by side, Maggie and I left one of the outbuildings. I ignored the look of utter surprise on Charlie and Ronan's faces. I had found two sets of white overalls that we'd had to roll not only the legs up but the arms as well. We had wedged our feet into wellies and tucked the excess leg length in. On our hands we wore chemical grade, industrial rubber gloves, way too big, of course. They were the kind of gloves a farmer might use when dipping sheep, I imagined. The *pièce de résistance* were the hard hats with attached plastic face guards that would stop any nasty coated material clogging our respiratory systems, or getting into our eyes. Mine was fogged up because I'd forgotten to spit inside it and rub to stop any condensation.

A voice said, "A long time ago, in a galaxy far, far away…"
I pushed the mask up to see Ronan lounging by the open
door way.

"Huh?"

"You look like a Stormtrooper," he explained. The skin
beside his eyes crinkled as he held in his laugh.

"Rather that than diseased," I replied.

Maggie and I spent the rest of the day stripping the interior
of Christine. I was sure she needed decontamination as well
as a bloody good clean.

Dust particles floated around the small space as we ripped at
old and stiff material. The inside of my plastic screened mask
fogged up with each breath I released, to the point I couldn't
see anymore and I stood, wincing at the ache in my back.

I clapped my hands to rid them of the dust and stepped
outside. Only then did I push the mask up to my forehead.

I panted a little, gasping in some fresh air. "I think Christine's dirtier than I imagined."

"Mmm, I like the sound of a dirty Christine."

I slapped Ronan on the chest. "If you helped it would be
quicker," I said, sweetly.

"And my payment for that would be?"

Before I had a chance to answer, Maggie pushed past us

both, also in need of some fresh air. "Dinner, you daft bugger," she said. "That's your payment, *dinner*."

She removed her gloves and slapped them against his chest. Laughing at her, he grabbed them before they hit the ground. With her oversized overall and mask on her head, she did look a little peculiar. Particularly because she wasn't quite five feet tall. Ronan donned the gloves and helped me.

By the end of the day we had removed all the cupboards— in fact, they just fell off the wall at the slightest tug—the built-in sofas, and carpet. Ronan, bless him, tackled the small shower room himself. I couldn't step through the door without constantly heaving at the sight of the stained loo. Charlie was charged with wheelbarrowing all the debris to a trailer that would soon depart to the local council tip.

I stood in the empty carcass and planned. "I love her," I whispered.

Ronan stood behind me, wrapped his arms around my waist, and rested his head on my shoulder. "She's going to be as pretty as you when we're done. No, not *as* pretty, nothing could be *as*... "

"Good recovery," I said, laughing. "She's going to be a stunner."

I had warmed to the idea that, when we weren't using Christine, we would park her up and rent her out in our camping field. I was sure others would find her as romantic as I did.

"Come on, let's go and decontaminate ourselves," I told Ronan, wriggling from his embrace.

While I spent a half hour in the shower, scrubbing my skin clean of all imaginary bodily fluids, Ronan stood by the sink and shaved. He wore just a towel around his waist and I admired his form. He caught me and winked at my reflection in the mirror. I laughed. I could stare at him for every minute of every day and still find something new about him, still admire and appreciate his body, and love him more.

I left the shower and he stepped in. Before he did, he kissed me briefly on the lips, leaving a little shaving foam around my mouth and I, stupidly, licked.

"Eeww, that's gross," I squealed, rushing to the sink to splash my face with cold water.

When Ronan finished his shower I was dressed and ready to leave the bedroom.

"Sit with me for a minute," he said, as he walked into the room.

"Okay, what's up?" I asked. Although he hadn't said there was anything *up* his tone of voice was slightly lower.

"I want to ask you something. I received a letter today, from Demi's parents. You know, my ex…" I was aware of who Demi was, of course, and encouraged him to continue.

"They want to come to Scotland and I wanted to know how you'd feel about that?" he asked, as he sat on the bed beside me. "For them, I guess, seeing where she lived is the last part of knowing her life before she died. Maybe it's that final piece of closure they need. I know it's been a few years since…but…well, I don't know why, I'm just guessing here."

"Ronan, I think it's a lovely idea that they've gotten in touch with you. You had a great relationship with them, and it's a shame that dropped. Invite them to stay here with us."

He looked sharply at me. "You'd be happy with them here?" he asked.

I nodded. "Why wouldn't I?"

"I don't know…I…" He didn't continue but shrugged his shoulders instead.

"You can spend some time taking them to the places that you and Demi visited. It would be nice for them, and it would be nice for me to meet them. She, and they, were, and still are, an important part of your life, Ronan. Now, ring them, invite them to stay, but be aware of when we're filming unless they might like to see that, of course."

I left him smiling and shaking his head. "You're more wonderful than I realised," he said as he rose from the bed.

"I know, I'm fabulous. Now get dressed because right now, my stomach is only marginally winning the battle for food over my hooha for you."

He held up his hand to stem my words. Hooha was his trigger word. I had vowed not to use it often but every now and again, when I wanted to see that smile he tried so hard to quell, I said it very slowly.

I left him laughing to himself.

3

Panic took over.

The film crew started to arrive; Maggie was in a flap baking for the fifty thousand people she thought she *ought* to feed. Charlie was walking around with his *spiffing cane,* accompanied by Max, who was meant to be my dog but had abandoned me the minute we had arrived in Scotland. I took a few photographs of Charlie, without him knowing. I wracked my brain for the name of the character, an old 1970's cartoon in a newspaper. That guy was in a flat cap with a scarf but, I thought, always had a cigarette in his mouth. Still, Charlie was having fun and even after learning he'd only be in the background, he was super pleased to be part of it all.

Ronan and I sat with the film director, set crew, and others while they detailed the filming plan. We really didn't need to do anything other than keep out of the way and bank the cheque when it came. It was easy money, for sure. It was, however, one of the most interesting things I'd watched. To be behind the scenes and see how a movie, or mini-drama was made was so very different to how I pictured it. Nothing was in order. They filmed all the scenes they needed in the library, in the parlour, as they called it, and in the hallway. They brought in their own furniture, carefully removing ours. Switched paintings but we were pleased to see they left just enough for us to actually prove it was our home it had been filmed in.

Ronan loved the experience, despite his earlier reservations. And I immediately loved Demi's parents when Ronan returned from collecting them from the airport.

"Lizzie, thank you so much for having us," Aoife said, as she wrapped me in an embrace. She told me her name. "Pronounce it Eefa," she added without being prompted and I laughed.

Both Aoife and her husband, Jack, were wonderful, elderly but very spritely. We spent the first day showing them around the estate, Maggie couldn't stop feeding them, and I, pretending I needed to work, left them with Ronan. He took them off to see where Demi had lived. I thought it nice for him to spend some *alone time* with them to reminisce, without feeling uncomfortable about doing so in my presence. Twice, Aoife had asked if I felt awkward and twice I assured her that I didn't. Ronan had loved Demi, I'd told her, she was a part of his life and therefore a part of mine. Tears had welled up in her eyes at that.

That evening we were using the dining room and the family crockery for the first time in years, according to Maggie. Between us, we had cleaned and polished the most wonderfully decorated plates and bowls, each of which contained the family crest. We laid the table with glasses that had discoloured with age, their mottled sides casting rainbows as the sun bounced off them.

"Will you look at that?" Maggie said, quietly. I could hear the nostalgia in her voice.

"It looks amazing," I said, stepping back from the table to admire it.

Venison was being cooked slowly and we had prepared a starter of salmon from the river, all to be followed by a selection of mini desserts Maggie had made earlier.

"I've missed this," I said.

"What?" she asked.

"Entertaining. I don't want to do it as frequently as I used to, but this room looks wonderful. It has a purpose. I wonder how you'd feel if we did a monthly dinner club here?"

"I'd love that, not sure about Ronan though."

Ronan was adamant that all business activities, other than the filming, were to be kept outside the property, and I understood that. The house was his home and held both sad and wonderful memories for him. He said he'd never want that tarnished with unruly or unappreciative guests.

I tripped over some cables as I left the room, closing the door behind me. "Sorry," I called out in case I'd unhooked it.

"Not a problem," came the reply.

When Ronan, Aoife, and Jack returned, Aoife and Jack decided to have a nap before preparing for dinner. They had been given one of the grandest bedrooms. It housed an ornately carved, wooden four-poster bed with gold brocade drapes that matched the curtains and the chaise. Maggie had been in sewing goddess mode when she'd made those. Under the window, in the bedroom, was a claw-footed bath with gold taps and a shower room was situated opposite, across the hall.

"They're wonderful people," I said, as I joined Ronan at the kitchen table for a large mug of tea.

"I know. I've missed them." He reached over and took my hand. "Thank you."

"What for?"

"Allowing me to reconnect. There aren't many who would be happy about that," he said.

I scoffed. "Then those *others* are simply selfish and insecure in their relationships, aren't they!" It was a statement, not a question, and he smiled at me in agreement.

"I saw the dining room, it looks amazing. Where did you find all those old plates?" he asked.

I told him Maggie and I had reorganised one of the loft rooms as storage and we'd come across them in a box some months prior.

"I don't think my mother ever used them, they go back to my great-grandparents, I think," he said.

"Maybe we shouldn't be using them, then," I replied.

"I never saw the point of owning something just to look at. They look great and I'm sure Charlie and I will be happy to handwash them when we're done."

I wasn't sure I wanted Charlie handwashing them. I noticed he had started to shake a little and wondered on his health. I filed that away for a conversation with Ronan on another day. I had learned that Charlie had never visited a doctor; didn't trust them with their *modern poisons,* preferring to pick God knows what from the land and eat it. Still, he was in his eighties and prancing around like the Lord of the Manor, so there might have been something in his herbal remedies.

————

The thing I loved the most over dinner was listening to Charlie and Jack converse. Both spoke in Gaelic interspersed with English, Irish, Scottish, and something unknown to us all. They laughed constantly and it was the kind of laugh that made everyone smile, even if they had no idea what was being said. Occasionally, Aoife reprimanded them, reminding them that I didn't understand but I waved her complaints away. I was enjoying myself. I'd started to learn a few words, but I was more than happy to sit and watch people come alive, who hadn't in a while, and to have the flames of the open fire reflect off generations old glassware, as the candles burned down.

What I was more than happy about, was Ronan. The expression on his face as he listened and laughed, as he relaxed and joined in, all the while holding onto my hand and giving me a squeeze to let me know he hadn't forgotten I was there. I believed that, for the first time, I was seeing the real Ronan, the man who didn't have the world on his shoulders. He would argue I was seeing a Ronan in love and settled, and he might be right, also.

The evening wore on and fire burned down until everything had been eaten and drunk, and we retired to the library to sip on coffee.

There was a pause in conversation, the laughter had tailed off. "I can't thank you all enough for giving us this glimpse into Demi's life," Aoife said, quietly.

I took her hand in mine. "I'm pleased that we've been able to, and it doesn't end here, Aoife. You're both welcome back whenever you want."

"Ronan, you'd better marry this woman before someone rushes in and swipes her from under your feet. I don't think I've ever met anyone with as much empathy and love as her," Jack said, startling me. Ronan simply smiled and gave him one nod.

Jack turned to me. "Demi would've loved you. I think you two would have been great friends had the situation been different."

I wasn't sure how to answer, so I simply smiled. Had Demi been alive, the chances are we would never have met but I understood the sentiment.

"I think it's time we retire," Aoife stated, as she placed her cup and saucer on the coffee table. We hugged as they left the room, leaving just Ronan and I.

We sat in silence for a little while, holding hands and watching the fire as it clung to life on the embers of what were once logs. Ronan looked at me.

I straightened myself up. "If you're going to thank me one more time, I'm going to punch your nose."

He laughed, and held up his hand, palm facing me in submission "Let's clear this away and go to bed." In silence, we washed the last remaining cups and saucers and left them on the drainer for packing away.

Aoife and Jack were leaving in the morning; they wanted to tour other areas of Scotland before heading back across the sea, and Maggie wanted to set them off with a hearty break-fast. I could imagine her up before the larks to prepare.

I took hold of Ronan's hand and we left the kitchen to head to our bedroom.

"Do you remember when you first came here?" he asked, as we climbed the stairs.

"I do, it was cold and stunning but sad as well. If that makes sense."

"Now look at it," Ronan said.

He had paused halfway to look back down to the hall. Flowers stood proud in a vase on the hall table. Although not real, the fake lilies were the only ones my allergy could cope with and they looked amazing. Just a change in light bulbs to low energy and warm white gave a cosy and welcoming feel.

"You've done this," he added, turning to look at me. "And when we get married, we'll stand in this same spot with all our guests looking up at us."

"When we what…?" I gasped and my heart skipped a beat. I wasn't sure that was in happiness or fear, though.

I was silenced by a kiss, then Ronan laughed as we continued to walk the upper hallway. I shook my head, unsure if it was a joke in response to what Jack had said, or not. Still, it wasn't a proposal, that was for sure.

4

The house felt quiet and empty after Aoife and Jack had left. Maggie was in town, Ronan and Charlie were out with the farming students doing something or the other; he had told me but it had gone over my head. I walked from room to room on my own, marvelling at the very fabric of the house. The walls and woodwork, the paintings and the repairs still needed. The film crew would be packing up that day, having gotten the shots they needed. They had said they doubted they would need to return but that option was always left open, of course.

"Someone could die and we'd have to film their replacement," the casting director had laughed, alone, no one else had found that remotely funny.

I pulled on an extra jumper and my walking boots and decided Christine needed my attention. Ronan had marked out where the new kitchen cupboards, the U-shaped sofa that doubled as a bed, and the shelving were all going. He was going to make it all himself and I loved that he would. I had picked out material from the surplus in the storeroom and was being taught how to make curtains. My first attempt was a mess; I'd cut through the hem in error before hand-sewing it to my jumper without realising. Perhaps sewing wasn't for me. I'd do well to leave it to Maggie, who could knock up a pair of curtains in a half hour, so she constantly told me.

I had painted all the walls with a base coat, rubbed it down as instructed, and was going over it with a second base coat before the duck egg blue went on. I had laughed while in the hardware store, having never seen a blue duck egg. Of course, the cashier was stumped. Charlie reliably informed me that some ducks do lay light green or blue eggs. I wasn't sure if he was pulling my leg or not. I wouldn't put it past him to send me to the hardware shop to ask for a left-handed screwdriver.

I was lost in thought, humming tunelessly as I painted.

"I have the curtains," Maggie said, as she hauled herself into the caravan.

"Are your knees okay?" I enquired, as she had huffed and sighed at the relatively small step up.

"It's the weather. The colder it gets, the more my joints play up. Now is the time I regret not stealing some of those herbs from Manuel's house." She laughed as she hooked the new curtains on their poles.

"*Cannabis*, Maggie, not herbs. And it's illegal, although I do believe CBD oil is okay to buy. You should ask in the chemist when you're in town next." I regretted what I'd said as soon as I had because it wasn't beyond the realms for Maggie to ask for cannabis and not cannabis oil. I added, "I'll ask for you when we're next in town." Thankfully, she nodded.

"They were lovely, weren't they?" she said, and it took me a moment to realise she was speaking about Demi's parents. "Mind you, she was a lovely girl as well."

"They were, I'm so glad they came and stayed. It'll be nice to keep in touch, especially for Ronan. Do you remember the photo that got broken? I thought I might reframe it for him. I don't think it's nice to hide her away, what do you think?" I asked.

Maggie pursed her lips and frowned. "I don't know. I think you should ask. It might be that he doesn't want to be reminded."

There were a million questions that ran through my mind where Demi was concerned, but I swallowed them all back down. It wasn't my place to know about her any more than I had already been told. I was sure that the rest wasn't being hidden from me, it just wasn't necessary for me to know. Only, curiosity sometimes got the better of me.

"What did Demi think of the house and Ronan's mum?" I asked.

"She said it spooked her, if I remember. I'll tell you a secret, I think Verity embarrassed her, and that was a shame. Demi was a lovely girl, but I don't know that she knew how to handle Verity in the end."

I was somewhat surprised by that statement. "How bad did Verity get?"

"She was nuts," Maggie said, and then laughed. "And I mean that in the kindest way. She was born a rebel and died a rebel and we all loved her, even if we didn't understand her at all."

"Ronan thinks I'm a little like her," I replied.

Maggie gave me such a kind smile. "You have the same heart, that's for sure. I don't know many who would welcome an ex-partner's family into their home. And this is your home as much as his now."

I shrugged. "It just seemed the right thing to do," I said, as I scraped the excess paint off the brush and replaced the lid. I stood stretching my back. "I think that's all the undercoat done."

Maggie stood back to admire the little curtains that would go over the sink. They were just a light blue with yellow humming birds printed on them. Perfect for the summery feel I wanted. We were going to cover the sofa in the same fabric and then have yellow scatter cushions. Ronan had suggested a lino type of floor covering; easier to keep clean, and I agreed with him. He was meant to measure for that so I could get it ordered.

As I thought of him, I heard the sound of a quad bike come into the courtyard. Maggie left the caravan to see Charlie on the bike, towing a trailer with a deer on the back. Hunting season had ended so I could only suspect the deer was sick or injured. I stepped closer to look at it and smiled sadly.

"Poachers, again," Charlie said, in his usual clipped and *only-use-the-necessary-words* way.

"Poachers?" Maggi enquired and her voice rose in surprise.

"Yes, we heard them shoot this hind, but we got to it before they did. Ronan managed to grab one of 'em, he's waiting on the police."

"Is he okay?" I asked, hastily.

"I doubt it, took a good right hook to the nose, he did." Charlie cackled as he spoke.

"What?" I asked, shocked that my man might be hurt laced my voice.

Charlie's eyes glinted with mischief. "The poacher, you fool, not Ronan." He cackled again that I'd thought Ronan had taken a punch to the nose.

I helped unload the deer and we carried it into one of the outhouses which stored a large freezer, stainless steel benches, and butchery equipment. Neither Ronan nor Charlie butchered the meat from the estate; a local came in to do that so the deer was laid on the bench to wait for him. Charlie locked up the door so nothing could get in and feast on it beforehand.

"Ah, Max, you've finally remembered me," I said, as I leaned down to pick up my dog.

Although only a year old, with one operation on a broken leg under his belt, he was small for his age. He licked my chin and wagged his tail.

"He did good, chased the wee scunners off, he did," Charlie said, roughing up the fur on his head. Max gazed lovingly after Charlie and wriggled to be put down.

"Traitor," I whispered, as he trotted off after him. "Who picks up your shit, huh?" I called out.

"Who does what?" said a voice behind me.

I spun on my heels. "Ronan! Are you okay?" I rushed over to him and picked up his hands. One had slight grazes over the knuckles. "What happened?"

"I punched him, the gobby shite thought he could intimidate me. He couldn't have been more than six stone soaking wet! Anyway, the police have him now."

"You're not hurt, are you?"

Ronan laughed. "Do I look hurt? I'm pissed he shot one of my deer, though."

"I bet. Charlie put her in the outhouse."

Ronan nodded at my statement and slung an arm over my shoulders. He leaned down and kissed the side of my neck. "How about a nice cup of tea?" he asked. I nodded and led him to the kitchen door.

Ronan rinsed his grazed hand under the cold tap while telling Maggie and me of his citizen's arrest. He told the police that he thought the poachers could well have been the two I saw some months prior. I'd managed to take a photograph and, although grainy and slightly out of focus, I forwarded that to Ronan's mobile so he could show the police.

"Is poaching taken seriously up here?" I asked.

Charlie, with a mouthful of cheese sandwich, answered. "We should be allowed to shoot the glaikit wee bastards." He nodded to himself, as if his method of punishment was acceptable to all. I had a tendency to agree with him; but not to kill, just harm a little.

"It's not taken nearly as seriously as it should be, but that's because there aren't the resources. Too many police cuts, and it's the rural communities that suffer the most," Ronan said.

I remembered it had only taken half an hour for the police to arrive at Manuel's drug factory, and I didn't want to tell them that was a normal wait time in London for a stabbing, let alone a *non-emergency.*

"Anyway, it's done now," Charlie added, washing his sandwich down with a cup of tea, which he then also proceeded to swish around his mouth as if cleaning his gums as well.

I winced. "What will you do with the deer?" I asked.

"Eat it," Maggie answered with a shrug before anyone else could. She even rubbed her stomach to emphasise the point.

As if to distract me, Ronan sat at the table and slid a mug of tea over. "We'll get your caravan fitted out this afternoon," he said, with a smile. "And we can plan a trial run out in her."

"I'd love if you could make me a nameplate for Christine," I said, with a smile.

Ronan jumped from the kitchen table and left me staring after him. "I need to get something for you, hold on." It was about ten minutes later that he returned. "Couldn't bloody find it at first. Here, read this, then decide if you want to call your caravan that."

Ronan handed me a tattered book by Stephen King. I smiled at the title, *Christine,* but my smile slipped when I read the back. "That blurb is odd," I said, flipping back to the front.

"It's about a possessed car called Christine," Ronan said, sighing with exasperation.

"I get that," I replied slowly and sarcastically. "I don't have a *car*, I have a *caravan* that can do nothing on her own.

She's called Christine," I said decisively, slamming the book on the table.

"Mumbo jumbo," Charlie said, or at least, that's what I thought he'd said. He picked the book up and placed it in his cardigan pocket. "I'll read it for ye, lass."

I slid my chair back from the table and laughed as I slipped on my coat and headed for the back door. "Possessed car," I said, giggling some more. "I'm going to wash down the floor, ready for your cupboards," I added, smiling at Ronan.

I cleaned up where I'd spilled paint, and used a Stanley knife to chip away at paint that had sploshed onto the window glass. I wanted Christine to be perfect. I partially screamed when a hand reached around and covered my mouth. I bit down, hard, and was granted with a satisfying squeal.

"That will teach you," I said, turning so fast Ronan had to lean back to avoid being slashed with the knife. "Oh, sorry," I said, looking at it and then placing it on the side.

"I wanted to scare you," he said, getting close enough for his words to become a whisper that ghosted over my cheeks.

"You didn't."

"Can I kiss you instead?"

I tilted my face to his and closed my eyes. His lips brushed over mine so gently until he reached around and cupped my arse. He squeezed and I chuckled, kissing him deeper.

"Uh hum," came a voice from behind Ronan. He laughed as he pulled his head away. "I hate to break up you love-birds, but you have a deer needs butchering?"

I looked over Ronan shoulder to see a slight man, already with a blood-stained apron covering a blue uniform. He waved a large carving knife around as he spoke.

"Jesus, you look like a mass murderer," Ronan said.

"I try to, at all times. Serves me well on occasions."

I was introduced to Sandy, the local butcher. He was someone I had met before when I'd popped in to the shop with Maggie, but we had never been formally introduced.

"Lizzie, I hope I didn't scare you," he said, very politely.

I laughed. "No, but I can imagine I wouldn't want to meet you in a dark alley."

He frowned, not sure if I was joking or not, and then straightened his brow. "She in there?" he asked, nodding his head to one of the outbuildings.

"She is, I'll come with you." Ronan left the caravan, and me to my cleaning up.

————

It took Ronan one week to complete the refit of Christine and a further week for Maggie and I to furnish and finish our decorating. When we were done, we had a grand opening. It consisted of tea with cake, as we sat squashed around the small Formica table using dainty floral teacups.

"Ye cannae get your fingers through this," Charlie moaned, trying to force his forefinger through the handle hole of his cup.

"And it's only one mouthful," Ronan joined in with Charlie's complaining.

Maggie waved a hand at them. "Away with you both, if you don't like it, go make your own tea."

I loved the caravan. I loved the colours and the smell of freshly painted wood. I loved the feel of the hard cushioned sofa. I loved the fact the tap twisted and lowered to be concealed in the sink when the chopping board was placed over the top. The two-ring burner sat above a neat little fridge, and in a cupboard, Ronan had placed a microwave. He had also created a snug bedroom.

Maggie and I had found the crockery in a local bric-a-brac store in town. We had gold-coated cutlery that matched the gold rimmed teacups and plates. Nothing was practical, of course, but after taking lots of photographs of the table set for afternoon tea, I was sure it would be a hit in our caravan park by the loch.

"So when do we take her out for her trial run?" I asked.

"Whenever you want, stock her up and we'll head to Skye tomorrow," Ronan replied, he then grabbed his laptop to buy a ferry ticket.

I was excited for Christine's first outing and possible photo shoot. "Tomorrow it is, then," I replied. "How far is Skye from here?" I asked. As we were in Mull, I thought it was hours away.

"Four hours, roughly, from memory. It's a beautiful journey, Lizzie. You'll love it."

5

Ronan and I were up early and discussing the route to take. I worried it was a little too far for Christine's first outing and suggested just driving to the next farm. Ronan laughed at the thought.

"What about the ferry?" I asked.

"Got a ticket online yesterday. It's not that busy at this time of the year."

Maggie had packed a picnic basket with freshly baked bread, rolls, and cakes. I had loaded the fridge and dry food cupboard. I'd placed Max's bed, bowls, leads, and towels in the bathroom, and a raunchy new range of underwear in the bedroom.

I intended to make sure that the first sexy times in the *new* Christine was on her maiden voyage. I had stocked the bedside cabinet with a range of my perfumes and body lotions, made sure to have sumptuous cotton bed linen over the fluffiest pillows, and added a dimmer switch to the *thousand-and-whatever-watt* central light.

A bottle of champagne was chilling in the fridge and everything was secured and ready when Ronan hitched her up to the Land Rover. Max jumped in the back, I climbed in the front seat and with a wave to Maggie, we were off. Ronan had decided we were heading to Skye, it wasn't too far to travel and it was somewhere I hadn't visited before. We intended to only be away for a couple of days, maybe two nights, at the most. We had another art sale to organise as soon as we got back.

If the weather had been better it would have been the perfect day to open the window and let the fresh air flow in. Although sunny, it was a bitterly cold day. The sun was low, never really getting to the heights we'd expect in the south for the time of the year. It was, however, stunning. The scenery was breathtaking and I began to wonder what still held either of us down in Kent; other than friends and Ronan's work–something he could probably do from anywhere. I smiled for hours.

"That's some view, isn't it?" Ronan said.

We had pulled over to the side of the road to allow a car to overtake. To one side was a valley down and then a mountain. The snow-capped black rock dominated the horizon.

"There's a campsite over there," Ronan said, pointing

towards the mountain range. "We can walk up to Rubh' an Dùnain from memory."

"What's…" I had no intention of even trying to pronounce the place name.

"It's a ridge, lots of archaeological sites up there, I think. It's interesting. I haven't walked it in years, used to take a couple of hours, I think, but we can do part and double back."

"Sounds like a great idea."

Although I didn't mind walking—I had been doing a lot since owning Max—I wasn't fit enough for any of that hill climbing or scrambling. Ronan's idea of a walk was often miles in length at a pace that had me semi-jogging to keep up. I wasn't up for any of that lark! However, a nice gentle stroll with the dog and holding hands sounded romantic. Ronan put the Land Rover in gear and we carried on. It was another half hour before we reached the caravan park, and because of the time of year, it was practically empty, save for the ardent hill walkers and mountain climbers.

We found a spot and unhitched. I was busy making us a cup of tea while Ronan stood outside with Max, who was sniffing to find a suitable place to pee. I'd never known a dog like him. He would take at least ten minutes to find his perfect loo and, more often than not, he expected one of us to be with him while he did his business. This was okay in the summer months, the spring, or autumn even. I could stand at the back door with my coffee and wait while he sniffed his way around a familiar garden as if it was the first time he'd entered it. But it was winter in Scotland and not the kind of weather to be standing outside without a coat. I called out to let Ronan know his tea was ready and if Max wasn't, to leave him, he would never venture far away.

I loved sitting at the little table with Ronan. Max was asleep in his fluffy bed, he had peed twice and I guess that had exhausted him. I'd relented and packed some mugs, large enough for Ronan's rough hands and for him to have at least five mouthfuls of the scalding liquid before he'd drained and refilled it. I'd never known anyone who could drink tea so hot. I was still blowing on mine while he was pouring his second. Something to do with being a builder he had assured me one time.

"I confess, this is rather pleasant," Ronan said, looking out the window at the mountainous backdrop.

"It sure is. I can't wait for our first night. I've splashed out on some sexy underwear," I smirked and gave him a wink.

"I hope it's easy to get off," he replied.

"We'll have to see. You have stabilised Christine, haven't you?" I asked, having a fleeting vision of us rolling down the hill mid-sex.

He rolled his eyes at me and I laughed.

We finished our tea and decided on a short walk to get our bearings. It had been many years since Ronan had toured the area and because of the time of year, the small campsite office was closed. I loved the honesty box that was mounted outside and allowed for campers to post their fee through the little slot. I wondered how many didn't, though.

I pulled my bobble hat down over my ears, wrapped my scarf tight around my neck, and covered the lower part of my face. I zipped my ski jacket up and slipped on my gloves, only to take them off again when I realised I hadn't tied my bootlaces. Then I unzipped the jacket when I realised I couldn't bend down enough to tie said laces. Ronan huffed and grabbed my foot. I laughed as he placed one, then the other on his knee and tied my laces for me. We were then ready to go.

"How long ago is it since you were here?" I asked, completely aware that my voice was muffled through the scarf.

"Iomadh bliadhna," Ronan answered in Gaelic.

I pulled down the scarf so I could speak. "Huh?" I said.

"Oh, I thought you were speaking a foreign language," he said, giving me a wink.

The one thing I loved the most about Ronan was his wit. There had been a time when he'd given me whiplash with his mood swings and insecurities, but as our relationship had blossomed, his fast wit and sarcasm had endeared me further.

"I said, how long since you've been here?"

"I brought my mum here years ago. She had come here frequently as a child, and I can't remember why. Something tells me she might have had a relative here. Anyway, that relative got sick, and, as you do, we all traipsed to sit by her bedside and say our 'goodbyes' to someone I don't think I'd ever met. Most strange."

I was tempted to ask what Verity had died of, not that it was my business, but in all the time we'd been together, it had never been spoken about. Maggie had told me she got depressed and simply gave up on life. I wasn't sure if that was exactly true or just Maggie's interpretation. Ronan rarely spoke about his mother, and other than explaining who he was one time, he never spoke of his father.

I thought it a shame. I took hold of his hand in mine. "It's beautiful," I said, stopping near a ridge to take in the view.

"In the right time of the year, which is about now, you can see the Northern Lights," he replied.

"Now *that* is something I'd love to see. Did you know I went to Norway once, on a ship, to see the lights? Didn't see a bloody thing, and all we were told by everyone we met was to *head to Scotland*!" I laughed at the memory. Harry had been so cross to have spent all that money on a Norwegian cruise, with its awful food and even worse entertainment, and to not even see the lights.

"We'll camp out and watch for them."

Another thing I loved about Ronan was his knowledge of

his home country. I'd be lost if someone asked me the history of London. I knew about heads of traitors being put on poles at the 'gates' of London as a deterrent, but that was about it. I was ashamed when I compared myself to him.

It was lunchtime when we returned to Christine. Max drank a gallon of water, dribbled everywhere, and then flopped onto his bed for the rest of the day. I thought we might have overdone his walking of late and I had to remember he still had a dodgy leg.

I laid out some bread and cheese, home-made chutney, and yet more tea. We ate, we snuggled on the sofa with our books, and we dozed. It was bliss.

That evening, with Max in tow, we left Christine and headed a little north into a village for a meal in a pub that Ronan had mentioned. We had taken the chance it was still there, and that it was open. He hadn't visited it in years. Although under new ownership, the atmosphere was warm and friendly and the home-made steak and ale pie with horseradish mash was perfect. I even ventured out of my comfort zone and took a half pint of the local beer. Well, they said it was local but I wasn't so sure. Perhaps the wink to Ronan was a clue. Wherever it was from, it was pleasant. Ronan opted for a soda.

"This is a lovely place," I said, as we sat after our meal on a sofa in front of the fire.

"This is my kind of pub. It's what I wanted for the Kings

Arm's," he said. I frowned. "Our pub. The one the estate owns," he clarified.

"Oh, I don't think I ever knew the name," I laughed as I spoke. After the incident with his ex-wife, Carol, and then the run-in with Maggie's ex-foster child, Gregg, both of whom had decided the pub was the best place for either a showdown or a snipe at Ronan, we didn't really venture in there much.

For a couple still in the prime of their relationship, we sure had it tested from members of Ronan's *family*. We still bumped into Carol, she still sniped at us both, and it annoyed the shit out of her that neither of us rose to it anymore. I was pleased; Ronan was finally letting go of the anger he harboured towards her.

I shook my head to rid me of the nasty memories. I was in love with an amazing man; we were sitting in a beautiful pub, in a wonderful place. I wanted to enjoy this private time with him.

"What are you smiling at?" he asked, reaching forward to take my hands in his.

"You, us." I clasped my fingers around his.

"I love you," he whispered.

I leaned closer to him. "I love you, too."

He chuckled as we sat back. "So, are we still calling the caravan Christine?" he asked.

"Yep, all the mumbo jumbo about possessed cars is just fiction."

He nodded slowly as he finished his soda. I drained my half pint and was ready to leave. We waved goodbye to the landlord and with Max by our side, we walked to the car park. Before we got back into the car, we stood and scanned the sky. The clouds were low and plentiful, masking any light we might have seen.

"Did you leave the caravan door open?" Ronan asked, as our headlight swept across Christine.

"No, I take it you didn't, either?"

He pulled the vehicle to a halt and told me to wait in the car. I ignored that, of course, and he huffed as I stepped beside him. I watched the hackles on Max's back rise and he emitted a soft, warning growl. I reached down to stroke his head and calm him.

Ronan approached the caravan cautiously, and poked his head through the door. "What the fuck?" I heard, before he turned to me with wide eyes.

"What?" I asked.

"There is a llama in the caravan."

I frowned. It wasn't that I disbelieved him, but...I disbelieved him. I pushed past him and flicked on the light, to see a cream and dirt coloured llama standing in the caravan eating bread from the side.

"What the fuck?" I echoed Ronan's initial thoughts. "What do we do?"

"Get it out!" Ronan pushed me to one side and climbed into the caravan. He whooshed and waved his arms; the llama wasn't remotely afraid of him and stood there chewing, its lower jaw moving from side to side.

"Are they related to camels?" I asked.

"What?" Ronan's frown was deep; his eyes screwed up as he probably wondered what on earth I was on about.

I shrugged my shoulders. "They eat the same way. Don't frighten her."

He shook his head and delivered a concussion inducing eye-roll. "I'm not going to frighten *her*; I'm trying to get it out the bloody caravan." He pushed past the llama and I worried it might kick him. He gave her a slap on the arse and she finally, nonchalantly, walked towards the door.

I laughed at the shock of cream curls on top of her head and the swing of the jaw as she continued to eat the bread. "Come on, llama," I said, encouraging her out but she stood in the doorway.

"Put Max in the car," Ronan called out. Max was growling, having never encountered a llama before so I shoved him in the Land Rover.

Still the llama stood in the doorway. It had managed to jump up but seemed very hesitant to jump back down, not that there was a large step to take.

"Get some rope, or something. You might need to pull it out," Ronan said.

I was busy laughing at how obnoxious the llama was being. "I have Max's lead," I replied. I tied it around the llama's neck and pulled. Ronan gave her one last slap to the arse and she jumped out. She stood there, staring at me, a death stare that must've taken ages to perfect.

"I'm going to call you Colleen," I said, stroking her neck.

"You're not going to call her anything because she's not *yours*," Ronan said, taking the lead from me.

"Where do you think she came from?" I asked.

"There's a petting zoo here in the summer, I'm guessing from one of those barns."

We led Colleen down to the barn but found the doors locked. "You hold her, I'll ring the farmer," Ronan said.

Beside the honesty box was a telephone number in case of emergencies. I guessed an escaped llama was an emergency.

Ronan was back in a couple of minutes. "No answer, but I left a message." He took the lead from me and started to walk towards a small paddock. "Open that gate, will you?"

I leapt forward to grab the metal gate and lifted it off its bracket. Ronan led the llama in, removed the lead and then came back out; we closed the gate making sure it was secure.

"Do you think Colleen will be okay?" I asked.

"You can't name *every* animal you come across. And yes, I'm sure she'll be okay. What's with the Colleen anyway?"

"Hoover."

"Huh?" His frown lines were as deep as the Grand Canyon, such was his level of confusion.

"Colleen Hoover. She's one of my favourite authors and she likes llamas...or is it alpacas? I can't remember. Anyway, I've named her Colleen, they both have blonde curly hair."

Ronan had raised his eyebrows so high I thought they might meet his fringe. "What on *earth* are you on about?" He seemed to think better of his question and shook his head. "Forget it, come on, we need to figure out how she got in."

"Bye, Colleen, see you in the morning," I said cheerfully, as the llama continued to fix me with her death stare.

It was very possible I had forgotten to lock Christine's door, I was trying to remember if *I* was meant to, or Ronan was. I know I pulled it closed, I was sure about that. There didn't seem to be anything wrong with the door or the lock so we could only assume, in her curiosity, Colleen had wiggled the handle and let herself in. I was most thankful that she hadn't shit everywhere. I did, however, mop the floors and wash the countertops.

"It stinks in here now," Ronan grumbled, as he mopped the tabletop and anywhere he thought Colleen had ventured.

The bedroom and bathroom doors were closed so I was pleased she had been confined to the main area that wasn't large enough for her to leave too much mess. The remaining bread was crumbled up and left in a bag ready for the birds the following morning. While Ronan made coffee, I slipped into the bedroom. I wanted to change into my sexy underwear as a surprise.

I took a quick shower and slathered on a little too much body lotion. I was sure I might poison Ronan if he licked my skin. Still, I smelled nice. I picked up the black lace knickers and pulled off the tag, I heard an unsatisfying rip and cursed under my breath. In my haste, I had pulled the plastic tag through the delicate lace and it had created a hole. But that wasn't all I detected. While I was inspecting the small hole, I saw another.

"Oh," I whispered, sure it wasn't there when I bought the item online.

I held it up, turned it around, trying to decide where the hole was meant to be. I pulled them on and decided they had to be back to front. Whatever the knickers were, they weren't crotchless. It dawned on me, then, where the hole was meant to be.

"Oh!" I said, again.

"You okay in there? Can I come in yet?" Ronan called out; I'd asked him to wait outside.

"Erm, no, a bit of a technical issue in here," I replied.

I deliberated, should I wear them or not? Would I be inviting something I was absolutely not game for? I rifled through the drawer that I'd put my underwear in, for anything else black. Perhaps I could seduce with the bra, Ronan was more a tit man…no, he wasn't, he was most certainly an arse man from the amount of times he grabbed mine.

I sat heavily on the bed. The bra was strangling me and I was wearing the knickers on my wrist like a bangle when Ronan walked in.

"I didn't want to wait anymore," he said, and then paused, abruptly.

I held up my wrist. "They have a hole in a place I'd rather they didn't have a hole, and I wanted to surprise you with them," I said aware I sounded like a spoilt child. I was waving my arm and watching the delicate lace float around. However, by raising my arm I had caused one tit to pop out from under the tight bra.

Ronan laughed. "You look a little trussed up, like—"

I pointed my finger at him. "If you mention last Christmas's turkey then I might just kick you out for the night."

He held up his hands in surrender. "I wasn't going to mention the Christmas turkey that was very expertly trussed, to the point I thought you might be a Kinbaku expert."

The Christmas turkey *had* been trussed; it had to be, and it didn't fit in the oven. Ronan had mentioned this Kinbaku thing back then and I had been surprised to learn it was a type of Japanese bondage. I had questioned why he knew about it.

He sat beside me. "Trussed up or not, I want you so badly right now," he whispered.

Thankfully, the bra came off and I was able to take in a deep breath.

"Remind me to ask about your kinky knowledge," I whispered, and I was gently encouraged to lie back on the bed. Ronan laughed and I suspected he might have known what I meant. My stomach fluttered.

6

"Colleen!" I shouted.

Ronan, without even opening his eyes fully, leapt from the bed. His hair was standing on end and he turned from side to side. "What?" he said, blearily. I guessed I'd startled him when I'd shouted.

"Colleen, she's looking in the window."

"What?" he repeated, still not with me. I wanted to hold him still, stop him turning so he could face the window and see the llama looking in at us.

"She's been watching us have sex," I squealed.

Ronan slumped on the bed. "For fuck's sake, Lizzie, you near on gave me a heart attack. Who's been watching us?"

"Colleen, the llama." I pointed to window. The cream puff

of curly hair atop the creature's head was bobbing in time with the side to side grinding of her jaw. She still gave us her death stare.

"Her name isn't…never mind. I'll get rid of it."

Ronan stood and retrieved his jeans from the floor. He slipped them on, tucking his *bits* inside, before giving a little jump and zipping them up then tightened his belt. There was something in his actions that had me stirred all over again. I sat up in bed, holding the duvet to my neck. I didn't want Colleen to see my boobs.

"Don't be mean to her," I called out as Ronan left the bedroom.

He grumbled. "It's a fucking llama," he said.

"Still, don't be mean."

I didn't understand the reply. Ronan had the annoying habit of answering back in Gaelic when he wanted to score a point or get the last word, knowing I'd be stumped. I'd vowed, one day, to learn at least some curse words so I could swear at him.

I watched as Colleen turned her head. By the gust of cold air, Ronan must have opened the caravan door. She didn't budge when he waved a tea towel at her. She just fixed him with her death stare instead. I could hear Ronan swearing at her and I giggled. After a minute, she casually walked away and Ronan returned, kicking off his jeans as he did.

"Where did she go?" I asked.

He sighed and ran his hand through his hair in tiredness. "I don't care where she went, she's gone. Do you want a cup of tea?"

"Get back in bed, I'll make it," I suggested. "You're my hero, did you know that?" I said, patting the sheet beside me. He laughed.

I slid out and padded barefoot to the kitchen. "I wonder how she got out of the field?" I asked, as I boiled the kettle.

Max was snoring on his bed, oblivious to the drama the llama had caused.

"No idea, and I don't care," I heard. Ronan was such a liar; he was as much an animal lover as I was. I laughed and finished making the tea before I glanced at the clock to see it was only three in the morning.

As I snuggled down, I thought about the caravan door. "Did you lock the door?" I asked.

"Yes."

"Are you sure?"

"Yes."

"Should I check?"

"Yes."

"So you didn't."

"Yes, but you're gonna keep asking until one of us gets up to prove the door is locked, aren't you?"

"Yes," I replied.

With a sigh, Ronan climbed from the bed, yet again, and, leaving the bedroom door open so I could see, he rattled the front door. "Okay now?" he asked, I nodded. At that, Max woke. He stretched, whimpered, and then rose. He walked to the door and placed his paw on it, indicating he wanted to go out.

"For fuck's sake," Ronan said, for the second time that night.

He grabbed a tea towel and held it over his crotch while he opened the door to let Max out. A cold blast of air had him hopping from foot to foot, and I wondered whatever someone would think should they walk past, seeing him in all his glorious nakedness but with a tea towel covering his modesty. Not that, I suspected, anyone would walk past at that time of the morning.

"Morning," Ronan called out and raised a hand in greeting.

"Shut the door!" I screeched, knowing no one could see me but panicking just in case. Ronan laughed and closed the door as soon as Max ran back in.

"Who was that?" I asked.

"No one, I was kidding," he replied. I shook my head at him, and to emphasise that I didn't get his *joke* I pursed my lips as well. A right old scold, he got.

Once he had slipped back in bed and we had finished our tea, I snuggled into his arms and it wasn't long before I was asleep again.

———

A wet nose poked under the duvet and a tongue licked my cheek. "Max," I murmured knowing it to be him...*hoping* it to be him. I was licked again. I opened my eyes to see his head resting on the mattress under the duvet with me.

"Hello, baby," I whispered, conscious Ronan was still asleep. I glanced at my watch, it was still only seven. "You want to go out?" I asked, half expecting the dog to answer me. A thud as his tail hit the floor was the reply I needed.

I quietly slid from the bed and dressed in jeans and a jumper. I grabbed socks and, with Max behind me, I left the bedroom and Ronan still sleeping. I closed the door and set the kettle on to boil. I pulled on the socks and my boots, grabbed my jacket and opened the caravan door. I would take Max for a pee and then come back to make the tea.

Max jumped down and ran straight to the first tree he could find. I followed a little more gingerly. It appeared to have rained in the night and the field was a little muddy and slippery.

Max galloped off into a wooded area and I called after him. It was most unlike him to run too far ahead. He would normally pause and wait for us to catch up, but something had his attention. I guessed a squirrel, since he was fond of chasing them. I wasn't overly concerned; he was good with recall. As I zipped up my coat, I followed to the tree line. I could hear him scrabbling among the fallen leaves and his little whimper of excitement when he found the most perfect stick that would become his bestest friend until he'd chewed it to nothing.

It was very quiet, not even the birds were tweeting. Even in my coat I shivered. My exhaled breath froze in the cold air but it felt wonderful to be outside. I remembered back to winter days in London, in the smog that was a mix of fog and fumes, tripping over rubbish left on the streets, and elbowing my way through throngs of people. When I thought back, I wondered why I'd suffered it for so long. Standing there, in the wilderness, as such, felt like home. More so than Kent even. I thought I heard a noise behind me and waited for Ronan to do something stupid like creep up on me. I smiled as I felt a breath on the back of my neck but frowned when it became wet. I reached up to touch a green sticky substance and then spun on my heel.

I squealed.

Colleen was standing right behind me, still chewing her fucking grass and drooling. Her shock of blonde curls seemed even frizzier in the morning mist and I nodded in sympathy.

I reached up and stroked her neck. "I know, Colleen, my hair is just as mad on days like this. You need a hat, my girl."

She seemed to like me, I thought. When Max returned she made a hissing sound so he gave her a wide berth, and I chastised her for it. She had to learn to get on with all animals and considering she came from a petting zoo, I was surprised.

"Och, there she is," I heard a rough voice say. I peered over her body.

A man, who could only be described as a farmer, was walking towards me with a halter. He wore so many layers of clothes, topped with a red-checked shirt, that it was hard to determine his size. His jeans were too short and held up with braces and his green woollen socks were visible, wedged into dress shoes, completely inappropriate for the environment. He had the jolliest face though, and his broad smile was infectious.

"Good morning," I called out.

He raised a hand in greeting. "Ah've been searching all over for her," he said, breathlessly and I wondered if he'd been out all night.

"We put her in that field over there but she seems to have escaped," I replied.

"Aye, Houdini she should be called. I'll take her back to the barn." His accent was different to Charlie's, not as broad, softer, but it still took a trained ear.

Colleen had other ideas. As soon as he got close enough to slip the halter over her nose, she was off. Max decided it was fun to run with her so I shouted for him, and the farmer shouted for...I had no idea what he'd called her but it didn't sound nice.

All the shouting had Ronan at the caravan door just in jeans and his walking boots. "Sam?" he asked.

The chap looked over. "Ah, Ronan, here to help, are ye?"

It appeared they knew each other. Ronan slipped a coat over his bare chest and joined us.

"Colleen went that way," I said, pointing down towards the barn. Both the farmer and Ronan looked at me with crumpled expressions. "Don't worry. *She* went that way." I gestured again for emphasis.

We walked down to the barns but Colleen was nowhere to be seen. I suspected she was enjoying her little game of chase. Even Max was stumped as to where she'd gone, but then he hadn't been brought up as a working dog so had no real tracking skills beyond what was normal for a pet. We turned a corner and I thought I caught a flash of cream; she was toying with us.

"I'll go this way," Ronan said, doubling back.

"You open that barn door, then run to the back and open that as well. We'll trap her inside," Sam told me, while he carried on.

I did as I was instructed and opened the barn door enough for me to squeeze inside, then ran to the bottom door and opened that; no Colleen, nor Ronan nor Sam. Then I thought, I ought to shut the top door in case she did come in and run out the other end, so I ran up and closed it.

Outside I could hear, "No!"

I opened the door and peeked out to see Ronan waving his arms. I guessed they'd corralled Colleen to the top door. "Jesus Christ," I whispered, unsure what door to leave open and which one to close. I ran back down to the other end and as I did I passed a pen of little goats. "Oh, look," I said, jogging over. "Oh, fuck!" I added as one fell over with his legs stiff in the air. "Ronan!" I called out.

"What?" he shouted from the bottom door.

"I killed a goat." My voice was muffled by my hands covering my mouth and I had genuine tears in my eyes. "I must've frightened it, it's had a heart attack…wait, oh, it's getting up." Confusion laced my voice.

"Lizzie, forget the goat, get the fucking llama." Ronan didn't sound overly pleased to be chasing a llama around a barn.

I guessed Colleen had decided she'd had enough and sauntered into the barn. The door was slammed shut after Sam and Ronan followed her in. She stood in the middle of the aisle with not a care in the world. I decided then, that I didn't particularly like her.

"Something happened to your goat," I said to Sam. "I think

I scared it and it fell over. This one…" I must have moved too fast toward the pen to point out the sick goat when it did it again. It keeled over with its legs stiff in the air.

Ronan laughed and I slapped him on the chest. "Don't laugh, do something," I said, panicked that the poor goat was sick.

"Myotonic," I heard Sam say.

"Myowhat?" I asked, with a sniff.

"They're Myotonic goats, they have a genetic disorder that makes them do that," Ronan answered, as he placed his arm around my shoulder. "So, no, you didn't kill the goat."

Relief flooded me. "Drama llamas and fainting goats! I don't think any day could top this one and all before breakfast as well," I said.

On cue, my stomach rumbled, reminding me I'd been running around a barn prior to even a cup of tea, let alone a biscuit or two. I wondered how many bacon sandwiches would make up for the calorie loss.

Colleen was ushered into a pen with an alpaca and two mini pigs. If I'd had my way, I would've ushered them all into a trailer and taken them home. Even Colleen, who, I swore, gave me a wink as we left. I laughed out loud; she was a character, for sure.

"How did she get out?" Ronan asked, as we watched Sam produce a padlock from his pocket and then lock the door shut.

"I dinnae ken. She jumps the fences, I know that much. I think she might need a new home before the season starts."

I opened my mouth and then found a masculine hand over it. Still with the hand over my mouth, I was ushered away and back to the caravan, all the while Ronan called for Max and assured Sam that we would check the barn was still closed later that day. We would be leaving the following morning. My mouth was only freed when we got back to Christine.

"That wasn't nice," I said.

"And neither would it be to try and transport that bloody escape artist back home. *No*, Lizzie, we're not having a llama, or a pig, or a fainting goat."

I raised my eyelids at him and opened my mouth again.

"No, Lizzie."

I closed my mouth. I'd let him have this round, this *one* time. I laughed.

"I'd love one of those goats," I said, quietly, and to myself as I slid my coat off and kicked off my boots.

Max jumped into the caravan equally as exhausted by the morning's activities.

After two cups of tea and a bacon sandwich each, Ronan and I discussed what to do for the day.

Skye was probably the most amazing place I'd ever visited.

It's ruggedness and dramatic skyline was breathtaking. Every turn in the road we took brought another view that made me gasp. We passed people who raised a hand in greeting, sheep meandered along the lane, and eventually we came to a spot where Ronan pointed out the Old Man of Storr. A magnificent rocky hill came into view and there stood some pinnacles.

"The Old Man of Storr," Ronan said, as he pulled the Land Rover to the side of the road. "You can walk up to it but I don't think today is a good day for us."

There was a low lying mist rolling in from the sea that I thought might cause problems for the people I could see in the distance already making their way up.

"Do you know why it's called that?" I asked.

"I believe there's part of it that resembles and old man's face, not that I can see that," he replied, with a chuckle.

We sat for a moment just looking and I could have kicked myself not to have brought a decent camera with me. My phone wouldn't be good enough to do the image justice, but I snapped away just for my memories.

"Honestly, Ronan, how can you leave Scotland for Kent?" I asked, quietly.

"It's hard, and getting harder," he confessed. I turned to him. His brow was furrowed as he stared out through the windscreen, looking troubled. I covered his hand with mine.

"Do you have something on your mind?" I asked.

"Yes, and no."

He finally turned to me and smiled. "No, not for today, anyway. Now, let's find a nice pub for some lunch."

I settled back in my seat and mentally said goodbye for now to the Old Man of Storr. I knew we'd be back at some point. I'd fallen in love with Scotland as hard as I'd fallen in love with Ronan. If it was getting hard for him to leave, there was a large part of me that agreed with him. Maybe we were getting close to a decision.

————

The pub was just perfect, small, warm, and cosy, with metal bowls of water for the dogs dotted around. We laughed as we remembered that morning and the *drama llama* as Ronan had named her. In fact, he told me she reminded him of me. I laughed out loud and raised my glass to him in thanks. We then just sat for a few minutes in silence, absorbing the atmosphere.

"This time last year I buried my mother," Ronan said, staring into the fire.

"I know, I didn't want to bring it up in case it upset you," I replied.

The *anniversary* we had celebrated had been the day of our non-date, the time our relationship was meant to start, and it was from that point Ronan wanted to recognise, not the point we actually made a commitment to each other. But it coincided with the death of his mother, her funeral, and sad times for him. It was a bittersweet week and I was glad to be by his side.

"The firsts are hard," I added.

Ronan nodded. "I feel guilty because I stepped away from her for a while. I was embarrassed by her lifestyle but I was also mortified by her depression because I didn't understand it."

Ronan's statement surprised me. "You can't understand everyone and everything," I replied, gently. "Mental health is a difficult one."

"I know, I just thought I might be able to do more, save her. You know she took her own life?" He didn't look at me while he spoke, and I desperately held in the gasp of shock.

"I didn't, I thought she was ill."

"She was, mentally ill. She had tried to take her own life many times, it was just a matter of time before she managed it. Here's the shocker, though…I don't blame her. She was so depressed that, for her, the only way out was death. I loathe people who say that suicide is selfish. Making someone live because it makes *you* feel better is selfish." He had a bitter tone to his voice, and I wondered if he was speaking about someone he knew. Perhaps Rich had been the one to call their mother selfish.

"I don't really know what to say to comfort you," I said, reaching over to take his hand in mind. I wanted to touch him, for him to feel me instead of hear me.

He finally turned to smile at me. "Just being with you is a comfort. And here I am bringing it all down, again."

"Stop that right now. You're allowed to remember sad times, okay?"

He shuffled in his seat, as if sitting in a different position would change his mood and perhaps it had. He smiled some more and decided we'd have lunch, even though it was only a couple of hours since we'd eaten breakfast. I opted for a sandwich, something light. I was conscious of the weight I might be putting on each time I was in Scotland. Maggie did love to feed us all up.

It was early afternoon before we started to make the journey back to the campsite for our last night. Before we headed to bed, Ronan took Max for a walk around the barns. The padlock was still intact and we assumed Colleen and her friends were snuggled up for the night.

It was with a little sadness that we left early the following morning. I settled into the passenger seat of the car and watched the campsite as we left. I chuckled as I remembered our lovely couple of days.

———

We pulled into the courtyard and Maggie and Charlie stood to greet us. Charlie, I imagined, just wanted to see if Christine had managed her maiden voyage in one piece. We watched as he rushed to unhitch her and then did a circuit as if inspecting. I laughed at him.

"Welcome home," Maggie said, as if we'd been away for weeks. "How was it?"

"We had the most eventful time," I answered, climbing down from the Land Rover and tripping over Max who spotted his best friend, Charlie, and abandoned us immediately.

"Oh, that sounds interesting. I'll pop the kettle on and you can tell us all about it," she said, and then scuttled off to the kitchen.

Ronan and Charlie manually pushed the caravan over to the side of the yard, to allow the Land Rover to be returned to the garage. I'd replace all the crockery with cheaper ones and give her a good clean, and then she'd be ready for the campsite. I knew Maggie had taken a booking for her the previous week. That reminded me, we would need to start interviewing for staff soon. We had promised Maggie the cleaning and change over of the lodges, and caravan, in the newly formed camping site by the loch wouldn't be left to her.

Later, as we sat around the kitchen table, Ronan had both Maggie and Charlie in stitches as he regaled them with an embellished story of Colleen the llama and the fainting goat. I sat back in my chair and held a mug of tea between my hands. As I gazed around at their faces it dawned on me.

Those people were my family, and I loved them all.

7

Following three days of hard labour in the drizzle and cold, we had completed our campsite. There was a team of builders connecting the small lodges we had bought to the services, and Christine took pride of place among them. I'd had a small plaque made with her name on and Ronan had secured it just above the door. He still laughed at the thought of her name; I still dismissed his idea that it was wrong.

"It looks amazing," I said, as I pulled off my workers' heavy-duty gloves and picked a mug of tea from a tray.

"It sure does. And it was all your idea," Ronan replied, slinging his arm over my shoulder. He smiled down at me. "Now we just have to get it staffed."

"I have news on that. Angie has agreed to come and man

the office and the young girl in the hairdresser? She's going to be a *chambermaid* as she calls it."

"What about the bakery, she has to keep that running as well?"

Angie had been one of Maggie and Charlie's foster children and she owned the bakery in town. I'd had a conversation with her about putting a notice in her shop window for staff when she offered to come and set up the office. It wasn't long term, but she was willing to get it running, and then hand it over to a suitable replacement. I thought that a great idea, especially when she didn't want any form of payment for it. I explained to Ronan what had been decided and we agreed it was immensely kind of her. As a return favour, we offered to stock her goods in the small on-site shop.

Since the entrance to the campsite was at the other end of the estate, it wasn't much for Angie to pop in on her way from the bakery with fresh breads and cakes. I could picture my hips expanding at a rapid rate.

With more filming booked for later in the year, I could see Ronan and I spending much of our time in Scotland. I wondered if it was time for *that* conversation.

Later that evening the opportunity arose.

Ronan and I were sitting in the living room—a room we didn't use that often—because there was a documentary on the television we wanted to watch. We had snacks and a bottle of wine, and I retrieved a woollen throw from the kitchen as our backs were to the windows and a gentle draft chilled my neck. The fire was roaring and the lights low as we snuggled up.

"You know, we might have to make a decision about what to do with commuting soon. We're going to have to spend a lot of time here this year," I said, smiling up at him.

He returned my smile but sighed. "How do you feel about that?" he asked, his brow creased into a frown, and I wondered if the question had been playing on his mind.

"I love it here." I smiled softly at him, wanting him to believe me. "I really don't mind locking up the barn in Kent for the year. I'm sure Joe and Danny will make use of it for weekends, and there are enough people in the village to look out for it when it's unoccupied."

I knew Pam and Del, our neighbours there, were about to start building an extension. If it got too much to stay put, I could offer them the barn for the length of time it took for their build. We were all in touch in a village WhatsApp group and although I missed them, I loved being in Scotland with Ronan more. I enjoyed the business we had started to develop, sitting in our cosy and organised little office in the courtyard as we sorted invoices and sales receipts together. It was nice to answer the phone with the estate name and discuss opportunities or take bookings.

Despite Ronan's initial trepidations, the butterfly garden was going great. We'd had experts come and document, we'd had amateur photographers come to practice macro shots, we'd had enthusiasts come just to admire the collection, particularly when it was discovered we had a rare butterfly that had made its home there.

Ronan rubbed his chin and nodded. "I've been thinking about whether we need to make a more permanent move, but I don't want to force your hand," he said.

"Perhaps we need to think of the barn as our holiday home and this as our residence," I said, shrugging my shoulders.

Over the months, I had duplicated my home essentials there at the house in Scotland. I didn't need to travel with a suitcase anymore, just a holdall of anything I wanted for the journey.

Ronan kissed the top of my head. "I don't think you understand just what you've done to me, do you?" His face softened as he spoke and, unusually, his eyes brimmed with tears.

I sat back so I could fully face him. "Are you okay?" I asked, as I reached out to touch his arm in comfort.

"Yeah, just being silly. I love you so much, Lizzie, sometimes I find that a little overwhelming."

His statement took me aback; although it wasn't the first time I'd heard it. I guessed my insecurities forbade me from fully believing I could have that effect on someone, and I wasn't sure how to respond.

"That's put you in panic mode, hasn't it?" he added and then laughed.

"No, not panic mode, I just…I just don't always think I deserve you." It was the best I could come up with to explain how I felt.

Ronan wrapped his arm back around my shoulder and I slunk into his side. He kissed the top of my head again, and, in silence, we watched the documentary. It was ironic, the documentary followed a presenter, one who had found fame in a reality show based in Scotland, as he spent time with people living in remote areas and often off-grid.

By the time the programme had finished, Ronan was snoring softly beside me and I had a stiff neck. I laughed, hardly the party animals we sometimes thought we were. I reached for the remote, turned off the TV, and sat for a moment, just enjoying the feel of him, and watching the flames die down.

I hadn't heard from Joe for a couple of days, he had been planning on taking another trip to see Danny's parents, and I wondered if they'd come and visit us at some point. It had been hilarious the last time. Neither Joe nor Danny could understand a word Charlie said, and of course, Charlie had liked to emphaise his accent to such a degree even Maggie couldn't translate. I made a plan to give him a call the following morning. We were such good friends it didn't matter if we didn't speak from one week to the next, we always just picked up where we'd left off but I did miss having him close.

Ronan stirred, he stretched and his T-shirt rose showing off his muscled stomach. I ran my fingers gently over his skin, tracing the outline of his six-pack. He smiled, even though he kept his eyes closed. Up to that point we hadn't *made out* in the living room. I thought perhaps it was a good time to rectify, so I unbuckled his belt and then his jeans, and his smile spread further.

"I'm sure this is sexual harassment or something," he said, pulling me closer.

"Should I call the police?"

He laughed as his lips closed in on mine and my hand slid under the waistband of his jeans.

———

Post had arrived and was left on the kitchen table for me. Pam had collected it and put it all in one large brown envelope for ease before forwarding it to me in Scotland. I smiled as I recognised her handwriting. I emptied the post on to the table as I sat with my tea in an empty kitchen. I was having some difficulty sleeping, getting very hot in the night and kicking the duvet off, only to freeze a few minutes later. It was disturbing us both. So, when I opened the letter from my doctor to remind me I needed a mammogram, I was pleased. I was sure I was in the menopause and that would be a great opportunity to ask some questions. I could book the *titty squish* at the same time as a doctor's appointment. However, my doctor was in Kent and I was in Scotland.

It seemed daft to go back just for the appointment, but

that's what I would have to do. I pulled Ronan's laptop towards me and logged on. I could book the appointment online and then plan to head back for a couple of days, catch up with Joe and Danny, and call in on Ronan's neighbour.

"Hey, you're up early," Maggie said, as she came into the kitchen.

"I couldn't sleep. I think I might be menopausal."

"Ouch, you'll be going all nuts on us soon. I have some herbs for that," she added, opening and closing cupboard, I assumed, looking for the *herbs*.

"Maggie, last time you had *herbs*, it turned out to be cannabis and you drugged Saggy Tits and Limp Dick!"

Her laugh was infectious and she soon had her hands on her knees as she tried to catch her breath.

"Anyway, I've made an appointment with my doctor because I have a mammogram to attend. I'll have a chat with her about it."

My mum had constantly told me her, *man-o-pause,* as she called it, was, thankfully, very brief. She had a few nights of hot sweats and had gone off sex completely. She'd then proceeded to tell me how she and Dad made up for that *off* time, much to my disgust. I had absolutely no desire to know the intimate details of my parents' evenings/days/mornings/afternoons/anytime/anywhere activities. The last FaceTime conversation I'd had with them, they'd threatened to come and visit. They were intrigued with the naked art group. I shuddered at the thought.

"Hopefully, if I take after my mum, this will be a brief ordeal," I added.

"I think I never came out of it," Maggie said, to emphasise the point, she pulled the neck of her T-shirt away and fanned cool air down her front.

"I suspect that has more to do with the fact you now have heat, and lots of it, rather than the menopause," I said, doing exactly the same.

Since the Aga had been repaired, the kitchen often became a hothouse, so much that Maggie was able to just leave bread to prove on the side.

As I sat, Maggie set the table for breakfast and made tea. I felt guilty since I could have done that myself, but I was still a little foggy headed after a poor night's sleep. "Maggie, I'm sorry. I could have helped."

She waved her arm, her way of telling me not to worry. Instead, I grabbed a mug of tea to take up to Ronan.

For a moment I stood and watched him. He was lying on his back and he had one arm slung over his head, the other rested across his stomach. The tattoos I'd admired over the months ran from wrist to shoulder but nowhere else. I often asked him why he'd stopped at that point; they looked unfinished. He would shrug his shoulders and tell me he just grew out of wanting more. I'd always wanted a tattoo and maybe, if I was menopausal I could use that as an excuse to get one. Something small and dainty.

I sat on the edge of the bed. "Good morning," I said, gently.

He didn't stir so I jiggled around. Ronan could sleep like the dead when he wanted to, and I guessed, that morning, he wanted to. I was about to stand when Ronan decided to turn, and in doing so, he swung the arm that had rested on his stomach my way. His hand caught the mug and it, and the tea, flew across the room startling both him and me.

"What the…?" he said, sitting up quickly.

"You knocked the mug out of my hand," I said, laughing. I headed to the bathroom to grab a towel to mop up the tea.

"I bet that was my favourite mug as well," he said, looking over the edge of the bed.

"The mug is over there." I pointed to a rather unimpressive blue mug. He often used it because it was large, I had no idea it was his *favourite*. "Who has a favourite mug, anyway?"

"I do," he replied, swinging his legs over the side of the bed. He sat in all his naked glory, smiling at me. His hair was standing on end, his eyes still sleepy, and he had a five o'clock shadow that seemed to have developed overnight. God, he was sexy!

"I have to head down to Kent for a couple of days. I have a mammogram and I thought I might speak to the nurse about the menopause," I said, as I cleaned the spilled tea from the floor.

"Okay, I'll come with you," he replied, rising and making his way to the bathroom.

"There's no need if you'd rather stay here. I can catch up with Joe and Danny as well."

"That sounds like you'd rather go alone," he called out.

"No, don't get all insecure on me," I chuckled as I spoke. "I'm simply saying, come if you want, stay here if you need to. I'll be two, maybe three days."

He poked his head around the door with a toothbrush in his mouth and winked. "I liked being all needy. But, I'll stay here, on my own, alone, and I'll miss you like mad. Maybe we can have Skype sex or whatever the modern term is," he spluttered.

"FaceTime sex, I think. And yes, that would be fun," I replied, as I placed the broken pieces of mug inside it and left the room.

Ronan was laughing as I made my way down the hallway and back to the kitchen. By the time I arrived, Charlie was tucking into toast slathered with inches of home-made raspberry jam and Maggie was busy mixing something that smelled delicious, despite being uncooked.

"I'm off back to Kent tomorrow, if I can get my train booked," I said, as I threw the broken mug away and pulled another from a cupboard.

"I'd love to head south one day," Maggie replied, and I was surprised.

"You've never been?" I asked.

She shook her head in response and then frowned. I watched as she stopped her mixing and then reached into the bowl to retrieve a piece of something that looked remarkably like a strand of wool from the jumper Charlie wore. She threw it into the sink and carried on as normal.

"You're welcome to come with me," I said with a smile. It would be nice to show her the sights.

"Another time, this one here would never manage without me," she said, flicking some batter at her husband.

Ronan entered the kitchen. "Maggie, you should go. Charlie and I can manage. Remember that time you were in the hospital? We were fine then," he told her.

"Why were you in the hospital?" I asked, taking a seat at the table. Maggie's stories normally warranted a seat, and a cup of tea or two.

"Well, this is an interesting story," she started, placed the bowl on the side, pulled out a chair, and as expected, poured a cup of tea. "When I was a child I had a twisted gut," she said, and that wasn't what I expected to hear at all.

Maggie went to tell me about the numerous operations she'd had when she was young and even offered to show me her scars. I had no desire to see them, and politely told her that. She went on to say, as she got older she'd had the odd bout of unexplained stomach pain resulting in a stay in hospital. One day, they decided to take her in, *cut her open like a fish to find out she didn't have a hernia all along.*

I was a little baffled considering no one had mentioned a hernia and could only surmise the doctor thought that's what it was but it turned out not to be.

"So what was it then?" I made the fatal mistake of asking.

She sat back and folded her arms under her boobs.

"I think I have something to do," Ronan said.

"Aye, lad, we have that…thing. Wait for me," Charlie added.

Maggie snorted her displeasure. "I'll tell you what was wrong. It was a bloody mistake on the doctor's part, that's what was wrong. I told him I didn't have a hernia and that the pain was adhesions, but what do I know? It's just my body!" Her indignation at not being believed caused her cheeks to flame red and her brow to furrow so much she looked demonic.

I was still none the wiser but wished to end the saga of her non-hernia. "So, do you want to come to London?" I asked.

Slowly, she started to smile. "Why not! I'll go and pack a suitcase."

"Maggie, we'll only be gone a couple of nights. An overnight bag will probably do."

She widened her eyes as if what I'd said was ridiculous. "I might need a posh dress."

"For what?"

"You might take me somewhere nice in the *big smoke*." She scuttled off and I wondered what on earth I'd just signed up for. More so when I heard her start singing, "Maybe it's Because I'm a Londoner."

"I think I've made a terrible mistake," I said to myself, since I'd been abandoned by everybody.

I poured my tea and sighed.

———

"What time is the train?" Maggie asked, for the third time. Instead of telling her, I wrote the time on a piece of paper and handed it to her.

We were in the Range Rover on our way to the station and Maggie—bless her—seemed nervous. I was excited for her, as was Joe when I'd told him. He had decided we were going to do some sightseeing in London, maybe a hop-on-hop-off bus if the weather was okay.

After a quick goodbye, Maggie and I left Ronan at the roadside and entered the station. We bought coffees and Maggie was mortified at the price. She tried to barter with the barista, until I informed her he just worked for a large American chain of coffee shops and he was unable to change any prices. I paid and ushered her to the platform.

"How can they charge that kind of money?" she asked, sipping the coffee and then screwing her nose up at the taste. "It's not very nice, is it?"

"Have you ever been to a *high-street* coffee shop before?" I asked.

"No."

"You'll learn to love it. Our train is due any minute."

Maggie dragged the suitcase behind her as we stepped forward on the platform. Once the train arrived, we walked up a little to our carriage. A porter offered to take her case and I wanted to laugh as he exhaled loudly with exertion and his face reddened.

"Wait, I need things in there," she said before he could manhandle the case into the storage area.

Without much effort, Maggie dragged the case to where we were sitting. She crouched down and unzipped it. I rolled my eyes and looked around, hoping we were the only ones in the first-class carriage. She placed a picnic on the table, which included bread, cheese wrapped in greaseproof paper, apples, tomatoes, juice, and cakes. She also had teabags and a small plastic container of milk. Once satisfied she had placed a week's worth of food on the small table, she allowed the porter to store her bag.

"Maggie, what on earth is all that?" I asked.

I watched as she shuffled into the seat nearest the window and I sat opposite. I hoped that we had the whole four seats with table to ourselves and even if we didn't, I hope the conductor would allow them, or us, to move.

"We're not eating all that plastic crap," she said, then proceeded to organise the table, and I had to admit, my stomach had started to rumble. I was sure there was plenty of food to not only last the journey, but the following day as well. I was tempted to text Pam and tell her not to bother with the usual milk and bread she normally left for me to arrive home to.

When the server arrived to see if we wanted snacks, Maggie instructed her to provide us with proper mugs, not the miniscule cups and saucers she had on her trolley, and hot water. Somehow, the young lady, much to our delight, was able to produce corporate mugs. Maggie made tea and settled back to enjoy the journey. For a little while we read, then we chatted about the house and Maggie's childhood on the farm her father owned. Her mother had been a seamstress and had taught her all she knew, she told me.

I watched as she dozed, and was tempted to video her snuffles and the twitching her nostrils made as she dreamt. I had to cover my mouth to stifle the laughter when her teeth—obviously false and detached from whatever glue kept them in place—clacked together. I pretended to be reading when Maggie woke with a start and fiddled them back into place.

I had no idea she had false teeth and I didn't want to make a deal of it.

"I don't think I've ever just sat for this long before," Maggie said, standing to stretch and wander a little up and down the aisle. "I don't think it's done my joints any good."

Before I could comment, she proceeded to raise her arms and point her fingers to the ceiling, she executed the perfect squat and slowly stood, as if she attempting Tai chi but had no idea how to go about it.

"Wax on, wax off," I said, giggling at her stretches as she waved her arms around.

"I do this every morning, keeps me supple. You should try it," she said with her eyes closed. "Mind you, you have Ronan for that," she added, and I spluttered into my company-issued mug of tea

"Maggie!"

She giggled as she finished her morning suppling up routine. Once done, she retook her seat and smiled at me. I sighed and shook my head, my eyebrows raised as I held back the laughter.

"What happens when we get into London?" she asked.

"We get another train to Kent, then a neighbour, Pam, is going to meet us. You'll like her, she loves baking and all that stuff."

By the time we arrived at the barn, I was exhausted and Maggie was still hyper. She was like a child allowed out of school for the first time. She dropped her bags in the hallway and gave a huge, theatrical sigh. She outstretched her arms and turned slowly. I thought, any minute, she'd give a rendition of *The Sound of Music*. I laughed and picked up her handbag, the picnic we'd packed up in a carrier bag, and then wheeled her case to the bottom of the stairs.

"Cup of tea?" I asked.

"I'll do…" she started, and then smiled.

"I'll do it," I corrected her. I had no doubt she would take over the kitchen but at least I could offer her a cup of tea.

"I stole the mugs, Lizzie," Maggie whispered, looking around the kitchen as if a hidden camera might capture her confession.

"I think we were allowed to keep them anyway," I answered, trying not to laugh. I'd started to believe Maggie had a little naughty streak in her.

The disappointment in her face that she hadn't committed the crime of petty theft made me regret my comment. I was sure, for her birthday, Ronan and I might be able to arrange some artificial *crime* she could get away with. I smiled as I finished making the tea and brought it to her in the living room. I stood in the doorway and watched her sleep, assuming the journey had taken its toll on her. I placed her tea on the side table, picked up a woollen throw, gently placed it over her lap, and then adjusted the thermostat in the hall. The heating had been left to tick over and it was a little chilly in the house.

Quietly, I reacquainted myself with the barn. I loved the feeling of returning there and comparing the vastness of the castle to the barn. Although not small, it felt tiny and cosy in comparison. I totally understood what Ronan had told me one time; he had bought his cottage because it was the opposite to his home. I agreed. The castle was wonderful but hard work. The barn was wonderful and easy. It was like having a little holiday home. I unpacked the picnic bag and chuckled again at the amount of food Maggie had packed. I carried her suitcase to one of the spare rooms, a lovely one at the back of the barn that overlooked the garden and the woods beyond. I checked the radiator, placed clean towels on the end of the bed, and made sure to have some nice toiletries in the bathroom. It felt nice to have a house guest.

I sat at the kitchen table and opened what post had been left for me. Usually it was junk mail that Pam didn't think was important to send up to Scotland. She was correct, of course, and I placed it all in the recycling bin.

It was quiet, except for the snuffles from Maggie. There was no clanking of water trying to force its way through furred up pipes. There was no creaking of wood as it shrank and expanded with heat and cold. There was no barking from dogs or revving of quad bikes. There was no chatter from the students as they sat in the office with their gloved hands around mugs of tea and discussed their day's activities. As much as I loved the quietness, I realised I didn't love it as much as I loved the hubbub created by the castle and its occupants. All of a sudden I was longing to return.

"Oh, pardon me," I heard and then a giggle. "I just passed wind," Maggie shouted.

"Well, I hadn't heard but now you've alerted me to the fact, I accept your pardon," I replied, laughing. I stood to put the kettle on as Maggie came into the kitchen.

"It's so quiet, I can't believe it," she said.

"I was thinking the same myself. I'm not sure I like it."

She smiled as she sat. "There's something to be said for having a conversation with a building hundreds of years old."

Maggie had it spot on. The building was communicating with its creaks and groans, reminding us of its age and condition and, I hoped, those complaints would lessen the more we got on top of its maintenance.

"Where's Ronan's cottage from here?" she asked, as I placed a mug of tea on the table.

"The other side of those woods. We've walked back and forth a couple of times, it's an hour on foot but only twenty minutes in the car. We'll drive there when you've had your tea."

8

"Oh my Lord, Oh my Lord," Maggie muttered.

I looked at her, my eyes wide with both amusement and astonishment. "Are you kidding me?" I asked, still reversing from the drive in my little Honda.

"Watch out, there's a…"

"There's a…what?" I asked, slamming my brakes on, not that I was going fast enough to warrant it.

"Nothing, I thought I saw something," she replied. She had both hands on the dashboard as if preparing for an almighty crash. It occurred to me that, other than when Ronan drove, she hadn't been a passenger.

"Sit back, will you! I can't see," I said, backing out into a completely empty lane, and one where I had full vision in both directions. "I think we'll get a train into London," I said, chuckling. That drive would just about finish her off.

I took it slowly, so as not to overly stress her, and made a point of chatting about the countryside; how wide the lane was compared to where we lived in Scotland, and how unlikely it was we would hit a deer/badger/fox/rabbit/cat or any other animal she cared to mention.

Blow me, if a bloody squirrel didn't just then decide to leg it across the road.

"You hit it!" Maggie said, her voice fearful.

"I didn't, it jumped into the hedge. Look behind, no squashed squirrel." I laughed. "Let me tell you about a squashed squirrel."

It had occurred to me just then I'd never told Maggie about Pat the Cat or the squirrel with its innards removed in Danny's old flat. It did the job. She let go of the dashboard and turned in her seat to face me. Her mouth was a perfect O and her eyes streamed with tears of laughter, particularly when I told her about calling Ronan to remove the dead body.

"When you're celebrating your wedding, we should remember that story. Maybe have dead Pat as guest of honour," she said, wiping her tears with the hankie she had stashed up the sleeve of her cardigan.

"I don't know that there'll be a wedding, Maggie. I think

everyone is jumping the gun a little. I'm not sure I want to do all that again."

She peered at me, cocked her head, and frowned. I wasn't sure whether that was a look of confusion or pity.

"What?" I asked.

"I thought you'd love to get married to Ronan, be Lady of the Manor," she replied softly.

"I love Ronan, I'm not sure a wedding is needed to clarify that. As for *Lady of the Manor...*" I laughed. Surely one had to be born into that title? It had a nice ring to it, of course. "Do others view Ronan as a Laird?"

"Of course, because he is, with a coat of arms as well! Verity's family is very old and very Scottish."

"Well, it's not on the cards as far as I'm aware."

Would I marry him? I thought. Of course, if he asked, I would, I guessed. But it wasn't something I was actively looking towards. I hoped we'd stay together for the rest of our lives, but maybe I wasn't considering Ronan's feelings in my thoughts on marriage. I shrugged my shoulders as if my internal dialogue had been spoken out loud and I was ending it.

Maggie settled back in the seat, not clinging on for dear life, while we drove at around twenty miles per hour past the green and pub. We left the village and entered the next. All chat about Ronan had ended, until we pulled up on the cottage drive.

"Oh, that's not good," Maggie said.

I sighed heavily as I noticed a smashed front window. The cottage hadn't been let; Ronan wanted to give it a good repaint but hadn't got around to it. It had stood empty for nearly a year and I'd nagged him repeatedly that he'd end up with squatters. It was being looked after by one of his builders, and, of course, Mrs. Sharpe, Ronan's closest neighbour, was back and forth regularly.

"I assume this must have happened recently," I said, flicking through the keys in my hand to find the right one.

"Should we call the police?" Maggie asked.

"I will, let's get in first."

"Won't we disturb evidence?"

"I highly doubt the police will even attend to be honest, but we need to register it, I guess."

I opened the front door that led straight into the room with the broken window. The room had minimal furniture dotted around and nothing seemed to be out of place. The pieces Ronan loved he'd brought to the barn, and what was left was a sofa with a chair and matching footstool, and an old coffee table that I loved and thought would be a great upcycle project, but Ronan scoffed at. I'm sure he said he had found it roadside himself.

I walked close to the window; it was obvious it had been broken from the outside as the glass was scattered over the floor. At least I didn't have to worry about anyone inside the house creeping up on me. I shuddered; I really needed to change my night-time reading. The ghost story on my bedside cabinet would have to be switched to a daytime read. What was missing, however, was any evidence of what had broken the window.

We wandered into the kitchen and it was only there that we realised the house had been occupied. There was a range of fast food wrappers on the kitchen table, a mug in the sink, a bin nearly overflowing, and a man's coat draped over a chair. I placed my finger to my lips to indicate to Maggie to stay quiet. I pulled my phone from my pocket and dialled for the police. I whispered that I believed we had an intruder who might still be in the cottage and was advised to leave immediately. I nodded, for me, that gave the police—who would have no idea I'd just nodded—the confirmation I'd adhere to their recommendation, when I knew I wouldn't. It was a *fingers crossed behind back* type of thing.

If I gave an affirmative action and didn't speak, it didn't count that I was lying, did it?

"Do you think someone is upstairs?" Maggie whispered.

"They could be. The mug in the sink is warm. Whoever put it there, did so recently. Let me get you in the car," I insisted.

"If you're staying, so am I!" she hissed. Maggie folded her

arms over her ample bosom but at less than five feet tall, she didn't really scare me.

I raised my eyebrows at her and glanced from her to the front door, using the jutting of my chin to signal that I meant business. She huffed and left.

I followed. "I'm not staying in the house, and neither are you. What if it's some drug addict or someone violent? Now, get in the car." I felt horrible speaking to her that way, but she was certainly too naïve, thinking it would be okay to investigate.

I didn't move the car, I didn't want any engine noise to disturb but I did lock the doors and call Ronan.

"I think there's someone in your cottage. I've called the police," I said when he answered.

"Huh?"

"There's someone in your cottage, they broke in, smashed a window. I think they might be upstairs, the police are on the way…Oh, they're here, I'll call you back."

I heard Ronan calling out to me as I disconnected the call and stepped out of the car. I met with a police officer that, I thought, looked just out of school. His squeaky voice didn't help or give me any confidence that he was up to challenging our intruder. I explained about the window, who I was, the warm mug, and the fact I thought someone might be upstairs. The officer dialled down his walkie-talkie and told me to wait outside. Ideally, he wanted me off the drive but that would mean him moving his car as well and the lane wasn't big enough for us both to stop in it. I left my phone on the car seat.

It was like an episode from an old comedy. The officer crept to the front door and gently opened it, I crept behind him. I had an idea I might be of use should he get attacked. He didn't look the kind to be able to defend himself even with his little truncheon. He started to walk up the stairs and halfway, I thought he might have realised I was behind him; he stopped. I stopped, but there was a creak of wood. We both turned around to see Maggie with a saucepan held aloft. I scrunched my eyes at her, frowning hard, she copied me. I didn't want to speak for fear of alerting our intruder, but I wanted to tell her to get back outside. It was too late, however. We heard footsteps, and the cheek of the intruder as he hummed to himself.

With the policeman frantically waving at us, and Maggie angrily gesturing back, we weren't getting anywhere. I prodded PC Plod in the back to encourage him up, and just as we reached the rather small landing, we heard the toilet flush and the bathroom door opened. A confused looking man stood there. He was wearing wool socks that came halfway up his shins and a T-shirt with another shirt over the top. He was naked between the hem of the shirt and the tops of his socks. Maggie screeched. I wanted to turn to cover her eyes but then remembered; she'd seen way more from the naked art group.

"What the fuck?" he said.

"What the fuck?" I replied, indignant. "What are you doing here?"

"Taking a shit!" he said.

Maggie lunged forward with her saucepan. It was only then that I noticed it was a milk pan and highly unlikely to cause any damage to our intruder, or be of any use as a weapon of defence.

"Ma'am, put down the saucepan," the officer said. He turned to the intruder. "Can I ask what you're doing here?"

"I've told you once, taking a shit," the intruder replied. At that point his phone starting to ring. "Am I allowed to answer that?" he asked.

"No!" I said.

"Yes," said the policeman.

I glared at the officer, thinking him rather accommodating to someone who had broken into my boyfriend's property. I clenched my jaw closed; it would do us no good if I were hauled off in handcuffs.

The intruder handed his mobile to the policeman and I watched as he replied 'yes' and 'no' to the caller. He handed the phone to me.

I frowned as I took it. "Hello?"

"Lizzie, that man standing there is one of my builders," Ronan said.

"Why is he using your bathroom?" I asked, not thinking about the broken window.

"I don't know, maybe he needed to piss! He's meant to be there. He broke the window by mistake, he's going to replace the glass today and then give the place a repaint. You cut me off before I could tell you."

"Oh."

"Yes, oh."

"He has no clothes on other than a T-shirt, shirt, and socks," I added.

"Well, maybe you want to let him get dressed and then he can explain what he's doing there, yes?"

I nodded. "I'll call you later."

I disconnected the call and then stood with my hands on my hips. "Well, you need to get some clothes on and then explain what you're doing here," I mimicked Ronan's words, trying not to look like a complete numpty and saving just a little face.

"What's he doing here?" Maggie asked.

"Fixing the place up," the intruder…builder said, as he walked into the bedroom. He returned a minute later with jeans on.

"Why didn't you have any clothes on?" Maggie asked, a question I wanted to ask but was too embarrassed to.

"Because I spilt paint down them so decided to change."

"You said you were…" She waved the saucepan in the air, pointing towards the bathroom.

"And I was. Is there a law against that?" He turned to the policeman.

"No, you carry on." He turned to me and said, "I'll be leaving now unless there's anything else you need me for?"

"No, and thank you. And…sorry for calling you. I honestly thought…well, I didn't know he would be here," I stammered through an apology and the 'police child' left.

The builder held his hand out to me, his smile made his ruddy cheeks plump up and his eyes sparkle.

I took it. "I'm so sorry. It's the menopause," I said, and pointed a finger to my head, twirling it around. "Doesn't let me think straight." I laughed, and thankfully, so did he.

"Yeah, my wife is having all the flushes at the moment. Now, Ronan wants this place painted, and I'm afraid a pane of glass broke when I slipped and knocked the paint over me. You'll actually find my boots and jeans outside the front door." All the while he spoke, he continued to shake my hand. I wondered if my carpal tunnel might flare up.

"This is Maggie," I said, introducing her while she still waved the saucepan.

"Maggie, Ronan has told me a lot about you. About you

both, it's a pleasure to meet you, even if the circumstances are somewhat strange."

"I've seen more willies than you've had hot dinners, laddie," Maggie said, reaching out to take his hand.

I rolled my eyes. "I wouldn't ask her to expand on that, if I were you," I said, for clarification.

It was decided that a cup of tea was in order, that also allowed Maggie to put the saucepan back where she'd found it.

Tony, as he'd introduced himself to be, told us he'd worked with Ronan for years as a self-employed contractor but was a stonemason by trade. "Not enough work in the South East for that anymore," he said, sadly.

I was sure there was plenty of stonework needed on the castle but I didn't mention it. If Ronan wanted that done, I was sure he'd ask Tony himself.

"Well, Tony, it was nice to meet you and I'm sorry it was in such…bizarre circumstances." I drained my tea and left the mug in the sink.

Maggie and I stood and Tony walked us back to the car. "You'll make sure to clean that bathroom, won't you?" Maggie added, wagging a finger at him.

"I hadn't really used the toilet, I just washed the paint from my hands and thighs," he said, laughing at us.

Maggie and I were still giggling as we drove up the lane and made our way to the doctor's.

"Are you sure you don't want me to drop you off at home first?" I asked, as I neared the surgery.

"It's okay, I'll wait in the car. That poor man must have thought we were nuts."

I nodded. "And Ronan! God, he's going to be laughing about that for weeks."

I was still laughing when I walked into reception.

The doctor's had inserted a new machine to check in. On the wall was a display screen and I had to select my sex, date of birth, and then confirm if it was me or not. Except, it wasn't. Instead, a gentleman called Trevor appeared on the screen but with my appointment time and my nurse. I knew men had mammograms of course, but there had to be an error. I queued for the woman on the desk. When it was my turn, she peered at me over her glasses, she reminded me of the bookings clerk from *Monster's Inc.*

"You can use the machine to book in," she said, pointing in the direction I'd just walked from.

"I did but it brought up the wrong name," I replied.

"It can't do that if you input the correct details."

"Well, even with the correct details it brought up a man and last time I looked, I was most certainly female."

She huffed. "Name?"

"Mine or the person in the machine?"

She peered at me over her half-specs. I gave her my name slowly, gritting my teeth.

She tapped angrily on her keyboard. "It says here that you've booked in," she said, not looking at me.

"I probably have, but the machine—"

"Why are you trying to book in twice?"

I thought I might have to ask to speak to another receptionist. I wasn't in the mood for *Miss Roz*. Instead I placed my palms on the counter and leaned slightly forward. "I booked in using the machine, so yes, I've booked in twice. Possibly under my name and then the gentleman's name that came up with my details. So, when that man comes here, you're going to assume he has been seen because he checked in but he hasn't."

She looked blankly at me. I didn't think I was making myself clear so decided it was best to just mention to the nurse. My name flashed up on the board and I left reception. I tapped on the nurse's door and was called through.

"Ah, Lizzie, if you don't mind removing your top and bra," Nurse Sarah said.

While I did as instructed, I explained about Trevor and hoped he had managed to get his appointment sorted. Sarah said she'd deal with it and joined me in a sigh when I got my bra off.

"No better feeling in the world, is there?" she said. I laughed.

I was positioned in front of the titty squish machine, my boobs were manhandled and I was ordered to stand absolutely still. The trouble was, I was that person who, when told to stand still, either falls or moves, or wobbles without realising. Worse than that, I needed to sneeze. I was gripping the two handles and hoping to hold the sneeze in. No chance, though. Just as the plate came down to squish the soft flesh, out came a sneeze and my boob slid off. Except, the plate was mechanical and still lowering. Instead of trapping boob, it caught on my nipple and I yelped.

"Oh shit," Sarah said, I wanted to chuckle but didn't dare open my mouth in case something worse than *shit* escaped.

I was set up again and although very uncomfortable, the image was taken, and I shifted into a different position.

When I had originally joined the surgery I was thrilled to learn it had a mammogram machine in situ. Often, the titty squish was in a van in a car park somewhere. Cold and miserable, with a line of women all with folded arms because they had removed their bra but left their tops on, and wanted to disguise erect nipples from the cold.

Ten minutes later and it was done. I was invited to take a seat once I was dressed.

"Now, menopause?" Sarah asked.

I raised my eyebrows. "Can you tell?"

"The fact you're rather hot and sweaty probably gives me an idea," she said, and laughed.

"Am I?" I was mortified she had been handling my sweaty breasts.

"No, you're in your fifties, Lizzie, there's no doubt. Are you feeling any effects?"

"Well, now that you ask…" I went on to tell that I was feeling a little dry *down below* during sex and the hot flushes. I also mentioned that I seemed to have trouble sleeping right through the night. Sarah nodded along and smiled.

"Obviously, I'm getting some hot flushes but they don't seem to last too long," I added.

"I think we could offer some oestrogen for now, in pessary form. It will improve your vaginal health."

"Vaginal health?"

Did I need to concentrate on vaginal health now, on top of mental health, boob health, heart health, and all other healths?

"Buzzword. Lubricate and loosen you up a little. You should be enjoying a sex life, not worrying if you're going to set the bed on fire from friction. Got to take care of the lady downstairs from now on," Sarah winked and I laughed. As nurses went, she was about the best I'd ever met. Always positive and jolly.

"I see you had your smear a year ago, how was that?" she asked, twitching her nose so her glasses slid up a little while reading from the computer screen.

"My doctor then said I had vaginal atrophy. She didn't really go into detail, to be honest."

"Well, I think this will do the trick for you. I'm going to give you enough for eight weeks, twice a week, and then we'll make another appointment to see how your symptoms are."

I thanked her and took the prescription. There was a dispensary on-site and I decided to queue instead of driving around to find a pharmacy. I knew I could have my medication delivered to me, but that wouldn't be practical considering I never knew where I was going to be at any given time.

The problem with queuing in the doctor's is the risk of infection from all the spluttering and coughing, and the risk of having to listen to old folk detailing all their ailments and treatments. I kept my gaze firmly on the wall above the dispensary counter to avoid any form of eye contact. It wasn't that I didn't want to chat, or hear what the old folk had to say, I simply wasn't open to discussing my own *vaginal health.*

"How did it go?" Maggie asked, as I placed a large white bag on her lap. She started to open it.

"That's my medication," I replied, wondering why she, Charlie, and Ronan for that matter, never had any sense of private space.

I pulled out of the car park into the main road as she opened the box and pulled out a strip of long blue *things*.

"What are they?" she asked.

I glanced over quickly. "Maggie! Put them back," I said, forcibly. "I have no idea," I added, glancing again at the blue stick. I thought I was getting a pessary. Whatever that was wasn't going to fit inside me. "Open one."

I knew I shouldn't have, but I was as curious as Maggie at the blue item. I should have waited until we were home. I should have told Maggie off for delving into something so personal. There was a lot I *should* have done…

Maggie held the blue applicator—as we discovered it was. She didn't just hold it, though, she pressed the plunger and a little white pill shot out the end, bounced off the windscreen, and hit me in the eye.

"Ouch!" I yelled, swerving.

"Look out!" Maggie shouted.

"I can't, you bloody blinded me!" I shouted back.

I pulled up in a passing point and rubbed at my eye. "You want to wash that out," Maggie said.

"No shit, Sherlock."

I grabbed a bottle of water and attempted to flush my eye by bowing my head and lining my eye up with the opening.

I tipped my head back but the neck of the bottle was wider than my eye socket and water ran down my cheek.

"Oh, for fuck's sake," I said.

"Is the pill in your eye?" Maggie asked.

"Of course not...I don't think."

I pulled down the sun visor and peered at my eye in the mirror, pulling my lids up and down to inspect. Satisfied I had no vaginal pill in my eye, I sat back.

Maggie giggled. "Where does that go, normally?" she asked, waving the blue applicator around.

"Where do you think?"

She looked at it and then dropped it into the paper bag as if it had already been used. "Eeww."

I laughed as she scrunched up her nose in disgust. "It's clean, for Christ's sake."

"It shoots out rather fast," she added.

"I'm sure it needs to." I took the box from her hand to read. "What if I cough? Will it shoot out just as fast?" I mumbled.

I had visions of little white pills flying around the bedroom, or the bathroom, wherever they were going to live.

"What if...?" I started. No, I wasn't going there with Maggie. In my mind, I was convulsing with laughter. *What if, during sex, the little white pill frothed up with the friction? It would be like I had an Alka Seltzer in me!*

"What's funny?" Maggie asked, laughing with me but having no idea why.

"Nothing, let's just get home. Then we need to find that pill. I don't want Max eating it."

It took a half hour of shaking out mats before the little white pill, and it was tiny, fell on the drive. I crushed it under my boot. Still chuckling, Maggie and I walked into the barn.

"What a bloody day," I said. "Put the kettle on while I put these away."

While Maggie walked to the kitchen, she called out, "Did you know you can buy crystal dildos?"

I stopped mid-stair and looked over the balustrade at her. She hadn't flinched in what she'd said.

"What?"

"Yes, crystals are good for you. I might buy you one. I saw them in a magazine."

"I do *not* want a crystal dildo!" I stomped up the rest of the stairs with her cackle following me. "Crystal dildo," I mumbled to myself, shaking my head as I placed my vaginal health pills on my bed.

I grabbed my phone and searched the Internet. I was that sucker who believed in everything, and I did know that crystals were very good for…I wasn't sure what, but I had a crystal lamp somewhere.

I changed into a vest top before I ventured back downstairs. Maggie was sitting at the table holding her mug with both hands, as if she needed the warmth.

"It's so hot in here," I said, walking to the doors to open them a fraction.

"It's bloody ten degrees, Lizzie. It's freezing out."

It was unlike Maggie to feel the cold, especially considering for years she'd lived in that huge house with hardly any heating or hot water.

"Are you sure?" I asked.

"Yes. You're the one who's hot, not the house. Sit and have your tea, I'm sure I read somewhere that tea was cooling. And we'll stop at a health food store to get some supplements."

I left the door firmly closed and joined her. "Yes, supplements," I mumbled, blowing on my tea to cool it.

I wasn't a believer in supplements but it wouldn't hurt to investigate.

9

———————

The following morning Maggie was up and dressed way earlier than necessary.

"I'm excited," she told me as she paced the kitchen. "I've never been to *The Big Smoke* before."

"Maggie, I don't know anyone who calls London that and I've lived there most of my life."

Neither Maggie nor Charlie had left the Inner Hebrides, let alone Mull, so they told me. The busiest places she'd ever been to were the town high street, the out of town industrial park, and a cattle market. I told her I thought she'd love London and its landmarks and I was excited to show her around my *home* town.

I drove to the international train station and we took the fast train into St. Pancras. Maggie walked out of the station with me and then stood still.

"Oh my Lord, look at all the people!" she said, her eyes wide in shock. I frowned at her.

It wasn't overly busy that time of the day, or rather, it wasn't as busy as it *could* be. We had no queue at the taxi rank, which was good seeing as it could usually take a good twenty minutes to get to the front in rush hour.

I gave the cab driver instructions to take us to Harrods. Maggie had told me she'd always wanted to get a Harrods tote, one of those green plastic ones.

Maggie sat the whole journey looking out the window and exclaiming constantly how busy London was, how grimy the streets were, and how sad the people looked. I couldn't disagree with her at all. I questioned, again, what on earth had attracted me to living in London for all those years?

"There's no colour, Lizzie," she said sadly, as she turned back in her seat to face forwards.

I hadn't noticed the bland greyness of the buildings— although the architecture was magnificent—until I spent time in Scotland. Every time I returned to London, I thought the same but felt disloyal to my place of birth.

Maggie visibly lit up when Harrods came into view. It was a stunning building and one that Joe often admired or referred to when he spoke about architecture.

We were deposited outside entrance three and the dapperly dressed doorman doffed his smart green cap and opened the heavy glass and brass door for us. The scent as we walked in—although I knew it was pumped around the store—reminded me of days gone by when I'd regularly shopped in the food courts or *nipped in* for a pair of shoes or repair of a broken nail, while tutting at all the tourists blocking my route.

I took Maggie's arm and escorted her through to the section that sold the branded items. I smiled at the cute teddy bears with the date embroidered on their feet. I'd collected those for a while. Maggie marvelled at the items on offer, until she picked up the green tote that she wanted and saw the price tag.

"Thirty-five pounds for a plastic bag!" Maggie exclaimed. I heard a couple of women beside her chuckle and saw them nod in agreement.

"I put that straight back," one said. Maggie and the woman then engaged in a short conversation on how the store could justify that kind of money on a plastic bag.

"Do you want to look for a cheaper one?" I asked.

"Oh no, I'm having this, and I'm leaving the price tag for all to see. You wait until Ann finds out I have a Harrods bag. She'll be the same colour with envy."

By the time she'd added a pen, a key ring with a plastic fob showing a picture of the famous Harrods Westie dog, a small notepad that she was sure she'd have a use for, and a mug, she'd spent close to one hundred pounds. I laughed as she grumbled while counting out her notes that had been screwed up in a ball in her pocket.

Maggie was as pleased with the carrier bag her precious items had been placed in, as she was with the items themselves.

We took a wander around and there was something very satisfying in seeing her amazement at the expensive items on sale; the designer concessions, and eventually, my favourite place, the food court.

"Can we get a coffee?" Maggie asked. I think she was overwhelmed with the general busyness of the place. Twice she had complained about being bumped into even if she was apologised to.

"Too busy for you?" I asked, as I led her up some metal stairs to a mezzanine floor that housed one of the many coffee shops.

"A little, it's not the high street, is it? But I do love it, Lizzie," she said, smiling at me as she took a seat.

I ordered our coffees and we sat and people watched.

"See that couple there? That's an affair," Maggie said, I followed her gaze.

"How can you tell that?" I asked.

"He keeps looking around and he's sitting on the edge of his seat, as if about to get up and run. I bet he's worried his wife might be local," she explained.

"Your observation skills are to be admired," I replied, staring at the couple. It might explain why the man picked up his mobile every thirty seconds, why he scanned the room constantly, and why his companion seemed to get stressed with him. However, when he ducked at the sight of a blonde woman carrying at least eight designer carrier bags, Maggie and I nodded at each other and then laughed.

I hadn't seen Maggie smile for so long and I wondered if both Ronan and I had been remiss in not offering to take her and Charlie down south a little more often. She was like a kid in a candy store and it was infectious. We absorbed all the sounds and smells of the food court; the bells ringing for various reasons and staff calling out to one another. It was like being in a market, albeit very upper class.

Once we had finished our coffee, I suggested we did a little sightseeing. By the time we got out I was having another hot flush, to the point I really needed to just sit. In the foyer were a couple of wheelchairs, I collapsed into one and started to shed layers.

"Are you okay, Ma'am?" I was asked by a rather attractive security guard. Maggie, initially, just stared at him, ignoring me.

I nodded, panting and fanning myself. Maggie decided to help and grabbed my jacket to waft. All she achieved by doing so was catching my chin with the zip and scratching me.

When I thought I had embarrassed myself enough, I grabbed my jacket from Maggie and ushered her outside.

"You look very red," Maggie said.

"Thanks. I felt faint in there, Mags. Is that normal for the menopause?"

"I had a hysterectomy so a forced menopause. I had the hot sweats but that was it." Maggie's voice was laced with concern.

I welcomed the chill in the air and just stood for a moment taking in deep, cold breaths. I coughed when the pollution hit my lungs, forgetting the level of carbon monoxide was probably twenty times higher than I had been used to recently.

We decided on a *hop-on-hop-off* bus tour. Maggie wasn't sure she was up for any kind of walking, and climbing in and out of taxis would cause her too much stress. I was thrilled with the idea of sitting up top and cooling down.

———

"Oh my Lord," Maggie stuttered. I was smiling as I listened to the narrator telling us all about St. Paul's Cathedral. I turned to her. "It's bloody freezing!" she said with a chatter of her teeth for emphasis.

"Maggie, how on earth are you cold? You're the one who moans that Ronan has gone all soft because he wears a jumper in the snow!" I laughed as I spoke.

She pulled her coat around her tighter and I handed her my scarf. "Do you want to go downstairs?" I asked.

"No, I'm loving it," she said, even though she visibly shook.

Although cold, there was no better way to see the sights than from the upstairs of an open top bus.

By the time we got to Buckingham Palace, Maggie had snapped so many pictures on her phone that she'd used up her meagre storage. I promised to find some postcards she could take back. We decided to get off the bus at that point and stand in front of the gates. She posed with her Harrods bag held to her chest while I took a photograph, making sure to have a Coldstream Guard in the background.

When she was done posing, we hopped into another taxi and made our way back to the station.

"I've had a wonderful day, thank you," Maggie said, a little sleepily, as we slowly made our way through London.

Once we'd boarded the train, I watched as she rested her head back and closed her eyes. We were only two stops, twenty minutes, away from home so she wasn't about to get any meaningful rest but I envied her. The past couple of weeks had seen me taking a *nanna nap*—as I liked to call them—each afternoon. I seemed to be so overly tired all the time. I guessed all the tossing and turning at night, the waking up with a hot sweat, wasn't allowing me to get any decent sleep.

I started to think about the llama and wondered what the farmer had decided to do with her. While I checked some messages on my phone, I remembered the name of the camping site and searched the Internet. It was slow going considering I only had limited mobile range and no Wi-Fi but eventually I found it. I saved the number, just in case we wanted to return and book a pitch...Or, more's the point, if I wanted to check in on Colleen and her fainting goat friends.

"Maggie, what do you think about getting a petting zoo to go alongside the campsite? Something to entertain the kids?" I said, as we pulled up on the driveway of the barn.

"I don't know. Won't that be too much work?" she asked as she, and what had become a permanent fixture to her chest, the Harrods bag, climbed from the car.

"A llama maybe. Don't they just eat grass?" My knowledge of llama husbandry was a little limited.

"We had some goats once, and a few sheep, to keep the grass down. Verity thought it was better for the environment than the old lawnmower. I think she changed her mind when she kept stepping in shit with her bare feet," Maggie said, and then laughed out loud.

I chuckled along with her. "Yes, I can imagine animal faeces would be a problem for the naked artists."

We were in the barn and sitting at the dining table with a nice hot cup of tea. Maggie had placed her Harrods carrier bag in the centre and was admiring that. I thought she might blow a gasket by the time she actually took the tote out.

"There was this llama, when we took Christine for her first run," I started, and then proceeded to tell Maggie about Colleen.

When I finished the story Maggie said, "I don't think Ronan will be too pleased with an escaping llama."

"No, but I feel sorry for her. I think the farmer is going to get rid of her."

"Well, I'm sure he'll find a good home for her." Maggie grabbed a packet of biscuits from the centre of the table, and, although tutting they were not home-made, she proceeded to devour three or four, or five!

"I might just ring the farmer and check she's okay. That won't be doing any harm, will it?" I said, picking up my mobile phone.

Maybe Maggie had her mouth stuffed full of Hobnobs and couldn't speak or had decided not to. She did, however, raise her eyebrows at me as high as they would go. It was the same look she often gave Ronan before she whacked him with the broom. Thankfully, she didn't have one to hand and by the way she was gripping the biscuit packet, I doubted she wanted to let go and use that as a missile.

"Oh, hello? Hello, can you hear me okay?" I said into a squeaking and static phone. "It's Lizzie, we helped to catch the llama. I just wondered if you'd found a nice home for her." I wasn't sure if he could hear me or not. I heard him say Ronan's name so I continued, "I'd hate for her to go somewhere horrible, or…" I didn't finish my sentence for fear of putting the idea into his head.

What if he put her to sleep? I thought. "I hope you can hear me. I just wanted to check whether she had gone or not."

"…home…trailer…" were the only two words I could understand from Sam.

"Yes, okay, well that would be good," I replied while shrugging my shoulders. I was that person that always answered with a positive, even though I had no idea what had just been said. I usually had to rely on facial expressions to see if I'd got it right, but since Sam was on a very disrupted line, I had no idea. The phone call ended.

"What did he say?" Maggie asked.

"I have no idea. I couldn't hear him; the line was terrible. I guess he'll do the right thing, he's a farmer after all," I said, convincing myself he'd want a nice home for his llama rather than a bullet.

That evening we met with Joe and Danny for dinner. Maggie proudly displayed her new Harrods tote and carried it on her arm, even though it only contained the new pad and pen and her purse. Still, Joe and Danny made a fuss of her and *cooed* over the bag as if it were the latest Louis Vuitton.

We had decided on a gourmet pub in Kent that Joe had taken a fancy to. It was also close to a property he said he had his eye on. I had often wondered if there was anything that would take Joe out of the city and maybe Danny could be it. In addition to having his mum locally, he could jump on the high-speed train and be in London in no time. If their relationship was to progress, so he told me, it was time for them to live together.

"I'm so pleased for you," I said, and I raised my glass in a toast. It was handy, because either one of them could look after the barn and Ronan's cottage a little easier.

"Did I tell you about the builder on the loo?" I asked Joe.

Maggie and I were like a tag team. As quick as I got one sentence out, she got the next. We laughed and Joe and Danny, in sync, kept turning their heads from one to the other of us.

"God, are they always like this?" Danny asked, watching us laugh at the story we'd just told.

"Yes, now, let me recap for Daniel here. You thought someone had broken in, but it turned out to be a naked builder from the waist down who was using the loo?"

I nodded and Maggie laughed further at the summing up!

"And then, Lizzie got a fanny pill and it pinged off the car windscreen," Maggie screeched and I stared open-mouthed at her in utter shock.

Joe held up his hand, Maggie continued to laugh.

"I got a prescription for *vaginal tablets...*" I whispered the word. "And Maggie decided to muck around with one."

"I'm really not sure I want to hear the rest of this," Danny said, still, even though it had been nearly a year, not comfortable with how open Joe and I were.

"Oh, you do," Maggie said.

"No, he doesn't," I replied.

When we had all calmed down, I realised it was the most I'd ever heard Maggie laugh. She was so animated. She continued to regale Joe and Danny with stories of Verity and the estate, Saggy Tits and Limp Dick, and even Manuel/Derek.

"She's fabulous, isn't she?" Danny said. We stood and watched as Joe helped Maggie into my car.

"Honestly, she's like a second mother to me. In fact, she probably cares more than mine ever could." I hadn't wanted to be critical of my own mum, but the time I spent with Maggie highlighted all that I seemed to have missed out on.

I gave Joe and Danny a hug and we went our separate ways. The following morning we were due to head back to Scotland.

10

"Lizzie!" Ronan's voice over the airwaves didn't sound happy. Unfortunately, the Wi-Fi on the train was intermittent and the signal just as bad. "Lizzie, a llama has turned up here; not only a llama but a fucking *goat* as well. Apparently, the llama is better behaved if she has company."

I pulled the mobile away from my ear and stared at it, as if by doing that some clarity would form. Maggie frowned and then mouthed some words, asking me if all was okay.

I shook my head. "A *what* has turned up?" I asked, even though I had heard quite clearly the first time.

"The llama? You know the one, the *escaping* llama? Colleen, your favourite author llama!"

"I honestly do *not* know what you're talking about. Obviously, I know *who* you're talking about but not *why* you have her," I said, and then cursed because we were about to enter a tunnel and I knew I was going to lose signal. "Let me call you when we're on the second train," I shouted, as if that would make the signal strong enough so he got the message.

"What's happened?" Maggie said, her voice was laced with concern.

I scrunched my brow and stared at the phone. "The llama and a goat have turned up at the estate."

She cocked her head to one side. "A llama and a...?" she enquired.

"Goat," I said.

"How?"

I shrugged. "I have no idea. I didn't ask the farmer to bring me the llama; there was no mention of that. In fact, I doubted he could hear what I was saying anymore than I could hear him. And how would he know where we lived?"

Maggie folded her lips inside her mouth and her eyes widened. She let out a little squeak of a chuckle.

"It's not funny, Mags, I think Ronan's going to go ballistic at this."

I was worried, even though at my age I shouldn't be. I was way beyond the *get a telling off* stage. If, somehow, I'd given the farmer the impression that I wanted the llama, then I'd call and tell him he was wrong and he'd have to collect her. Or I'd find her a home somewhere. It couldn't be that hard to rehome a llama, I was sure there were plenty of those *come-and-walk-the-llama-and-do-all–the-hard-work-while-we-charge-you* type companies around.

"Oh, for fuck's sake," I whispered, still staring at my phone. There was no point in calling Ronan back until I was sure I'd have a better signal.

Maggie puffed out her chest and pushed her shoulders back defiantly. "I'll tell him *I* wanted the llama."

I laughed. "Maggie, you've made yourself look like a Weeble."

"We used to have a box of those," she replied then reached over to take my hand. "Ronan can't deny you anything, you know that." She smiled kindly at me.

I wasn't sure what had gotten into me, I was worried and anxious about his reaction and I shouldn't have been. I felt a little tearful and hoped it was just a menopause symptom. The last thing I wanted to do was start crying in front of everyone on a packed commuter train.

Maggie and I made our way through St. Pancras and over to Kings Cross. We stocked up on coffee and croissants, even though Maggie was mortified at the price. I hadn't allowed her to pack a feast for the journey back, insisting that she ate the meal we had chosen as part of our first-class package. She had reluctantly agreed only because it was part of the ticket price.

I felt my heart flutter in my chest, as if it had missed a beat, and I took in a deep breath, confused.

"Are you okay?" Maggie asked as we took our seats. "You've gone a little pale,"

"Yes, I feel a little odd to be honest. I'm wondering if I should have had a check-up with my doctor before we left." I had begun to wonder if maybe it wasn't just the menopause, maybe there was something more.

It was another half hour before I called Ronan back. "Hi, we're on the train, all settled," I said, once he'd answered.

"Hey, did Maggie enjoy London?" Since he hadn't started immediately with the llama drama, I hoped it wasn't such a big deal.

I told him about our Harrods trip, the hop-on-hop-off-bus, and then Buckingham Palace. Ronan laughed as I described how Maggie hadn't let go of the bag and I was sure she had even slept with it.

"Now, what were you saying about the llama?" I asked.

"Sam turned up with not only the llama but a goat. He said he had a conversation with you and that you'd said you wanted them. I'm sorry, Lizzie, I jumped down your throat before I got to the bottom of it all. After I spoke to you, Sam confessed to not understanding what you were saying on the phone because his signal was poor. I thought he was trying to pull the wool over my eyes, and I told him so."

"Good. I did call him, just to ask about the llama and I

didn't speak to him much because I couldn't hear him. Maggie can verify that," I said, not sure why I felt the need to have a witness.

"It's all sorted now. How long before you get to the station?" Ronan asked. I gave him the full train details and we said our goodbyes.

"Was he okay about the llama?" Maggie asked.

I gave her a pretend smile. "I'm not sure. He said Sam had tried to dupe him but he's sorted it now." I shrugged my shoulders, not having a clue what he meant by that. I'd actually be sad to know he'd moved the llama on.

Maggie started giggling at the book she was reading, taking great joy in reading passages out loud. I was thankful that, once again, the carriage was pretty empty.

"Lizzie, listen to this bit," she said, excitedly.

Once she had shared the passage from her latest raunchy book I told her, "Oh, you'll have to let me borrow that one after you."

Maggie did love her naughty books, but every now and again she'd surprise me by reading a biography or true life crime novel.

———

I had enjoyed spending quality time alone with Maggie; we learned a lot more about each other as England, and then

Scotland, sped past outside the train window. I confessed my upset over my parents' lifestyle and although I loved them, I tended to avoid spending any real time with them. Maggie likened my hesitation to Ronan's, although for different reasons. She said something I hadn't really thought about.

"You two have way more in common that you think. Both of you had strange parents and an odd upbringing, its no wonder you're so close." She smiled softly at me.

Tears brimmed in my eyes and I brushed them away.

She leaned across the table and squeezed my arm. "I didn't mean to upset you," she said, concerned.

"You haven't, honestly, I'm sure it's this bloody menopause!" I dabbed at my eyes to make sure my mascara hadn't smudged. I seemed to be crying at the drop of a hat.

I fidgeted and, although I'd done the journey before, it felt excessively long. I was desperate to get off and be at home. I couldn't seem to concentrate on anything for too long. My book wasn't entertaining me, the music on my phone was boring, and staring out the window gave me a crick in my neck. Instead, I decided on reading the spam mail in my email's junk folder.

In addition to the usual sex swaps, money laundering, penis enlargement, and offers of loans, I came across one from my ex. I guessed, since he had never actually emailed me before, my provider had assumed his message was spam. I chuckled at the thought; I doubted he'd be happy to know he wasn't important enough in the provider's mind to enter my inbox. I laughed out loud.

"What's funny?" Maggie asked.

I explained the situation to her.

The *double entendre* went straight over her head and wasn't half as funny by the time I had to break it down and explain what I meant.

"What does he want, anyway?" she asked, waving away my explanation.

"He's married, he thought I might like to see a picture. I didn't click on the link in case it's not really him but a virus."

"How would the virus know he was married?" Maggie asked.

I hummed at her and nodded slowly. "Good point," I replied. "I'm still not opening it, I don't actually want to see."

"I thought you were over him?" Maggie asked, quietly.

I hadn't thought about him in a long time; months. Joe brought him up every now and again. Danny hated him and I loved him more for that fact. Danny also thought it terribly disloyal that Joe kept in contact and regularly told him so. According to Joe, it was business. The ex had bought his house through Joe and it seemed, because of their interaction, Joe had signed up a couple of neighbours to sell their mansions.

"I thought I was as well." I deleted the message without reading further. "Bloody menopause!" The over fifty-year-old affliction was going to get blamed for all sorts of emotional turmoil.

I read out a couple of emails. Maggie and I laughed that one day that poor Nigerian man was going to be found dead atop a mattress ten feet high; piles of dollars, millions in fact, would be stacked underneath. All the chap had wanted to do was share his wealth, and we all thought him a scammer. The laughter cheered me up, somewhat.

Before boredom or anxiety got the better of me, we were pulling into Oban station. I spotted Ronan before he saw us, and my smile widened. He was carrying a brightly coloured bouquet of blooms. He'd never presented me with flowers before and I laughed as he spotted us and held his arm out as if to present them to Maggie.

"We haven't eaten for days, and there's no clean underwear," he said, dramatically. Maggie swatted his arm away and he turned to me. "For you, the pain in my butt I've missed," he said, handing the fragrant bunch to me.

"What have you done?" I asked, suspiciously while sniffing the posy.

"It isn't what *I've* done, Lizzie. Now, those flowers weren't actually *bought* for you, but—"

"They're from my pots, aren't they?" Maggie said, snatching them from my hand.

"They are, and thanks to Lizzie, the fucking llama has eaten them all. Those are the only ones I managed to salvage," Ronan said, beaming a smile at me.

I took in a deep breath and pursed my lips while I thought of a response.

"The llama ate all my flowers?" Maggie asked in a small voice and I felt awful, not that it was my fault the llama had taken up residence in the estate.

"Not all of them, just some." Even Ronan hadn't realised how upset Maggie would be. "I'll get them all replaced."

"It's no bother. Let's go and meet the culprit, shall we?" she replied.

Maggie didn't stop talking the rest of the journey home. She told Ronan all about London as if he'd never visited and I lost count of the amount of times she showed him her tote. I decided I was going to buy her a nice leather one for her Christmas gift and have it sent up to us.

Max bounded up to the car when we pulled into the courtyard. I opened the door and he leapt in, walking mud all over my jeans. He licked my face and wagged his tail so hard he wiggled and fell back out the door. I laughed and climbed out, helping Maggie out from the back seat. She held her precious bag aloft so Max didn't scratch it when he jumped up at her.

"Down," Ronan said sternly, and Max immediately complied. It wasn't like him to jump up at people and I wondered what Charlie was allowing him to get away with.

Speak of the devil... "I'll get yer bags, eh?" Charlie said, as he appeared behind the vehicle.

Maggie stood with her Harrods tote still held to her chest. She smiled at him, gently shaking the bag.

He stared back at her. "What're ya daen, you daft coo?" he asked.

Maggie tutted. "Och, look at my new bag, ya bawbag." When Maggie was addressing Charlie her accent became stronger, but I certainly knew what *bawbag* meant and I laughed.

"It's as pretty as you," Charlie said, and then cackled showing an expanse of gum.

While Maggie and Charlie took our bags through to the kitchen, Ronan led me to one of the stables. We looked over the door to see the llama and a black goat munching on hay.

"Hello, Colleen," I said, reaching forward to stroke her nose. I was sure she remembered me when she curled up her top lip and then licked my hand. "We're going to have to do something with your hair," I added, with a laugh.

Ronan unbolted the door but kept his body shielding the gap. "Slide in but be careful, she'll make a run for it if she can."

I slithered between him and door; the feel of his body against mine was pleasurable and I guessed it was for him too as he gave me a wink.

"Don't move too fast, the goat will..." Before he could finish his sentence, the goat fell to the floor with his legs stiff in the air.

"Will he do that all the time?" I asked. It seemed a little silly and I wasn't sure he was going to be any good in our petting zoo, if we ended up with one.

"He's only supposed to do that when threatened. The vet's coming to look at them both tomorrow."

I turned to face Ronan. "I didn't think they were staying," I said.

"Yeah, well..." He laughed instead of finishing his sentence. I shook my head and smiled. He was a sucker for a sob story, as much as I was, and I bet old Sam had given him a great one.

"I missed you," Ronan said quietly.

"I've only been gone a couple of days."

"I know, but that's a couple of days too long."

I smiled lovingly at him. "I've got some funny things to tell you later. In the meantime, what will we do about these?" I asked pointing at our furry guests.

"I think we need a licence for a petting zoo, so for now, I guess they're pets," he said.

We left them munching away and headed for the house. "Max likes to leap over the door and sleep in with them," Ronan said, as we entered the kitchen.

"He'll teach that bloody thing to jump all right, you mark my words. You'll be out all hours looking for it," Charlie grumbled.

"I take it you don't like llamas, Charlie?" I asked.

"Good fo' nothing. Cannae eat 'em," he replied.

"I'm sure somewhere in the world they eat them," I said, with a chuckle. Not that I wanted anyone here to try, of course.

Maggie whipped up a cottage pie and while we sat and ate she regaled the lads, once again, with her story of *The Big Smoke*. She'd sigh as if it were a distant memory and one that she was never going to recreate. I shook my head and laughed.

"Now, let me tell you about Lizzie's fanny pill," she started.

Charlie spat out the mouthful of cottage pie he'd just taken and I winced at *that* rather than the statement. He started to cough and it was only when he turned a rather deep shade of red that we acted.

"I think he's choking," Maggie said.

"You don't say?" Ronan replied, while leaping from his chair and bashing Charlie on the back.

"You'll have to do that Himmler thing," Maggie said, her hands covered her mouth in panic.

"Himmler?" Ronan replied, still bashing poor Charlie in the back; he was now frantically waving his arms around.

"Squeeze his stomach," she shouted.

"No, don't squeeze his stomach. Out of the way," I said, pushing Ronan to one side.

I encouraged Charlie to sit up and I stood slightly to his side. I held one hand on his chest and used the heel of my hand to give five thumps between his shoulder blades. On the fifth a piece of half gummed carrot shot across the table. Charlie slumped forward raking in deep breaths.

Maggie rushed to the sink to fill a glass with water and Ronan knelt down beside him. "Are you okay, Charlie?" he asked gently, and I could see the worry lines crease around his eyes.

Charlie made a funny noise, a squeak of some sort, and then he laughed. I don't think I'd ever heard anyone laugh the way he did. It was somewhere between the noise a troop of monkeys would make to alert their friends of danger and a hyena. It was animal like and more worrying than the choking.

"If you had your bloody teeth in, that carrot wouldnae have got stuck," Maggie scolded, holding the offended piece of carrot between her fingertips and at arm's-length.

Charlie slumped back in his chair, he grabbed a rotten

hanky from his pocket and dabbed at his streaming eyes. "…fanny pill…" he whispered, his voice hoarse after his episode.

"See what you did?" I said, glaring at Maggie. She raised her eyebrows at me, like a nan might do to give that first warning to their grandchild. I took the warning and backed right the way down.

Charlie sipped at his water and his laughter was on the normal scale one would expect from a human being. Soon, Ronan and Maggie were laughing with him. I wasn't, of course. I had no desire for Charlie to know about my *fanny pills*.

Charlie pushed his chair back. "I think I'll take me sel' off to bed," he finally stated and then, mumbling to himself, he left the kitchen.

"Maggie!" I said, hissing her name through gritted teeth.

"Oh, I'm sorry, I thought it was funny. Do you think I should go and be with him?" Maggie replied.

"Yes. Who knows, he might keel over or something," Ronan told her, and I was sure it was just to clear the room so he could interrogate me.

Maggie left, then immediately returned. She grabbed the tote she'd left on the kitchen table and then scuttled off again. In the meantime, Ronan and I sat in silence.

"So," Ronan finally spoke.

"So?"

"Fanny pill?"

I started to giggle, and then told him about the box of pessaries and Maggie shooting one at the windscreen.

By the time I'd finished, Ronan was dabbing his eyes of the tears that were constantly falling. "God, only you, Lizzie, only you," was about all he managed to say.

"I do have to read the instructions because...well...something has just come to mind. I mean, if the pill is in there, we can't have..." I stumbled through my sentence but Ronan wasn't letting me off lightly.

"Have what, Lizzie?" he asked, staring at me. The corners of his mouth twitched.

"Well, if the pill is in there, you might, I don't know, fizz it up." I thought back to the Alka Seltzer.

"Fizz it up?" Ronan laughed again.

"Oh, I don't know. If the pill is there it has to dissolve and you..." I waved my hand towards his crotch. "Well, it might be your cock that gets the oestrogen and not me. And since it's meant to soften me up, lubricate me, I don't suppose you want that, do you?" I challenged.

"No, you're absolutely right." He chuckled while stacking the dishes in the washer.

I sighed and put the kettle on to boil and stared into space when I felt arms wrap around me.

Ronan rested his chin on my shoulder. "Are you okay?" he asked. I nodded and sniffed. "Are you crying?" he asked gently. I nodded again and he turned me in his arms.

"I don't know why I'm crying," I said, adding a laugh. "I'm hot and then I'm cold. I'm waking at night and peeing, and I'm getting hot flushes. I'm in the menopause and...well, it sort of surprised me, to be honest."

I wasn't sure why I felt surprised. I was the right age, my periods had slowed down, and it wasn't like I didn't know what the menopause was.

"How was the mammogram?" he asked, and I loved he was as concerned about my health as I was.

"Okay, I'll get the results in the post. The nurse said I could think about hormone replacement but I'm not sure, as it's maybe a little early. I'll see how I go with the *fanny pills* first." We both laughed and I made the tea.

"Let's head to bed and you can *show* me where this pill goes."

11

I woke with a start. Ronan snored softly beside me and I angled my wrist so my watch face caught the weak light filtering through a gap in the curtains. I couldn't determine the time, but I was sure it was a shout that had woken me so suddenly.

I sat up and waited to hear the noise again. Instead of the shout I could certainly here rushing footsteps coming from the living room, situated directly beneath the bedroom. I slid from the bed and pulled on my PJs while cursing at the cold. I didn't think I'd ever get used to the chill of the rooms in the mornings. My body still shivered even after I'd pulled on the fluffiest robe.

I gently pulled open the bedroom door and heard Maggie. Although I couldn't understand what she'd said, she sounded in a panic. I ran down the corridor and came to a skidding halt at the top of the stairs.

"What on earth?" I said.

Maggie looked up at me. "Did I wake you?" she said, and then smiled.

"Not necessarily *you*, Mags. But *she* did," I said, and then stared accusingly at the llama in the hallway.

"I thought I heard someone outside, so I opened the back door and in she bloody barged. I can't get her out," Maggie said.

Thankfully, the llama had her halter on but no amount of pulling by Maggie was making her move.

"I didn't want to wake anyone," Maggie said, as she slapped the llama on her arse. All she got in response was a snort and a batting of large eyelashes.

I descended the staircase slowly, in case the fluffy slippers I'd put on caused me to skid down. While Maggie stood and held the llama, I headed to the kitchen. I was pretty sure that she was a little on the greedy side and maybe food would be the bribe we needed to get her back out.

Since Maggie hadn't been there, the kitchen cupboards weren't full of nice sweet things like buns and biscuits. I did, however, find a couple of oatcakes. *Llamas should like oatcakes,* I decided. Colleen had other ideas. If I could have filmed the response when I waved one under her nose, it would have gone viral. Her eyes grew wide, her nose scrunched in disgust, and she snorted, yet again.

"Okay, so she doesn't like oatcakes, fussy mare. What else do we have out there?" Maggie asked. I retreated to the kitchen.

I grabbed a plastic tub that we kept Charlie's chocolate stash in. I opened the lid and pulled out a small party-sized Twix and unwrapped it. I had no idea if chocolate was a favourite for llamas or if it was even safe. I hoped the scent would be enough to get her out the front door, and then we could lead her back around the house. I didn't think it wise to get her back through the hall to the kitchen and out the back door.

Colleen had other ideas.

Before I could even get into the grand hall she must have smelled the chocolate and by the time she came into sight, she was dragging Maggie towards me. Maggie was trying to hold on and not slip and slide on the polished stone floor. I decided to wave the Twix in the air and scuttle backwards.

"Let her go, Mags," I said, it was clear Colleen was after the chocolate so I turned and ran.

I could hear her hoofs slapping on the stone floor and started to giggle. The problem was, I had a full bladder. I tried to clamp my thighs while still keeping up the pace required to stop Colleen getting too close. By the time I was out the kitchen door, penguin style, Colleen's head was reaching over my shoulder. I could feel her hot breath on my neck, and I thrust my arm forward to keep the chocolate as far away as possible.

I decided that getting her back in her stable was more important than my leaking bladder so I legged it. I had the stable door open and threw the chocolate in. I had startled the goat so much that it hadn't just fainted but full on passed out. Colleen rushed in and kicked the straw to find the chocolate. I shut and bolted not just the bottom door, but the top one as well. I guessed we'd need to put some bars above the bottom door to keep her in.

I rushed to the outside loo ignoring the fact the light didn't work, it probably hadn't been cleaned, and was full of spiders so I hovered having no intention of sitting.

By the time I got back into the kitchen, Maggie was sitting at the table having mopped the floor of shitty hoof prints, and had a pot of tea waiting for me.

She shook her head as I entered. "I can't believe we've just spent a half hour enticing a llama from the house," she said, as she poured us both a mug.

"I can't believe the bloody thing managed to get over the stable door in the first place. She must have been an Olympic hurdler in her previous life."

"Well, if she doesn't learn to stay in her own home, I imagine she'll be seeing her next life sooner than she thinks," Maggie replied.

I laughed as I took a biscuit from a plate wondered when Maggie'd had the time to bake them. They were still slightly warm.

"Have you been up a while?" I asked, concerned.

"A little, I couldn't sleep. It always takes me a little time to readjust when I've been away. And Charlie's snoring like a train," she replied.

It looked like she had scrubbed the kitchen, made the biscuits, and I bet if I uncovered that dish on the counter, I'd see bread proving.

"Is there anything I can do to help?" I asked.

"No, get away to bed now. You've got a busy day trying to keep that pest in her stable," she replied with a laugh.

I did so, but reluctantly.

————

I stretched and rolled to my side. Ronan must have got up earlier as the linen was cold to my touch. I breathed in the scent he left on his pillow and smiled. Although I hadn't much experience where love was concerned, the tightness in my chest when I thought of him, the fluttering in my stomach when he touched me, was overwhelming some-times. For the second time, I climbed from the bed and slid on my slippers. It was too cold for a shower or bath so I dressed quickly and headed downstairs. I could hear Ronan in the kitchen and his laugh at something Maggie had said made me smile.

"Good morning," I said, as I joined them at the table.

"I hear you had quite an eventful early hours of the morning," he said.

"We did. We discovered that Colleen is quite partial to chocolate, particularly Twix bars."

"She didnae have my Twix, did she?" Charlie asked, as he came in through the back door and removed his gloves and scarf.

"No, I'm not sure which bar it was," Maggie lied, while giving me a wink.

"She looks sheepish this morning," Ronan said.

"I bloody hope she does," I replied, sipping on my cup of tea. "We're going to have to put bars or something on the top of the stable door. She must have leapt over it. How's the goat? I thought it had died when she rushed in after I'd thrown the chocolate in." I chuckled at the thought.

"He was up and eating when I checked," Charlie said. Then added, "He'll be good for keeping the lawn down instead of me mowing it."

I didn't imagine a foot high goat could manage his way around the half-acre of grass in enough time to make it look mown. Although, it would be a nice thing to see.

Later that morning, Maggie and I went to visit the new members of the estate. She decided to call the goat Gerald; apparently it was his beard that made the name fit. I had to shake my head at her on that one. After about ten minutes in the stable, *Gerald* had grown confident enough to stretch his neck forward and sniff our hands. I got a lick, which Colleen seemed a little jealous about. She barged him out of the way and stood staring at me.

"Don't be a misery," I said, scratching behind her ear. "And I think you could do with a bath."

"What are we actually going to do with them?" Maggie asked.

"I have no idea." I laughed as I spoke. If the camping took off then I suspected Ronan would section off a small area for them to roam when the weather was nice. "I guess we should take them for a walk, though. They can't stay cooped up in here all day and night."

I wasn't sure how to take a goat for a walk and while Maggie and I headed back for coats and gloves, I googled goat walking. I was stunned to see that there were plenty of companies offering goat walking, as well as llama walking, as a recreational activity for a fee. Not one of the goats in the images, however, wore any kind of halter. Although I did see a picture of a goat with a collar. Before I could switch to Amazon for a sparkling collar, Charlie had fashioned one from baler twine. It wasn't as pretty, but it would do the job. He was also confident the goat would follow Colleen since they were friends, but it was decided that Maggie would lead Gerald just in case.

The four of us set off for a walk down to the artists' campsite.

For the first half an hour it was pleasant. Maggie and I

chatted about the estate, what filming was coming up, how to increase the events, and all the things left to do for the art exhibition. The animals walked nicely beside us. Occasionally, we'd stop and let them graze. Gerald was very much like a little mower, moving as he gulped down grass. Colleen was more refined with her munching. She took a mouthful and then raised her head to chew, gazing either at me or off into the distance wistfully. At one point I thought she might have spotted some deer, she came to an abrupt halt and held her head high, sniffing the air and looking to the trees.

I began to see why people would pay for the experience. There was a therapeutic quality about it. That was until we decided to turn and head for home.

"Oh my Lord," Maggie said. I had been looking into the woods beside me, and not paying attention to her. She scuttled past at a pace I was sure she wasn't used to, being dragged along by Gerald. He was off, and as tiny as he was, he was clearly a strong bugger, pulling her with him.

"Let go!" I shouted after her.

Colleen was hopping on the spot and I hoped she wasn't getting ready to take flight. I snatched on the lead rope to remind her I was in charge. She looked at me as if to question that.

"Let go, Maggie!" I shouted again. For some reason, she was still clinging on.

Maggie stumbled and I could see it happen as if in slow

motion. She fell face down in the mud with her arms outstretched. Only then did I see that she'd wrapped the lead rein around her wrist, which was probably why she couldn't let go of it.

All the time Maggie was on her feet, Gerald could pull her along, but not when she was lying like a dead weight on the ground. He came to a skidding halt and then turned to face her. I watched as he backed up slowly and then charged at her, lowering his head to butt her side.

"Gerald!" I scolded, trying not to startle Colleen as we made our way towards them carefully. I didn't want her stepping all over Maggie in her excitement.

"Mags, are you okay?" I asked, concern at her silence was evident in my voice.

She raised her head, and then laughed. "What a little bugger," she said, and laughed again.

I helped her to her feet all the while Gerald was headbutting her. "I think we'll have to get some pool noodles on his horns when they grow," I said.

"Pool what?" Maggie asked, while attempting to brush some of the wet mud from the front of her jeans.

"Never mind. Now, unwrap that lead rope from your hand. If he does that again, just let him go," I said.

Before we'd managed to take a step, he was off, as was Colleen. We let them go, thankful they at least headed back to the house. I began to think they were going to be way more trouble than we expected and Gerald was most probably the ringleader.

"He's a sod that one. All that fainting as if he was a dear little thing," Maggie said, shaking her head at the thought.

"I think you might be right."

By the time we cornered into the courtyard, Charlie was locking the stable top and bottom doors. "Get away from yous, did they?" he asked. I raised my eyebrows at him.

"No, thought we'd let them have a run, you silly old fool," Maggie answered before I could.

He chuckled and mumbled under his breath. I thought I heard the word, 'edible' but wasn't sure.

Maggie headed for the kitchen, no doubt to wash her hands and change her clothes and I walked to the office.

We had two desks in there and Ronan was sitting at one. "How was your walk?" he asked, as I slid off my wellies and placed my feet into the slippers I kept in there.

"Gerald, that's the goat, did a runner. Maggie fell over because she'd tied the leash around her wrist, in the end we decided to let them go and run on home. Which, thankfully, they did."

"Sounds fun," he answered, chuckling.

"We'll have to make a paddock for them. They were fine going out, it was the coming back they were keen to do the fastest."

I then had him howling when I told him that Gerald thought he was a tough goat and kept butting Maggie.

"Small man syndrome, that one," I said, before taking my seat at my desk. We had an art exhibition and sale to get finalised.

Ronan continued to chuckle as we got on with our work.

12

Maggie and Charlie were directing the marquee company on the erection of the huge tent to be placed on the front lawn. It had been decided that the art exhibition would be outdoors, despite the cold weather. Ronan was reluctant to have people *traipsing all over the house being nosy*, as he believed they would. The marquee was to feature a seating area at one end with a champagne bar, this had been insisted upon by Joe, and the other held easels with paintings and photographs. I had found a beautiful photograph of Verity, with clothes on, that I'd had blown up and was going to place on an easel at the entrance. I'd typed up a bio to place with it, so buyers could get to know the artist. Ronan had been reluctant on that as well at first. I had thought the photograph to be stunning. Verity was sitting on a bench; I wasn't sure where but the loch was in the background. It was sunny day and she held her hand above her eyes to shield them from the sunlight. She was laughing and there was something so joyous and youthful about the image. Her sheer dress allowed the sunlight to filter through, giving just an outline of her long legs and her bare feet nestled in the lush green grass.

Ronan had no idea who had taken the photograph and doubted it was his father, as he believed it to be post him leaving, but he also didn't remember her being so happy. I hadn't wanted to ask if Manuel/Derek could have taken it.

"Helloooo," Joe called out from the opening of the marquee. I looked over to see him with a holdall in one hand.

I walked over and gave him a hug, it had felt too long since I'd seen him last even though it was just a month.

"So this is the great lady?" he asked, staring at the image of Verity.

"It is," I replied.

"She was pretty, wonder how come Rich didn't inherit her looks?" Although he laughed I did detect a little bitter undertone.

"How's Danny?" I asked, wanting his attention back to his long-term partner, the man he had decided to marry but hadn't asked yet.

"He sends his apologies. He has a super job, Lizzie, and he just couldn't get the time off."

I was pleased to hear the pride in his voice. "Another time. Now, help me place all these frames."

Stacked on a table were framed paintings and photographs ready for display. I had a plan of how I wanted them shown. There was a natural flow to the images we had decided to sell that day. They started with Verity partially clothed; she was kneeling on the canvas and spreading the paint with her hands. Her bare back was to the camera and her blonde hair curled down to her waist. By the time the last one was up, she was naked and covered with paint. It wasn't until you stared for a minute or so that you could actually pick out her body. I loved the image and I would actually be sad to see it go, but it wasn't something that Ronan wanted to keep around. He believed the sale of the images was necessary for the next phase of the renovations and projects to keep the estate profitable. What I had done, though, was keep one of the professional photographs we'd had taken for the brochure. I had it framed and hidden, ready to present to him when the time was right. I believed there would be a right time, and that he would miss the images once sold.

Joe chatted as we arranged the marquee, laid out chairs and small bistro tables, as well as placing the heaters where we believed them to be the most effective. He told me about the houses he had on his books at that time and that he had employed a full-time assistant, as he couldn't keep up with the paperwork. He had to credit his recent influx of clients on my ex. Since he'd sold a house to Harry and Pete/Saucy

Sally, he'd signed up most of their neighbours, who hadn't realised the price of their property and wanted to cash in.

It was nice just to listen to him, to work side by side as we had for many years when I'd needed a job. I wasn't sure I'd told Joe how much I appreciated him back then.

I placed my arm around his shoulder. "You know, I miss you so much, so it's nice to have this time together, isn't it?" I said.

"Are you getting all sentimental on me? Are you sure it's sincere or is it the menopause talking?" he jested, and the skin around his eyes crinkled with mirth. I pulled my arm away and punched him instead.

Maggie cooked the most amazing dinner for us. Venison steaks, sautéed potatoes, buttered greens, and glazed carrots.

Charlie moaned about the posh veg and wondered where his *neeps* were. "And, what's with the flat chips?" he asked, waving a potato on his fork.

"Charlie, ever since I've been here, we haven't eaten *neeps*," I said, raising my eyebrows at him and he chuckled. "I wouldn't mind, though," I added, I quite liked turnips.

Ronan kept Joe entertained with stories of me adjusting to Scottish life, and as I sat back and watched the people I loved more than anything in the world, I smiled. Everyone got on so well, Maggie and Charlie had always been so welcoming to Joe. I often wondered if they missed the days when the house was full of guests.

"So, are we all ready for tomorrow?" Ronan asked. We were waiting on a pot of coffee.

"We are. Everyone has their lists, don't they?" I stared at each of the 'team' around the table, daring them to contradict me.

"Aye, we do," Charlie replied on their behalf.

The local hotels brimmed with guests attending our art exhibition and sale. The format had been decided right from the beginning. Guests would arrive to champagne and canapés, have time to check out the paintings, and mingle. An hour or so later, when he deemed it the right time, the auctioneer would bang his gavel on his podium to start the auction.

Each painting had a reserve and it was considerably higher than the sale we'd had in London. In one way, I could have kicked myself for letting that go ahead without checking other valuations, but to be fair to Joe, who introduced the gallery owner, neither of us knew any different. It was only when we were constantly contacted by buyers of Verity's art, and magazines wanting article material, that we decided to hold the auction ourselves.

After one more bottle of wine between us, we decided to head to bed.

"Did you tell Joe about the water in the bathroom?" Ronan asked, as I cleaned my teeth.

I nodded and spluttered a reply, "I told him to turn the shower on for a couple of minutes before he got in."

"I wonder if he'll remember." He chuckled.

"I'm sure we'll hear if he hasn't."

I was snuggled under the covers by the time Ronan finished in the bathroom and came to join me. Instead of lying beside me, he held himself over my body. He smiled wickedly and then lowered his head to kiss my chest. He kissed all the way down to my navel.

"Did you do your thing?" he mumbled into my skin.

"My thing?"

"Yes, the tablet thing."

"Oh, no, not tonight."

"Good."

"Why?" I asked, as he lowered his head further.

"I don't want a mouthful of your hooha happy pill."

"My wha...?" I started to laugh so hard tears leaked from my eyes.

"I'm about to forage in your lady garden, I don't need any more hormones," he said, teasing me.

"Lady..." I laughed even harder.

Hooha happy pill was the perfect description of the pessary, and I decided I needed to tell the nurse we'd renamed it when I saw her next.

———

I woke to see Ronan lying on his side and smiling at me. I smiled back. Before either of us could speak, we heard a scream.

"I guess he forgot," I said, assuming Joe had stepped under the cold shower.

There was no point in rushing to shower until Joe had finished or we'd hear the rattle of the pipes to indicate the plumbing was protesting. It was the next thing on the never-ending list to upgrade and we were hoping that the profit from the art sale would cover it. The quote had made us all wince!

Half an hour later, we were showered and dressed in our smart outfits and ready for the snobs and well-to-do, most of whom Joe had invited.

"Jesus, Lizzie! Do you have any of those nipple things?" Joe said as he came into the kitchen.

"What are you wearing? And *what* nipple things?"

Joe had decided on *arty* as he called it. He looked more like an extra from the film, *Austin Powers*.

"Those nipple covers," Joe explained while also holding his

palms over his. "I have a serious case of cold nips and don't get me started on what's going on below!"

"He has what?" Charlie asked, cupping his palm around his ear, although I had no idea why. He wasn't hard of hearing.

"He has cold nips and frosty bits," Maggie translated.

"Frosty bits?" Charlie asked. Maggie pointed to Joe's crotch. "Ye want to get yersel' some wee panty hose," Charlie said; or at least I though so. We all stared at him.

Charlie reached under the waistband of his faded green corduroy trousers, his best clothes he'd told us, to pull up a pair of black tights.

"What on earth…?" I started.

"Naethin' warmer than my Mag's tights." He chortled as he spoke.

"Jesus," Joe exclaimed. "Now, do you have those nipple things? Or those new bras without straps, the ones you'd tape under saggy tits and hoist them up?"

I stared at him wondering at what point he'd lost his mind, or if the cold dousing that morning affected his rationale.

"Since I have no idea what you're talking about, let's assume I have neither and why not just put on a vest."

"I'd look ridiculous in a vest," he stated. It was on the tip of my tongue to tell him he did anyway; the vest was likely to be an improvement such was the sheerness of his flouncy shirt.

We settled down to a breakfast of tea and pancakes.

Once breakfast was over, Maggie started to lay out the canapés she had already made.

"We need to move those *can-apes* to the marquee at some point," she said. I didn't want to correct her mispronunciation.

There was a small marquee attached to the main one that would act as a kitchen. The previous day, we'd stocked it with glasses and champagne, soft drinks, and beer from a local brewery. They had sent someone to set up a polypin and ensure it was ready to be poured into their branded glasses.

Carly, from the hairdresser, and a couple of her friends were going to act as waitresses. She had been a dream to work with and I was sure, if hairdressing didn't turn out to be her thing, we'd have her working with us. She told her friends what to wear, including the colour of tights, flat shoes, and when to be here. She had them practicing walking with a tray of empty glasses at one point. Maggie and I were most impressed. It seemed a lot of the local girls would pick up jobs at events for some pocket money.

Once we were ready, Maggie and I covered all the dishes with tin foil and transported them to the marquee. Carly and her friends were smoothing cloths over the bistro tables and Joe was organising the cloakroom area. A wooden desk had been placed to create a barrier and another of Carly's friends, Sally, was stationed behind with a book of raffle tickets, a couple of clothes rails and cedar wood hangers, supplied by Joe, of course. It wasn't the done thing to have good old metal hangers.

The auctioneer arrived and was met by Ronan; at that point I started to get butterflies in my stomach. I really wanted the sale to do well, the money was needed, but more importantly, I believed in Verity's artwork. I'd grown to love it and I just wished Ronan would appreciate it more. I had a strange notion that, should it sell well, it would validate it.

Some of the first to arrive were the art group. Thankfully, all were dressed and I hadn't recognised the tree hugger until Maggie pointed her out. She was a beautiful girl, very *soulful,* if that could be a description. She had a sad aura surrounding her to the point that I couldn't tear my eyes away and my heart lurched in my chest. I was only broken away from that thought by Maggie tugging on my arm.

"The Viscountess of whatever one square mile she bought has arrived," she said.

I blinked but didn't ask for clarification. Just the tone of Maggie's voice showed her disdain.

An elderly lady, escorted by a younger one, *wafted* into the marquee. She paused by the cloakroom, no doubt surprised to be asked if she'd like to check something in. We watched as she unwrapped a moth-eaten fox fur scarf from her neck; the thing still had the head and tail and I was itching to call for Joe to see if that had been one of Danny's creations. It was ghastly! Even from where we stood, we could smell it and poor Sally, who held it just with her fingertips had wrinkled her nose. An apologetic smile from Viscountess whoever's assistant was most welcomed by Sally.

"Ah, Margaret," the woman said as she glided towards us. "Who is this?" she asked, peering over half-moon glasses and waving an empty cigarette holder at me.

"The new lady of the manor. Lizzie, may I introduce one of your neighbours, Mrs. Hatheshaw," Maggie said in the poshest accent and accompanied by a wink.

I held out my hand for a shake and it was limply accepted.

"Perhaps we could take a seat and a cup of tea, Granny?" the young girl said. We had thought her an assistant but by the adoring look she received, she was well-loved.

"I'll bring some over. Would you prefer Earl Grey?" I asked. On her nod, I left for the kitchen area.

As I prepared a tray I could hear more voices. I peered through a small gap to see the parking area beginning to fill. I worried we'd run out of parking places but was so pleased the event was going to be well attended. I heard Joe laughing and greeting some of his friends and acquaintances, and I swelled when I heard him address one as a *prince*.

By the time I'd taken the tray with the finest crockery to the Viscountess, Joe was introducing Ronan to some people. He looked my way and gave me a wink, Joe was in his element. Ronan looked a little uncomfortable and I doubted that had anything to do with the company, more the images of his naked mother on display.

"Petal, it's so lovely that you could join us," I said. She and Eric were at another table and sipping on champagne.

"Wouldn't miss it for the world, my dear. Although, I feel very overdressed," she laughed and the twinkle in her eye suggested she was playing with me. "We can't wait to see what happens to Verity's paintings, can we, ERIC?" She shouted his name and a few people turned to look. He smiled and nodded.

For the next hour, people mingled, chatted, laughed, drank, and studied the artwork. There were a lot of hands cupping chins and tilted heads from the *arty* types, and then some that completely ignored the pieces, showing no interest at all, and I wondered if they were just along for a free drink.

Carly was marvellous, she and her friends circled the room constantly with nibbles or to refresh glasses.

"I've mixed some Prosecco in with the champagne, keep it going a little longer," she whispered as she passed me.

I chuckled at her ingenuity. "Clever girl," I replied, giving her a wink.

It seemed to me that the day sped by and soon it was time for the auction. Ronan and I were thrilled when we'd met the auctioneer at a local auction house; he was just the right person to *power up* the buyers as he called it. He spoke of Verity and her life, how her art became her desperate escape from her evil American husband. We weren't sure where he had come up with the story, but it had meant a couple of tissues were raised to eyes and if the prices went up, we weren't about to correct him.

He started with the first painting and then it was bedlam. I'd never heard someone speak so fast. There were obvious bidders and then ones so subtle I had no idea. I clamped my arms to my side for fear of waving accidentally and adding to the bids, not that I thought it would be taken seriously, of course.

Joe came to my side as the bids for that one painting—one not as magnificent as the rest—reached fifty thousand pounds.

"Bloody hell, Lizzie," he said quietly.

"I know! I can't believe this. I have no idea where Ronan is," I said, scanning the room. I found him beside the auctioneer, tucked just behind his platform and with his head bowed. It was too hard to pick out any expression on his face.

Maggie sidled up to us. 'This is blooming amazing," she said.

Before I could reply, Sally approached us. "The goat has the fox," she said in a staccato rhythm but with a deadpan expression. She reminded me of a character from an old TV show that I'd loved, something to do with the French Resistance but played by English actors with terrible fake accents.

Maggie's eyebrows shot up her forehead so fast I thought they might come off. It was then I noticed that her hair never moved. Before I could study some more, her mouth formed a perfect O.

"Is that code for something?" Joe asked, bringing both Maggie and I back to the current situation.

"Yes, it's code for you're in charge," I said, thrusting a glass of champagne at him. "And don't tell Ronan!"

Maggie and I subtly—well I was subtle, she power-walked with her arms fixed to her sides—left the marquee. Once clear of the door, we ran around the side and into the courtyard.

"Where's Charlie?" I asked to no one in particular.

"He's sorting the cars," Sally answered, having run after us. "What do we do?"

"Did you see where the goat went?" I asked.

"No. I turned around, saw a goat, it took one look at me, jumped up…those things can really jump high, can't they? Anyway, it jumped up onto the table and grabbed the fox. I tried, but I didn't get to it in time," Sally explained. Her voice cracked and she wrung her hands in worry.

"It's okay. One taste and I'm sure he dropped it some-where," I said and then called out for him.

Colleen poked her nose through the newly installed bars on her stall. Gerald had been in the newly fenced-off paddock, attempting to get the grass down. Clearly, the paddock wasn't Gerald proof.

"We'll not worry about Gerald, let's find the fox," Maggie said. We retraced our steps. It was only when we got back to the marquee that I thought I heard a figure announced by the auctioneer that was over one hundred thousand pounds.

Maggie did the eyebrow and O thing again, only this time I joined her. We had no time to think about what was going on, we needed to find the fox.

"Got it, I think," came a voice from behind us. We turned and saw Charlie grabbing Gerald by his horns as if he was wrestling a bull. Gerald held the fox tightly in his mouth.

Maggie tugged at the fox but the little shit wasn't letting go. I stuck my fingers in the side of his mouth and that did the trick. As he opened it, Maggie pulled but ended up landing on her backside, and Charlie let go of the goat. He made a run for it and we helped Maggie to her feet. She held a sodden and muddy fox fur in her hand.

"It stinks," Charlie said contorting his face.

I rolled my eyes. "We know, now we have to clean it," I said.

Maggie ran to the kitchen and I followed. She grabbed a cloth and sponged off the mud. She then spritzed it with Febreze and instructed me to get a hairdryer. The fox was dry and slightly better smelling in no time, but its pelt had gone from dull and flat to shiny and fluffy. There was no way the Viscountess wouldn't know something had happened to it.

"Can't worry about it now," I said. "We need to get back."

We rushed back to the marquee in time for Sally to rehang the fox and to see the last painting sell. I hadn't realised they would go so quickly and we'd missed most of the auction action. A large round of applause followed and the Prince nodded and accepted congratulations. He walked over to Ronan and shook his hand. They spoke and I saw Ronan smile. The Prince then shook hands with the auctioneer. Yet again, as he walked back to the entrance of the marquee he was stopped many times.

"What happened?" I asked, grabbing Joe by the arm.

"He bought them all," he said, excitedly.

"No way! How wonderful," I replied.

"And he paid three quarters of a million pounds for them."

I stood stunned and covered my mouth with my hands. The Prince had bought what I believed was a series of six paintings. Each one showed Verity in a different state of undress and position. I had no idea someone would think them worthy of *that* amount. More importantly, there were another ten in the house!

"He asked if you had more. I think Ronan intends to speak with him tomorrow," Joe added.

"I'm blown away, Joe. Thank you so much, this wouldn't

have been possible if it hadn't been for you," I said. It had been Joe's contacts that had made up most of the guest list.

It seemed that the unsuccessful bidders were also badgering Ronan; I could see him point to me. I guessed he wasn't sure what to say so I walked over to him.

"Good afternoon, gentlemen," I said. I wasn't introduced simply because Ronan had no time.

"I understand there are other paintings?" one asked.

"Yes, we will have another auction soon. We also have photographs that Verity took, those will be for sale. If you'd like to leave Joe all your contact details, we can keep you informed," I said, thankful Joe had placed himself beside me. He accepted business cards and promises were made.

Ronan looked as shell-shocked as I felt. He spoke to people and when the last of the guests and the auctioneer had left, he slumped into a chair. "What the fuck just happened?" he said, accepting a glass of champagne from Carly.

"I think your mum just paid for the plumbing with change," I said, sitting beside him.

He laughed and shook his head. Joe, Maggie, and Charlie pulled up chairs; Carly and the girls came to join us. We celebrated with more champagne and laughed. None of us could have predicted what a great event it was.

"Now, food for us all," Maggie said.

"I should get going really," Sally said.

"And me," Carly added.

"Not before you've been compensated, come with me," Maggie said. She had prepared a hamper for all the girls that included a bottle of bubbly, chocolates, cakes, and an envelope with money for their time from Ronan.

I guessed the girls were going to head on to somewhere trendier than a marquee on a lawn.

I laughed as Joe topped up our glasses. "Who would've thought, a year ago we were sitting in a bar sipping on champagne, and now this," he said.

I raised my glass to him. "If you hadn't wanted to get into Rich's pants so much, I'd have never met Ronan," I added.

"Am I glad for that...not the bit about Rich's pants, of course," Ronan said.

We were too exhausted to clear the marquee that afternoon. Instead, we headed back into the house, showered, and changed into comfortable clothing and sat with more wine and coffee in the living room after Charlie had lit a fire. I had offered to help Maggie prepare the evening meal, but she wasn't having any of it. She hummed and sang to herself, smiled, and laughed at memories of the day. I stood just outside the door and listened. As the months had moved on, she had become more animated and I was sure it was the changes in the house. It, and everyone in it, was coming alive again.

"So, do we know what happens now?" I asked, curling my socked feet under me on the sofa.

"The money will get transferred to the auctioneer, he'll take his fee and then forward the balance to us," Ronan said.

"Why not just pay you?" Joe asked.

"It has something to do with art royalties, he did explain. If your friend sells those paintings we get a royalty, but only if it's done through a proper auction company," Ronan explained as simply as he could.

We had discovered through Dave, the original gallery owner, that if we used an auctioneer rather than sell to an individual ourselves, there was the opportunity of royalty, depending on the buyer. We also thought it more professional to step aside and let the auctioneer do all the hard work. Of course, there would be his fee to consider but they had forgone the usual percentage because we were hosting the event.

Joe sifted through the business cards he had. "We could make more on the next sale," he said, handing the cards to me.

"I think I might need a little break before we organise another," Ronan replied. I wondered if the memories of his mother and her art had overshadowed the excitement now it was over.

"Let's have dinner, shall we?" Maggie said, popping her head through the open door.

In the middle of the table was a bowl of neeps and tatties and I laughed. I expected Charlie to pull the bowl towards him and spoon directly from it. There was a lovely leg of lamb from the local butcher and yet more fresh vegetables. As we helped ourselves, Ronan poured more wine. I guessed the steady drinking over the day and the copious amounts of canapés I'd eaten had kept me fairly sober. However, a wave of tiredness washed over me after my first glass of red.

"Did anyone find Gerald?" I asked, finally remembering the errant goat.

"Who is Gerald?" Joe asked.

"The goat," Maggie answered. "And no, but I highly doubt he'll go too far. It will be a cold night, I'm sure he'll be snuggled in the kennels in the morning."

"What was the thing with the goat and the fox?" Joe asked, Ronan raised his eyebrows in surprise and I remembered, he didn't know.

Maggie was the best to tell the story, she embellished and waved her arms for effect. By the time she'd finished we were crying with laughter. We all wondered if the Viscountess even noticed she was returning home with a cleaned fox instead of the stinking old one she arrived with.

"Who is she, anyway?" Joe asked, and it was a question I'd been itching to ask.

"Her husband used to be a large landowner north of here.

He died and sadly, like most of these estates, the taxmen wanted their share of a dilapidated property not worth much. She sold up and moved into town. She owns one of those town houses at the end of the high street," Ronan said.

"Dotes on her granddaughter, she does," Maggie added.

"Also, while I remember. The tree hugger? She looked super sad," I said. Joe looked sharply at me with a question in his eyes. I waved my hand at him. "I'll tell you about her tomorrow," I added.

"I don't think we've ever had a conversation with her. Petal looks after her mostly." Maggie explained that she believed the girl, Hailey, lived with them but wasn't sure why.

I stretched my arms above my head and yawned, trying hard not to have my mouth be a gaping hole in the middle of my face; instead I pursed my lips together and my open jaw stretched my face until it looked alien.

"I think I need to head to bed," I said. It was early but it had been a long day.

While I helped stack the dishwasher, Joe and Ronan headed to the living room with yet another bottle of wine. Maggie and Charlie left, and I decided I'd take a cup of tea up with me.

I had been asleep for hours, I believed, when I felt the bed dip and a cold body slid up alongside mine. I mumbled my complaint and heard Ronan chuckle before I must have drifted off again. I had a wonderful dream of goats and llamas running amok while a procession of models walked the catwalk on our lawn. I thought I might have even laughed out loud and was nudged by Ronan to quieten down. Or, I had started to snore, which I suspected more was more likely since I woke with a sore throat each morning.

As one does, I tried to convince myself to remember the dream as it was a pretty good idea, not the llamas and goats, but the fashion show on the lawn. I guessed, to have that idea I must have partially woken but was pleased when it all went blank and the next time I opened my eyes, it was morning. I was also happy to remember the dream and before I even glanced at Ronan, I reached for my phone and wrote in my notes:

Fashion show on lawn with Pimms and things

"Are you ready for today?" Ronan asked. I turned over to see him smiling at me.

"I am, although I'm nervous. You will come and rescue us if it all goes wrong, won't you?"

He laughed. "Of course I will."

That day Joe and I were taking Christine for a very short journey. It would be the first time I'd towed her out on the road, although I'd had a couple of practice journeys. I struggled with the reversing element of towing a caravan and intended to drive forwards only, as much as possible. Joe would be of no help whatsoever, but I wasn't going to spend time with him again for the next few months so I wanted to grab this alone time opportunity.

I snuggled into Ronan's side, wanting to grab as much warmth from him as possible before I slid from under the covers.

"Thank fuck we can get the plumbing sorted," I said, laughing as Ronan shivered when the duvet shifted to allow cold air in.

"I'm going to start getting quotes in today," he replied.

Reluctantly, we left the bed and rushed around to shower and dress. We were in the kitchen loading up provisions for the trip before Joe finally surfaced.

"Does my bedroom get heating before any one else's considering I brought the Prince?" he asked, wrapping his arms around himself and making his way to the Aga.

Ronan laughed. "You think *that's* cold, wait until you've spent a night in Christine."

He turned his attention to me. "Yes, I'm beginning to question my sanity on that one. Are you sure you can tow it, Lizzie?"

"You can always cancel but it's the last chance. She's going on the campsite forever after this. We owe it to her to give her one last trip out," I said, waving my hands around to add to the seriousness of my statement.

"I've packed plenty of food," Maggie said, as she walked into the kitchen. "It's all by the back door."

"Oh, thank you. I was about to raid the cupboards," I said.

Joe popped his head around the corner to look at the picnic. "Jesus, Maggie, we'll only be gone overnight," he said.

"You never know. You might get...hungry, or something," she said, and I just knew she was going to say 'stuck.'

The weather forecast had predicted snow later in the week and, if that came earlier, it would have scuppered our plans. It was the reason we were only staying away for one night, *and* the reason to stay local...ish. I'd found a lovely loch just ten miles away that allowed for camping. The trip was a two-fold one. I wanted to check out the closest competition and I genuinely wanted a little alone time with my best friend, Joe. We hadn't done that for over a year and I missed it.

"Right, are you ready?" I asked, gathering a small bag with extra clothes, nightclothes fit for Wee Willy Whatever his name was, and phone chargers.

The campsite was 'technically' closed, according to the owner, but we could have electric hook-up if we wanted. I wasn't convinced it would be available and wasn't overly concerned. The small stove ran on gas, as did the little heater. As long as we could boil the kettle and charge the phones in case of emergencies, we were going to be fine... Or so I convinced myself.

13

"Okay, I'm not going to reverse anywhere so you don't need to remind me of that," I said, as Ronan leaned in the wound down Land Rover window to explain how to reverse a caravan.

Joe was in the passenger seat with a throw around his legs, even though the vehicle had heating on full blast, Max was curled up on the back seat already snoring, and I was shivering in the driver's seat. I'd driven the Land Rover around the estate and even into town a few times, I was comfortable with its cranky gears and dodgy handbrake, in fact, I loved the vehicle as much as Maggie loved the old one.

"I'll call as soon as we arrive. I'm going take pictures of their set up and email them back to you, if I have signal," I said.

Ronan laughed and I wasn't sure if his mirth related to the

fact I thought we'd have signal, or that I was taking this *checking out the competition* seriously. With a brief kiss, he stepped back and I wound the window up. Then we were off. It was with a jerk and a crunch and the grind of metal on something that I ignored, however. Ronan wasn't running after us, he wasn't waving his arms, so I guessed we had started off without leaving Christine behind.

"Can you turn the heater up?" Joe asked.

"It's on full blast. You need to toughen up," I said, laughing at the same words Maggie often used to both Ronan and me.

"Jesus, I don't think I'll ever get used to this level of cold and it hasn't started snowing yet!"

"I can't wait for the snow to come. It's so beautiful, Joe. I can't tell you how refreshing it is to go for a walk. It's so silent, no birds, the only sound are deer—"

"And poachers," he cut me off, reminding me of the last winter I'd spent wandering the woods on my own.

"Yes, well, I take one of the guns if I'm on my own now," I said, sitting tall and showing how unafraid I was pretending to be.

Joe laughed. "Do you know how to use a shotgun?"

"Of course I do. Ronan taught me." I didn't confess to being thrown backwards on a couple of occasions because I hadn't sat the stock into my shoulder well enough. I also didn't confess that each time I fired, I jumped or squealed at the sound as cartridges flew in random directions. But, I felt safe with it slung over my shoulder, even if empty.

"We should have brought one in case of bears," he said, deadly serious I thought.

I frowned. "Bears? We don't have bears," I said, and then questioned myself. *Do we?*

"Or…what are those things called? One got Max."

"Wildcats? They won't come near us and they're not even meant to be on Mull," I said, although it was a contradiction because one had most certainly come far enough to attack my dog as a puppy.

At the sound of his name, Max yawned himself awake and stood with his front paws on the centre armrest. He licked the side of my face before continuing to watch through the windscreen but he startled me by barking when he saw some sheep.

"Max! Sit down," I said, panicking that I might have swerved and wobbled the towing caravan.

"He's a sheepdog, he's meant to do that. Aren't you fella?" Joe said, reaching behind to stroke the chastised dog.

"Not while I'm concentrating, he can't."

We drove along a road that cut around the base of a mountain. I pointed out places of interest, recited things that Ronan had told me. Joe was disbelieving that the field to one side was where great battles between clans had taken place and was therefore seen as sacred ground and couldn't be built upon. I had no reason to doubt Ronan; he wasn't a storyteller. Now, if Charlie had told me, of course, I'd take it with a pinch of salt. According to him, Robert the Bruce was an ancestor and it wasn't at the well-documented Bannockburn that *we kicked yer erses* but much closer to home. He'd point as he told a story, about his great-great-great-someone out to the woods, as if the battle had taken place in the back garden.

Maggie, Ronan, and I would laugh and nod as if agreeing.

"I think the place we're after should be coming up on the left soon," I said. I had consulted a good old-fashioned map book and written directions, not trusting the app on my mobile to work. I handed Joe the piece of paper.

I slowed alongside a gated field with a shack in the corner. Part of the roof had recently blown off due to high winds. I could see that, at one point, the field had been sectioned up and down. Along one side there appeared to be electric hook-up points, although the bushes and grass were doing their best to conceal them.

"Is that it, do you think?" I asked.

"I think so. I doubt you've much competition from this lot," Joe replied with an incredulous snort.

I scanned the area and had to agree. "It's out of season for here. But it doesn't offer much, does it?"

Down south the camping season was a lot longer than in

Scotland because the weather stayed calmer for most of the year. Even hardened campers, however, would be put off with what we were presented with. A man wearing blue overalls and large wellies left the dilapidated building.

"Lizzie, is it?" he called out, opening the gate to the field.

"Yes, it is. Thank you, Leith," I replied. I drove carefully through the gate until I was level with him. "I'm new to towing so are we able to leave her hooked up and in a position I can drive straight out again?"

Leith chuckled. "Of course, and don't worry. I'll be around. I'm knocking that old shed down. We're giving up on this camping field," he said.

"That's a shame. Can I ask why?"

"Not enough business to keep it going." With that, he stepped back so I could continue in and then he closed the gate behind us.

I drove to a pitch and parked sideways instead of reversing into it. I could use the electric, if it worked, and then, when we were ready to leave, simply drive a circle back to the gate again.

Leith walked over to us. "You'll have no trouble with holiday makers where you are," he said. I had been honest when I'd booked the slot and told him we were planning on opening up the area around the loch to campers. "You have plenty to keep them occupied," he added.

"I don't know about that, but thank you. Is there anything

we can do to help you?" I had learned over the past few months that all the landowners tried to assist each other.

"That's kind of ye, lass, but it's time for me to retire with my millions and take that world cruise the wife keeps nagging for." Leith winked, and I really wasn't sure if he was serious or joking.

He didn't have a particularly strong accent and I wondered if he'd moved into the area some time ago. Maybe he'd married a local woman. I didn't know him well enough to ask, of course.

"I'll leave yous to it," he said, walking back to the shack.

Joe and I blocked Christine's wheels, lowered her legs, and connected the electric cable. I was somewhat surprised to see an interior light come on and wondered if I'd done Leith an injustice when I'd criticised his field. On one side we had the hedge to protect us from the wind that came in off the sea and on the other there were open fields with a view to the mountains. It was a beautiful spot and I felt saddened that Leith hadn't made it work. If I were an avid hiker, it would have been the ideal spot.

"Let's have a cup of tea, shall we?" Joe said, he had been hopping about in the cold with a woollen hat on his head, his oversized Parker, and leather gloves.

It took him about five minutes to remove all the layers and, stupidly, he left his Parker on the one bed providing a nice cosy place for Max to snuggle up in.

"How are you not freezing?" he asked as I took off the one layer, which was my coat, and stood to make tea in a long sleeved T-shirt.

"Menopause. I'm like a little radiator at the moment." I laughed at the analogy.

It was true, of course. Whereas under normal circumstances, *he* would be the one in shorts and a T-shirt in all weathers, and I would be as round as the Michelin Man with layers, it had reversed. I often found myself standing at the back door or on the terrace to cool down; however, every now and again a coldness descended. All of a sudden, as if to remind me, a shiver ran over me and a *brrr* left my lips.

"Yeah, I can see that you're like a little radiator," Joe said, sarcastically.

I made the tea and we sat on the sofa around the Formica covered table. We chinked in a toast and I sighed. I loved Christine and to share her with strangers was going to be a wrench. However, the campsite was my idea; the posh yurts, Christine, the farm shop, and petting farm, and then the general camping area had been argued for and fought over. I'd won, and I could hardly take Christine out of the site since it was believed she'd be a real attraction.

I knew we'd already taken a couple of bookings over the next Valentine's period. Christine was to be decked out in hearts and flowers with champagne on ice for her visitors. Proposals would be made in that old caravan, I believed.

Romantic walks around the loch; which reminded me to mention to Ronan he had benches to cement into the ground. He'd made some *love benches*, as he called them; room enough for two, and we were going to place them in secluded areas for lovers to sit and watch the stars. I'd also had the idea of an outdoor telescope since the sky was so wonderfully clear most of the time.

"I had another fundraising idea last night. What do you think about a fashion show?" I said, as I opened one of the many Tupperware tubs filled with shortbread. I could live on Maggie's shortbread.

"It's not a bad idea, but... You know, what about the *Antiques Roadshow* or something like that?"

"You don't like my fashion show idea?" I asked, feeling a little disappointed.

"I do, but I'm not sure who you'll get to attend. You'd need to look at local designers, and do you have any there? You're a bit *back of beyond*, remember."

Joe had a point. Perhaps we weren't necessarily the fashion conscious type. More, fleeces, jackets, and wellies. I would investigate any local manufacturers of jumpers and socks, though. I knew, as did Joe, that townies coming for a weekend away to Scotland were often woefully underprepared for the weather.

"We have the house listed for filming, I wonder what we have to do to suggest it as a location for events like that as well," I mused. I typed the question into my notes section on my phone for another day.

"Now, tell me what's going on with you and Danny," I said. Joe had been super excited about asking Danny to marry him at one point, but all talk of that had disappeared.

Joe sighed. "I can't believe we found each other, to be honest. I just find it all overwhelming at times, you know?"

I did, I knew exactly how he felt and I wrapped my arms around him to let him know I understood. "It will all be fine, trust me and just enjoy it."

I unpacked the food basket and shook my head. Most of it would be travelling back with us. I filled a bowl with water for Max and placed his tub of dry food to one side. I'd hate for Joe to reach in and grab a handful thinking they were snacks.

We demolished the tub of shortbread, or rather, *Joe* did, and decided to take a walk before a late lunch. It took him all of about ten minutes to layer back up, and despite me telling him he'd overheat, he insisted on shoving a second scarf in his pocket. I slipped on my walking boots and pulled my woollen socks up over my jeans. I slipped my arms into a fleece jacket and then my waterproof over the top, then I grabbed my woolly hat and gloves, Max's lead, and we were ready.

"Jesus, the cold hurts my nostrils," Joe said.

"Last year, it got so cold my nose hair froze," I said, laughing at the memory of an itchy nose.

We didn't tend to venture out too much when the real snow came, if I remembered. And, not being from an area that receives much snow, I was in my element when the ground was covered in white. I'd gotten Ronan to make me a sledge for the next snowfall.

I locked up the caravan and we decided to head over the road to the mountain pass. There was no way we'd manage to get to the top, of course, even though it was a relatively small mountain. A walk to the first 'pit stop' as I called them, would do us just fine.

Joe had other ideas.

He stopped every minute or two to take pictures with his phone to send to Danny or store to show his mum. She had no idea he was in Scotland; in fact she had no idea, sadly, who he was anymore. We avoided talk of her because it upset Joe so much, but I knew he'd sit with her and scroll through the photos, telling her all about the trip.

Max leapt about and I worried he might fall over the side. Joe scoffed at the idea until I reminded him that Max had a deformed leg that wasn't as strong as the other three. I decided to put him on the lead and just hope he didn't pull me over the side with him.

It was a lovely walk, the pass was wide enough in most places for us to walk side by side and we chatted until we had to stop to catch our breath. Joe raved about his new clients and the new properties he'd taken on. I told him all of my ideas for the house. We laughed at old memories, particularly when we had to book a theatre trip as part of a school project. We'd ended up at a strip club and the teachers were not impressed. We hadn't intended to book a strip club, obviously, but we were so poor at organisation, everything that could go wrong, did. Suffice it to say we failed business studies.

"In your face, teachers! Look how far have we've come now!" I said, rather childishly.

"I wonder if we should get them together and show them just how wrong they were when they told us we wouldn't amount to much in the business world."

The criticism we'd received in school, the failings by our education system to catch Joe's struggles, were the driving factor in his constant need for success. Being gay in school actually wasn't a big deal, it was a novelty and the only thing that he faced was the boys' annoyance that all the girls wanted to be with *him* and not them. The teachers, however, were a different problem, some, to the point of homophobia.

"You don't need to prove anything to anyone anymore, Joe," I said, quietly while taking his arm.

"There's always something to prove," he answered. We fell silent for a little while and continued to climb the path.

When our legs were screaming in protest and our lungs stressed with the cold air *and* having to keep us alive while talking, we decided to sit for a while. It felt like—even though there was still a long way to go—we were on top of the world. We could see for miles.

"I don't think I like the look of those clouds," I pointed out. Ahead of us, to the other side of the caravan park.

"Rain, do you think?" Joe enquired.

"Snow," I replied.

"How can you tell?"

I shrugged my shoulders. "I don't know, I've just learned the difference between rain and snow clouds. Country living, and all that," I added, as if an explanation helped.

Internally, I panicked a little. The snow wasn't forecast for that day or the next, but those clouds were certainly looming our way. I pulled my phone from my pocket, took a picture and sent it to Ronan, marvelling that the upgraded phone worked in such a remote location.

Be careful. I'll check the weather forecast, was his reply

Joe was oblivious to the possibility we could get stuck if we had a huge snow dump, although the thought was also quite exciting. I'd rather be stuck with Ronan, though.

By the time we started to descend, it looked as if the clouds might blow away to the side of us.

We arrived back safely and disrobed. I put the kettle on and Joe was meant to make notes of what the campsite had that we thought might be useful for us.

"I don't think we need this, do we?" Joe asked, picking up the notepad from the table.

"I guess we could make notes of what we'd *like* to have, though. Think back to those days in the beach huts in Cornwall," I encouraged.

"Right, I'll add awful singer with a wig and fake tan to the list then," he replied and I laughed.

We curled up on the sofa and, as the temperature had dropped somewhat, I wrapped a couple of throws around us. We chatted more, reminisced about those holidays in Cornwall, and what he thought our future held.

"You're not coming home, are you?" he said, quietly, and I sighed.

"I don't know. There seems to be an endless list of things to do in Scotland and I must admit, I don't look forward to heading back down south. I miss you, of course, but I do feel like my life is here. Look, no jumper," I said, joking and holding out an arm. I wanted to lighten the conversation a little.

Joe chuckled. "You've definitely changed and it's all for the better. I don't know if you'll be offended, but you're *softer*, funnier. You're the girl I remember from school," he said. I wasn't sure how to respond. "But enough of that bollocks, what's for eats?"

Joe didn't often do sentimental. I shoulder bumped him and gave him a wink. "We have a whole chicken, some salad…" he screwed his nose up at that. "We have a meat pie, but I'll cook that later. We have…Jesus, a ton of stuff! Bread, cakes, rolls."

"Do you remember the chicken and salt sandwiches? I just can't face chicken after that," he said.

I started to laugh. Years ago, Joe and I had rented a little cottage in Bath. It was meant to be a shopping weekend that ended up being a drink-fuelled and accident-prone short break instead. We'd drunk so much wine throughout one day and into the evening that we hadn't cooked. Instead, we'd used the previous day's leftovers to make sandwiches. For some reason, Joe decided *one had to have salt with one's chicken sandwiches.* He hadn't checked the pot and when he shook, the lid came off and the entire contents poured onto his sandwich. Instead of binning it, he decided to brush off as much as he could, pour vinegar over the rest and eat it. I don't think I'd ever seen someone as sick before that day, and haven't since. He heaved his guts up for hours. It had nothing to do with the copious amounts of alcohol, oh no! Not according to Joe. It was the chicken and salt sandwich.

"Well, I'm having chicken so you need to come and look at what you want," I said.

We slid out from under the throws and I was a little concerned to notice it was colder than I was expecting. I checked the little fire to realise it had gone out and no amount of pleading was going to make it relight. I tried the stove, and that was working fine, so I could only assume the fire had a fault. Because it hadn't been that long since we'd used Christine, I didn't think to check the appliances, perhaps I should have.

"I don't want to leave the stove on for heat, just in case. I think we have an electric back up somewhere," I said, as Joe shivered in front of an open fridge deciding on what to eat.

I climbed on the bed and opened the cupboard above it and found the little fan heater, only I then realised it had no plug.

"Fuck's sake," I grumbled, searching the drawers for a screwdriver. I pulled out the second best thing, a knife, and decided we didn't need the radio. Once I'd swapped the plugs over, we had a little heat going.

Joe relented and we both had chicken open sandwiches with tomatoes and *greenery*, as he called it, on top. After checking the lid, I shook a little salt over mine and waved the cellar at him. He shook his head, as I expected him to.

"Wine?" I asked, and didn't wait for an answer before I poured a nice cold glass of white for each of us.

"It's gone very dull outside," Joe remarked. I had to agree with him.

It seemed those snow clouds had diverted back to us and the wind was picking up. The combination wasn't good. I didn't voice my fear, though. Instead, I checked my phone battery and once we'd finished our sandwiches, I made sure all the windows were securely battened down. Christine was vintage, and although recently renovated, she wasn't up for adverse weather, especially fierce winds.

"I can't believe you've stuck with the name, Christine," Joe said, with a chuckle.

"She won't hurt us," I replied, patting the countertop as if petting her. "She loves me. She could have been left rotting in an old field, the place for the herdsman and his lover." I shuddered at the thought. "Instead, she's magnificent, aren't you, old girl?" As I stopped speaking she groaned. Joe and I looked at each other. "It's just the wind picking up," I said, shakily.

Christine rocked a little as a gust of wind hit her side and I wondered if I should have parked into the wind. But then, I wouldn't have known, really, which way the wind would blow. We had the shelter of the hedge, I hoped, so if it was that bad, we couldn't blow over.

Within half an hour Christine was rattling like she was standing on one of the fat jiggling machines at the gym. I avoided those machines like the plague; I had no desire for my fat to jiggle for all to see. Anyway, Christine had no shame and shook her backside like a seasoned stripper. Joe managed to save the bottle of wine before it slid off the small table.

"Erm, Lizzie?" he said, although I wasn't sure what his question was meant to be.

"It'll calm down. She's perfectly safe, we supported all the wheels…didn't we?" I had a vision that the wind would roll us off our plot. It was impossible of course, the Land Rover was in front of her but that niggling doubt made me lace up my boots and pull on a jumper.

I opened the door and a gust of wind caught it so fast that I was swung out of the van. I let go of the handle and fell onto my arse, not happy.

"Oh my God, are you okay? That was the funniest thing I've seen in ages. You just lifted straight off the floor," Joe said, holding onto Max's collar, who was obviously way more concerned for my plight than my best friend.

"No, I'm not bloody all right. I have a wet arse now," I said, groaning as I climbed to my feet. The wind was swirling and it then occurred to me, the way the hedges were angled, the wind would be circulating around the field. No wonder no one wanted to camp here!

"Should we move the caravan?" he asked.

"No, I think she's in the best position. Now move out of the way so I can get in." I pushed past him and into the bedroom where I stripped off the wet and muddy jeans.

"We should get in our pyjamas," Joe said, excited to be inside rather than out. I already had one leg in my fleecy onesie.

"Ta da," I said, holding my hands out to the side, thrusting one hip forward and bending one leg at the knee as if I was on an old game show, showing off the prize car.

"Oh, get you!" Joe scuttled into the bedroom to change himself. In the meantime, I poured another glass of wine. If it was going to be a rough night, it was going to be a rough, *drunk*, night.

And a rough night it was. There wasn't enough alcohol to make it easy to sleep. In fact, Joe and I curled up in the same bed because the other end of the caravan was taking the brunt of the wind and rocked him off the sofa at one point. Joe, Max, and I snuggled under multiple duvets with our woollen hats on. The little heater was nowhere man enough to reach the bedroom and there weren't the plug sockets to move it. We did giggle though. As the wind battered Christine, we told ghost stories and silly memories of things that had scared us. We sipped on wine and, later, hot chocolate with all the curtains closed and just one over-head light for company. Max even refused to leave the bed for his food. At some point, gone midnight, I fell asleep.

———

"Lizzie, wake up," I heard Joe say, as he was shaking my arm.

"What?" I opened one eye and felt the blast of cold to my eyeball. I guessed I was over the little radiator part of the menopause. "Jesus, it's cold."

"I know, I think you need to come and look at this."

I climbed from the bed still with fluffy socks on, and slid into what became overly tight fitted slippers. I dragged my fleece from a chair and put that on, too. I walked the very short distance into the kitchen/living area. Joe was kneeling up on the sofa with the curtain pulled to one side.

"What am I looking at?" I asked, confused by what I saw, or rather, didn't see.

He tapped on the frozen window. "I can't actually open the door," he said. It dawned on me then. Snow had hit, and with the wind, had piled up as high as the windows.

"Oh my God," I said. The door opened outwards, as did all the windows. We were trapped! "At least we have a ton of food," I said, and then giggled.

"I'm not sure it's funny," Joe replied, letting the curtain go. "What if Max needs a piss?"

"Ah, yes, I see your point." I hadn't considered Max, who was still under the duvet. We had a toilet in the caravan, he didn't, and any minute he was going to wake up and start scratching at the door. "You'll have to go out the window."

I started to check them all to see which one had the least amount of snow piled up against it.

"I can't go out the window," Joe replied.

"Of course you can. It's not a long drop and you're hardly going to hurt yourself, are you?"

"What do I do when I get out?"

"Dig us out, obviously." I stared at him with raised eyebrows. He was such a townie, but even someone who had lived his life in London must have encountered deep snow somewhere. I was sure he'd been skiing at some point.

Joe placed his hands on his hips and I knew I was in for an argument. "I'm assuming you have a shovel?"

I mimicked his pose. "In the Land Rover. Do you think those of us who live up here would travel out without a shovel, a blanket, spare water, and snacks?" If I could have added a Scottish accent, I would have.

Joe shook his head. I thought I might be winning for once, although it seemed too easy. "Can't we shove Max out the window?"

My jaw fell open, appalled at his suggestion and convinced that would be animal abuse. "How does he get back in? Anyway, we can't stay here until it thaws. Trust me, that would be weeks from now." I had no idea how long it would take to thaw but I wanted to jolt him into action.

"What about my bad back?" Joe whined.

I rolled my eyes dramatically, opened my mouth, and let out a loud sigh. Perhaps I wasn't going to win, and in all fairness, he'd had back surgery a little while ago. Perhaps throwing him out in the snow wasn't the best idea. Although my knees were dodgy, I still pulled on my boots, decided on some waterproof trousers over my onesie, my waterproof jacket, gloves, and a hat. By the time I was dressed, Max was, as predicted, whimpering by the back door. If a dog could cross his legs, he was doing it. I wouldn't be mad if he had an accident, as long as it wasn't a full bladder, swimming in piss, type accident.

"You're going to have to help me open this window," I said, choosing the largest one, which, annoyingly, was over the sink area.

As Joe pushed, I cleared the countertop and prayed it would hold my weight. I could only assume it had been the driving wind that had pushed the snow up against the caravan. Joe swore as he reached through the window as far as he could and started to scrape at the snow. Each swipe allowed him to open the window a little more until, eventually, he cleared the top of the pile. I climbed up onto the counter and looked out.

"Jesus," I said. It was a white-out. I could see just a few feet as the snow still fell. I didn't think I'd ever seen as much.

"Is it bad?" he asked, I could only nod and wondered how the fuck I was going to get myself from the window round to the vehicle, then back to the front door.

"Right, help me," I said. I climbed up onto my knees.

The only way out was forward, there just wasn't the space to try and back out with my arse leading. I prayed I would —as I'd told Joe—have a soft landing. Just as I got myself to the window, I felt a barge and Max jumped through and totally disappeared into the snow.

"Max!" I called out in a panic. I could hear noises, snuffling and the odd bark but I couldn't see him at all, so I launched myself out after him.

Throwing one's self into a snow bank isn't as easy as you'd think. I was blinded, more importantly, I was upside down and I couldn't seem to move.

"Lizzie?" I heard, but I couldn't reply. I waggled my legs in the hope he might see them. "Lizzie," he called again, that time the voice held no sense of worry or urgency but laughter.

"Fuck off," I said, knowing he wouldn't hear me. "Fuck right off, and keep fucking off when you get there," I added, and then took in a mouthful of snow. I believed my friendship with Joe was going to be tested when I finally got back inside the caravan.

Before the blood could run to my head and I passed out, I decided I needed to right myself somehow. I curled up, hoping to get my feet on solid ground. It took a couple of times of falling forwards and getting more disorientated before I thought I was standing. I turned until I saw a track through the snow. Max! I called him and was so pleased to see him bound back to me. I guessed he'd pushed his way out and his tunnel would be my way out as well. I fell to my knees and crawled. If this had been a movie, Max would have been Lassie or one of the other many dogs that led humans to safety. Sadly, after tramping for what I thought might be way too long just to circumnavigate a caravan, I believed Max was more akin to Scooby Doo!

I cursed yet again, many times, as I fought to stand. Eventually, I managed to break the surface. The snow came to my chest but began to lower as I walked away from the hedge. Although the snowfall had been substantial, it had been wind, as I predicted, that had caused the depth built up against Christine. I turned to face her and saw Joe with his mobile. He had been filming me. I flipped him the bird with both hands.

Max was bounding around as if demented, flicking snow into the air and then leaping to catch it. I ignored him and waded to the Land Rover. Thankfully, the rear door was above the height of the snow. I grabbed the foldable shovel and slammed the door shut again. By the time I'd waded back I was getting hot. It had taken a lot of effort to get from one end of the caravan to the other. I started to drag the snow away from the door. It was going to take forever with the little shovel but I was determined to prove to Joe that *he* was the wimp and I was the superhero. He was still filming me and I was still swearing at him, telling him I'd bash him over the head with the shovel if I found that movie on social media.

I could see his mouth moving as if he was giving a commentary. I open and closed my mouth, not making any sound but, although petty, it was clearly irritating him because he thought I was talking to him and he couldn't hear. He put his hand to his ear but I just stuck my two fingers up at him.

A demented Max decided it would be fun to run around

and then leap up at me. I wasn't expecting the weight to hit my back and I found myself flying forwards. I could actually hear Joe laugh, that laughter slowed once I climbed to my feet and held up a broken shovel. It had been super flimsy anyway and totally inadequate for what I needed. Instead, I started to use my hands to scoop the snow away. By the time I got to the door I was crying. My hands were so cold I was convinced I was getting frost-bite. I wrenched the door open and only then, did Joe rush over to me.

"Oh, God, I'm so sorry. I thought it was funny. Come here, hunny," he said, and wrapped his arms around me.

He pulled off my gloves and my hands were red raw. He filled the small washing up bowl with warm water and encouraged me to put my hands in. I wasn't sure I wouldn't get chilblains. At least the water wasn't hot, that would be awful. Once they had slowly come back to life, I slapped him as hard as I could across the chest, then across the top of his arm. Had he not protected himself, I would have slapped him upside his head as well.

"You bloody bastard. You should have done that," I said. It was only then I realised Max was still outside. I pushed the door open and called for him. I took satisfaction that he decided to run in and shake right next to Joe.

Joe held his palms together and cocked his head to one side. "I'm sorry. Honestly, I didn't think it would be that bad." He smiled slightly and although I hadn't forgiven him, I shook my head and laughed. I seemed to forgive him for things I really shouldn't. "You need to see this video," he added.

"Not until I've changed clothes, you've made me tea and something to eat, and we've decided how we're getting out of here." In addition to the snow piled alongside the caravan, it had drifted into the gate and the road looked quite impassable. We'd need a tractor, I thought.

While Joe did as instructed, I headed to the bedroom. I could have stood under the shower but I wasn't sure the water would be warm enough. Instead I changed into dry clothes, wincing at my red and pimpled skin. My hair was wet; the woollen hat had given no protection in the snow. I dragged a brush through it and then wrapped a small towel around my head, more to keep it warm than to dry my hair. By the time I was back in the living area, there was a pot of tea on the table and Joe had muffins under the grill. I grabbed a pot of home-made jam, butter, and plates with two knives and I sighed as I found a second tub of shortbread and held it to my chest as if it would save my life. Only then, did I sit and when the muffins were grilled, Joe and I ate and then laughed at the video.

It started with me falling through the window and all that was left visible were the soles of my boots. When my feet wiggled in response to Joe's call, we burst into laughter. Although muffled, the video had picked up my cursing and we continued to laugh. The funniest part, however, was when I had decided to crawl through the tunnel I thought Max had made. Obviously, it wasn't as deep as I thought and Joe was able to video the two pompoms, that sat atop my woollen hat, moving as if on their own across the surface of the snow.

I leaned back holding my stomach and tears rolled down my cheeks as we watched. Joe rushed from one window to another to continue to video the pompoms getting further away. It turns out I had been heading out into the field instead of circling the caravan.

"If you put that on social media..." I started but didn't continue, his widened eyes and feigned innocence told me he already had.

My mobile started to ring and we both looked at it in surprise. I picked it up.

"Hi," I said, as I answered Ronan's call.

"Hey, how bad is it over there?" he asked.

"Pretty bad, I had to dig out the front door so Max could get out and pee," I laughed as I told him some of the story.

"Oh, for Christ's sake, Lizzie. Why didn't you call earlier? Why didn't Joe offer?"

"Because I had it under control. Not sure how we're going to get out of the field though." I didn't answer his second question.

"I've organised for a tractor to get you all to the main road. Might take a little time to get there, though. Seems tractors are out and about pulling everyone. You should see it here. I don't think we've had snow like it for years."

Ronan seemed as excited as I had been before the snow actually came. I laughed at this enthusiasm. "So, what do I do?" I asked.

"Just hold tight. We have more snow forecast for later today, tonight, and then tomorrow. So I want to get you out as soon as possible. You might need to leave Christine..."

I cut him off. "Nope. Christine comes with us, or we all stay."

His sigh meant he had chanced his arm with that statement and knew he wasn't really going to win. "The tractor will pull Christine out and you should be able to follow okay in the Land Rover. Just stay in the tracks. Once you're out on safer ground, you can hook back up and I'll meet you at that point to take over."

"I appreciate that, thank you."

I didn't relish towing Christine in the snow. There was no way the road would have been cleared. It was up to the local farmers to do that and since our one seemed to have disappeared—I would've hoped to have seen him that morning if only for him to check we survived the night— but if he was selling up, he might not have a tractor.

"I wish I could've got to you last night but we couldn't get out. I tried to call you but we had no signal."

"That's okay. We were fine, we had a couple of bottles of

wine and that was it, out for the count until this morning," I said, smiling at the level of concern he had for me. "Is everything okay there?" I asked.

"We've lost power, which is a pain, and I don't know when that will be back on, but we have a generator for the basics, heating, and candles. It's not quite the same cuddling up with Charlie though, so I can't wait to get you home." Ronan laughed and I joined in. He then thanked our lucky stars we ran on oil for most things.

"Hold that thought." I laughed again. "I'll pack up here and then see you soon."

We said our goodbyes and I relayed the message to Joe, omitting the part where Ronan asked why Joe hadn't gone out the window. Ronan had an old-fashioned soul. He would say it was because he was properly brought up. He would never have let me do the digging out. In fact, we'd have been dug out long before I'd probably woken to even know we had been snowed in. I had started to think Ronan wasn't the norm but then realised, I only had Harry and Joe as comparisons. Perhaps all good men were like Ronan. He'd fight for me, I knew that, and something inside swelled with pride and love at the thought.

Joe and I packed up the caravan, placing all the crockery back in its box for storage. I stripped the bed and balled the bed linens into a black sack for washing. I regretted putting everything away, once we had and the temperature got lower, we couldn't even make a cup of tea.

"How long do you think the tractor will take?" Joe asked.

"I don't know. I just looked at my phone and I've got no signal now. Have you?" I wanted to call Ronan to see if there was a time for the tractor.

"No, but I'm also low on battery."

As if to make our day even better, the electricity went off. I was surprised it had lasted as long; especially after hearing a power line was down back home. I grabbed the duvet off the bed and we wrapped ourselves in it.

"Sod it, I'll make tea," I said. I unpacked the necessary items, they could be thrown in the Land Rover when it was time to leave. We couldn't sit in the cold without a warm drink at least.

By the time we were on our third cup of tea and the snow had started to fall again, we could see our exhaled breath. Max was under the duvet with us and we donned our coats and hats. I didn't have a spare pair of gloves, mine were still wet from digging out the front door. Instead, I grabbed a pair of fluffy socks that had little ears above two googly eyes, and I shoved my hands in them. I waved my hands and laughed as it reminded me of the time Ronan thought I was about to dissolve a body and I wore pink rubber gloves with fur and a fake engagement ring.

"Sock puppets," I said, and made a mouth using my thumb and fingers. "Hello, Mr. Joe. How are you today?" I changed my accent to suit what I thought was perfect for a sock puppet.

Joe raised his eyebrows at me. "Either make more tea or get under the covers."

I made more tea and *then* got under the covers.

"My nips are bloody cold," I said, wishing I had another top to put on; my bra was chafing and it was uncomfortable. I threaded my arms through the sleeves of my top and whipped it off.

"Now, they'll be even more cold," Joe said.

"I'd rather they be cold than snapped off because of the lace," I said.

"Cold nips," Joe said, laughing. "Sounds like a dish from the local Thai restaurant we have back home."

"At least you don't have frozen bits! And didn't we have this same conversation back at the house?"

Joe continued to laugh. "I do now declare Scotland renamed the land of the cold nips and frosty bits." For emphasis, he waved his arm over his new domain.

For a while we talked but as time moved on, we stopped. We were cold and tiredness was creeping over me. I nestled into the crook of Joe's arm and closed my eyes. My face was cold, my nose running, but at least the rest of me was warm. I longed for the hot flushes to return. It seemed my menopause was on a cycle and since I'd had a week of the cold flushes, I knew it was still a way off. It was as if my body was on a month about turn!

I wasn't sure how long we'd both slept for but when I woke, before Joe, it was back to snowing hard. I checked my phone, no signal and low battery. I uncurled myself and slid out from under the duvet. I found one of the phone power banks and plugged my phone into it. I began to wonder if phones charged at certain temperatures. It was shockingly cold inside the metal container and I wondered if we'd actually be better off in the Land Rover. I could run the engine periodically to heat us up. Then I remembered something I'd learned as a child. Never run a vehicle stuck in the snow. The chance of the exhaust pipe getting covered and carbon monoxide leaking into the car could be deadly. Whether it was that thought or the cold, my eyes filled with tears. I thought they might freeze as they fell but it wasn't quite artic conditions. I grabbed a tissue to wipe my eyes.

As I stood, I thought I heard a shout. I looked out the window and saw someone by the gate. Whoever it was, was so covered up, it was difficult to see their face. The person climbed over the gate and as he got close, I ran to the door. I wished I'd kept my boots on so I could jump down from the caravan and throw myself into his arms.

"Oh, Ronan, I'm so glad to see you. What happened?"

I stood to one side to let him in. He wore ski clothing and had a backpack over his shoulders.

"Charlie drove as close as he could, then I walked. The bloody tractor is stuck back up the hill."

"Stuck?" I didn't think tractor could get stuck anywhere.

"Yeah, stuck. It's pretty grim out there."

He started to remove some of his layers, at which point Max climbed out from safety and whimpered with his tail between his legs. Joe woke with a start.

"Let me make you a hot drink," I said. "We still have gas but no electricity now."

"Oh, are we glad to see you," Joe said, straightening himself up.

Although Ronan looked his way and nodded, he didn't answer and I felt the frostiness in the air that wasn't from the cold. Thankfully, Joe seemed oblivious when he went on to tell Ronan about my leap through the window and it was then, I realised that was Ronan's source of annoyance.

"Please leave it for now," I whispered, as Ronan came to wrap me in his arms.

"Only for now," he replied. I kissed his neck.

"So what's the plan?" Joe asked. Ronan looked at me and frowned.

"I know, we're not getting her out, are we?" I said, stroking the countertop as if she'd understand my sadness at leaving her.

"No. I've spoken to Leith, he says she'll be safe and when the tractor can get through, he'll tow her back to us."

"Leith was the tractor?" I asked, not meaning 'he' was, but that he 'owned' the tractor.

"Yeah, he can't get out of his house at all. He thought he could but the tractor slid down the hill and grounded itself in the bank. He needs a tractor to get his one out."

"So we walk to your vehicle?" Joe asked.

"*You* can, for sure..." Ronan started to reply before I nudged him in the side. "No, I'll drive us out in the Land Rover."

"If the tractor can't get to us, how will the Land Rover get us out?" I asked.

"Because I can take that off-road but I can't with Christine on the back."

I didn't want to ask just how 'off-road' we were going, particularly since the snow was at least as high as the wheels.

"Pack as much as you can in the Land Rover, and don't worry. We restored this old girl once, we'll do it again if we have to."

It saddened me to think we'd have to leave her, and I wasn't sure for how long, either. If what Leith had said was correct, he was off on a world cruise at some point. The Inner Hebrides wasn't like London. It was highly unlikely we'd end up with squatters in the short time Christine would be stranded but I still worried.

We filled the Land Rover with as much as we could, Joe and Max got into the back still wrapped in the duvet, and I climbed beside Ronan in the front. He had already dug the snow away from the wheels and he'd laid an old blanket in front of them to give us the purchase we needed to get going. Although snow and not ice, he didn't want to take the chance that compacted snow would have the wheels spinning.

It was a hair-raising start with me holding on, Max still whimpering, and Joe with his eyes closed. Ronan got us across the field and into the next. He wanted to follow the road as far as he could before he needed to get on it, believing the vehicle better suited for the snow on ground rather than the tarmac. It seemed that Leith had opened gates until there were no more. A section of fencing had been removed and we bumped, at speed, over a bank, down a ditch, back up until we crashed onto the road. I screamed and Joe got himself into the brace position as if on an aircraft. Finally, we were back on the road.

It was then we saw the severity of the snow. "Jesus, this is bad even for Scotland, isn't it?" I asked.

"Yeah, the army has airlifted some people out of more remote places this morning. If this continues, we could be completely cut off. There are no trains out at the moment, Joe."

I didn't think Joe minded that much but would be awfully pleased to get back to the house and out of the vehicle; he'd never been 'off-road' with Ronan before. I'd had the benefit of many trips in one of the Land Rovers or on the back of a quad bike with him. He drove at pace, without worrying about other road users as if he was the king of the tarmac. It wasn't long before I began to recognise where I was. Soon, we were driving through the gates and up the drive towards the house. I had never felt such a sense of relief when I saw both Maggie and Charlie at the front door. It reminded me of the time I'd first arrived. Both came down to the car to help us. Maggie wore huge wellies and Charlie looked like he had fisherman's waders on.

"Oh, we've been so worried about you all," Maggie said, grabbing baskets and blankets from the back seat.

"There was no need to be," I replied, even though I had been worried myself.

I helped to unload the vehicle, and didn't correct Ronan when he shouted for Joe to come back out of the house to help. He had rushed in to get out of the cold. Sheepishly, Joe joined us. I loaded him up with way more than I would have normally and scowled at him. We would certainly be having words. Joe had often been a little selfish and I'd accommodated that for way too long. It was time to cut him down to size.

Once done, Ronan ran the vehicle around the back to the courtyard and parked it up. We were all in the kitchen with our hands wrapped around mugs of hot tea when he returned. Candles burned on all surfaces and the Aga pumped out heat. It was wonderful and cosy and I was glad to be home. I was looking forward to a hot bath even if that meant taking up buckets of boiled water.

Once I had finished my tea that was exactly what I did. Ronan and I took up two buckets of boiling hot water. I ran the tap until lukewarm water spurted out and we added the hot. It was pure bliss when I sank under the bubbles. Ronan sat on the closed loo and I told him all about our mini adventure.

"I know you're annoyed with him, and so am I. Will you let me deal with him?" I asked.

"If you insist. He shouldn't have let you go out that window. What if you'd got hurt?" Ronan took in a deep breath and sighed. "He's your best friend, you have words if you think he deserves them."

I smiled and reached out to take his hand. "I love you," I said.

"I should hope so." He gave me a wink and then left me to soak some more.

I never made it back downstairs. I was curled up in the bed when Ronan woke me and asked if I wanted dinner. I declined but a plate with a sandwich and tea, was placed on the bedside cabinet. I guessed the cold had rendered me exhausted. I didn't even hear Ronan come to bed later that evening. I felt his arms around me at some point, early hours when I needed to get up for a wee, but that was it.

14

I felt so refreshed the following morning. I'd gotten up and showered, dressed in snuggly warm clothes, and even applied a little mascara. I was down in the kitchen with breakfast on the go before anyone else appeared. I had decided to make pancakes. Not the kind that Maggie was famous for, but good old crepes. I chopped a lemon into sections ready for decoration and squeezing, I placed a bowl of sugar and another of jam on the table. I ransacked the cupboard for a jar of Nutella, sure that I remembered seeing one.

"Ah, there you are," I said, as I opened the lid to be sure I wouldn't see a layer of mould and then added the jar to the rest of the items on the table.

Maggie had every recipe ever written in her head, I had the advantage of a dying smart phone that lasted long enough for me to refresh on the ingredients. By the time Maggie shuffled into the kitchen, I was mixing the batter.

"What are you doing?" she asked, smiling at me.

"Making you breakfast for a change. Sit down and I'll get the kettle on," I said, placing the bowl to the side.

She couldn't help herself, though. Maggie inspected the bowl and dipped a finger in to test the mixture and nodded in approval. She circled the kitchen as I made the tea, as if she'd been outed from her domain and was readying herself for a takeover battle. I chuckled as she, finally and with a sigh, sat at the table.

"I'm making pancakes," I said, as if the batter wasn't obvious enough.

"I gathered that. Did you add two eggs?"

"I did. I highly doubt they'll be as tasty as yours, of course, but I thought it might be a nice gesture considering all you do for me." I smiled while I offered the compliment and that satisfied her. She sat back and sipped on her tea.

I found a tub of biscuits and placed that on the table. Charlie was a stickler for a biscuit with his cup of tea, even if that cup of tea was being drunk with his dinner. I guessed it was why Maggie made so many of them.

"I have to get some pies done for the bakery today," Maggie said, I wondered if that was code for *hurry up out of my kitchen* or *don't leave a mess* or *don't use all the utensils*.

"I'll help, I have a little paperwork to do but it will be too cold out there today."

The office was in the courtyard and although connected to the central heating, it was an old stone building with no insulation and single glazed windows. I wasn't taking the chance of freezing my fingers or the laptop. I'd move to the library for the day and set a fire going. It was going to be a pain not having Wi-Fi to check on emails, and I wondered if anywhere in town might sell a dongle.

"Oh, what's going on here, then?" Charlie said, as he came in through the back door. He dusted off snow from his shoulders and hung up his wax coat.

"I'm cooking breakfast," I said with a smile. I then turned to Maggie, "Don't you raise your eyebrows," I said in jest.

"I'm sure they'll be lovely. Now, is that pot still hot?"

Maggie slid the pot of tea to Charlie who filled his mug. I then decided I needed to call for Ronan and Joe; my stomach was reminding me that I'd missed dinner the night before.

"We need one of those bells to announce dinner, or a gong," I said, walking to the bottom of the stairs and screeching out their names.

"There used to be an intercom system but that broke years ago, long before our time," Maggie said when I returned.

I heated up two pans on the Aga and poured in the batter.

Years ago, I'd managed two pans and I was pleased I hadn't lost the knack. By the time Ronan and a grumbling Joe appeared, there was a stack ready to be eaten.

"I don't think I get up this early even when I'm at work," Joe moaned, squinting at his watch.

"It's half eight, Joe. Charlie has been out and about since six, isn't that right?" I replied, looking at Charlie as he stuffed a whole jam laden pancake into his mouth. He nodded in answer. "And I was hungry. I had a hectic day yesterday, remember?" The dig worked, I guessed. Joe smiled and apologised for being a grumpy pants.

"What plans do you have today?" I asked Ronan.

"We need to go check on the deer. Joe, you can come with us if you like. I think we'll take out some hay, Charlie, I doubt they're getting much to eat at the moment." He looked between the two for confirmation.

"Oh, do I get to ride a quad bike?" Joe asked.

"If you want to. If you're capable, of course," Ronan replied. I doubted Joe had ever driven before.

I was surprised Ronan had offered to take Joe out with him, he was still cross that Joe hadn't been much of a help and, once I saw the slight smirk, I began to wonder if he had something up his sleeve. I squinted my eyes at him, he raised his eyebrows as if in innocence.

"The MacCormacks have some sows that need housing.

Their barn collapsed, we can do that after sorting out the deer as well," Ronan added.

"Oh, I love pigs," I said, clapping my hands at the thought of baby pigs running around.

"We're not having them; they're not ours; they have names already; they're to be bacon not pets."

We all looked at Ronan. "Well, that was mean," Maggie said, and I laughed.

"I just don't want you getting any ideas." He gave me a wink and both he and I knew he'd do anything for me, even getting me a pig if I desperately wanted one.

Maggie insisted on clearing away the breakfast items and waved away my offer of help for her batch cooking. Since the snow was still falling and the lane outside impassable now, any idea of finding a dongle went out of the window. I'd be able to pick up any emails that had downloaded before the power went out, of course, but that was it. And I wouldn't be able to do any research, which was annoying.

"How long would it take to walk into town?" I asked Maggie, as I walked back into the kitchen with an empty mug for refilling.

"About a half hour, I imagine. Why?"

"I wanted to see if I could buy a dongle."

"A what?" she asked.

"It's a device that lets me connect to the Internet," I explained.

"But we don't have any power, although they've said it should go back on late today or early tomorrow."

"I don't need power as long as my laptop is charged. I might take a walk."

"I'll come with you. Be nice to get out in the fresh air," she said.

I wanted to ask whether she was able to walk that half an hour, especially since we would be walking in the snow.

"Oh, I've just had a great idea," she said. "Get yourself ready and meet me out the back." She winked and I frowned at her, wondering what on earth she was up to. She rushed off to change her clothes.

I was in the kitchen with my boots, hat and gloves, jacket, and scarf when Ronan walked in.

"You're going with her?" was all he said.

I frowned at him also. "Huh?"

"She hasn't driven that thing in a century. I've told her but there's no stopping her."

I laced up my boots. "I have no idea what you're talking about. I asked if Maggie wanted to walk into town. I'm hoping I'll buy a dongle and she had an idea she hasn't told me about yet."

Ronan started to laugh. "Well, welcome to Maggie's mad world of travel and if you're not back in two hours, I'll come and find you. You'd have been better off on a quad."

I hadn't thought about taking a quad but that meant Joe giving up his, we only had three.

"What do you mean?" I asked, ramming my hat on my head and holding out my hands for Ronan to help with my second glove.

"You'll see. Two hours, then I'll come and find you."

He started to laugh and I followed him outside. I came to an abrupt halt. Charlie was standing beside a rotten old tractor, the kind with the metal seat and the metal steering wheel. God knows how old it was but the engine was running.

Maggie was in the driver's seat and she waved over to me. "You'll have to stand, there's only one seat," she shouted above the engine noise.

"Are you kidding me?" I asked. She shook her head. I started to laugh. "Oh my God, this is going to be epic," I said.

I climbed up beside her. There had been a second seat at one time but it had rotted away over the years. I wondered just how old the tractor was. Rust had overcome the once red paint and black smoke billowed out of an exhaust that went up into the air.

"Do you know how to drive this?" I asked.

"Of course, it belonged to my father, I used to drive it with him."

"And your father has been dead how many years?" I asked, sarcastically.

"Must be like riding a bike, now hold on."

She ground it into a gear, the only one, I imagined, and we lurched forward. She shouted for me to hold on again and she pressed the accelerator. Off we went and I waved at Ronan who was still laughing at us.

"We should put a basket somewhere and we can go the shopping in this," I said, as a joke.

"Now that's a cracking idea," Maggie answered, in all sincerity.

We made our way out to the road and although Maggie stopped to look both ways, there was really no need. Nothing, other than the old tractor, hopefully, was getting up and down the lane.

There wasn't much opportunity for further conversation. I had to pull my scarf up over my face leaving just a small slit for my eyes. It wasn't that we were moving fast but we were driving into the wind.

"Oh, look," Maggie shouted and pointed.

Ahead of us was a man walking the lane towards the town. We slowed as we came level.

"Jump on," I said and moved over so the gentleman should stand beside me. He smiled his thanks, not able to speak as he had covered his face as well.

"We're heading into town," Maggie said, leaning over me. He gave her a thumbs up and nodded enthusiastically.

As we continued our journey I could hear him laugh, particularly as we levelled up beside another walker. A tourist by the looks of things. He had hiking sticks and although he looked perfectly capable of making his way into town, he hopped on as well. Maggie and I were squished and laughing like mad. I don't think I'd ever been in a situation so bizarre and I wished my phone had charge. A thought hit me.

"Sir, do you have a camera on your phone?" I asked the tourist. He nodded as a reply.

"We need some photos of this to add to our website," I explained. Not that we had a website but, in that moment, I decided we needed one.

I pulled on Maggie's arm for her to stop; he jumped off and removed one mitten that hung from the sleeve of his jacket. I remembered my mum stitching a piece of wool from one mitten to the other and threading it through my jacket so I wouldn't lose one. I doubt that was his motive but it made me laugh. He snapped a couple of images and climbed back on. I shouted my email address as we trudged on and although I wasn't sure of his answer, I hoped he'd manage to send them over to me. By the time we drove up the high street, we had an audience cheering us on. Maggie was like the queen, known and loved by everyone and it was as if her Majesty herself was driving up the high street, such were the level of waves and laughter. We parked outside the café, although we had the whole street to choose from, and debarked. We bade a farewell to our fellow passengers and pushed open the door of the café.

"I didn't think you'd be open," I said as I peeled off layers.

"Wasn't going to but we have a generator and I got the old town crier to get the word out we had free tea and cakes for those without."

The generosity and friendliness of fellow villagers never ceased to amaze me. The town crier, I'd learned, was Mrs. Marrigold, the local gossip and head of the W.I. If one wanted the whole place to know something, we told her.

A pot of tea was placed in front of us and I poured it into two lovely and dainty teacups. Maggie would've preferred a mug but I loved the little china, it was one thing that reminded me of London and afternoon tea at The Ritz. We wouldn't accept the free tea and cake, however, we had oil-fired cooking, heating, and hot water, which was a lot more than some had. There was no gas locally so oil or electric were the main sources of energy, and for that reason, we hoped the electricity companies made the area a priority. Most of the people we spoke to that morning had oil for their heating and hot water but ran an electric oven. They were super grateful for the free tea. Maggie and I left twenty pounds on the table under the pot because we knew a bill wouldn't be presented.

"Now, where do you think I'd get a dongle?" I mused to myself.

"What is it again?" Maggie asked. I explained, for a second time, what it was. "Follow me," she said, and then marched off up the street.

We stopped outside a hardware store, the kind I could spend hours in, and that sold brooms and paint, and hooks and wool. I doubted it would sell dongles, however.

"Hi there, Maggie," I heard over the tinkle of the doorbell.

"Johnny, glad to see yer open. My Lizzie needs a gongle," she said.

"A dongle," I corrected.

"A gongle?" he questioned.

I sighed. "Johnny, I need a dongle. It's a gadget that will allow me to…"

"I know what one is, my love. I was teasing Maggie, wait here."

"If he comes back with a dongle, I'll pay double for it," I said with a laugh.

I turned slowly to look around the store. I imagined Johnny should have worn a brown apron and the sign outside should have said *Open All Hours*. It, and he, were exactly like the TV show.

"There we go, last one. Had a run of them this morning." He slapped his hand down on the counter, and blow me, if it wasn't a black dongle in a clear plastic wrapper.

"Well, I never," I said, picking it up.

"It's a pay as you go," he added, and I was impressed by his technological knowledge. I wouldn't have thought to ask about the service provider. "And use my phone to ring though with your top up," he added, placing a very old and very dirty handset on the counter next to it.

While I did just that, Maggie and he chatted. I saw her blush a couple of times and chuckle. He leaned on the counter and I could imagine, sixty-odd years ago, he might have been quite a looker.

"All done, what do I owe?" I asked, having put fifty pounds on the dongle.

"Nothing. I owe Ronan for fixing my gate last summer. He won't take any money from me so that's my payment." He slammed his hand down on the counter yet again and I took it to mean, no further action was required.

"Well, thank you so much. I really appreciate it."

"So far, you two have brought a little life back into the old town, so we thank you as well." His smile was genuine but I was confused. I nodded and smiled, however.

"How did you know I'd get a dongle there?" I asked Maggie after we'd left.

"I didn't but he's a cutie and I fancied my Johnny fix," she said, laughing.

"Your what?" I asked.

"Johnny fix, that's what we used to call it. When we were all teenagers, he worked at the local café by our school. We went there for milkshakes and to ogle him." She started to laugh. "Dongle after an ogle," she blurted out.

She convulsed at her own humour and I had no choice but to laugh with her. Despite how silly it was, she was infectious.

"What are you two laughing at?" I heard. Maggie's ex-foster daughter, Angie, was standing in front of us.

"Maggie's been to ogle Johnny and I bought a dongle," I said, holding it aloft.

"Ah, you got the last one. Damn, I wanted that. I'll steal Gregg's," she said, and then gave us a wink.

"I'm sorry," I replied.

"Don't be. Daft isn't it? We run our lives online and then this happens. I can't get onto my bank to pay my suppliers today, not that they're worried, but I don't like being late. How did you get here, anyway?" she asked. I pointed to the old tractor. "You didn't? Oh, my lord," she said. I was reminded that Maggie used that same phrase all the time.

"I drove it, picked up some ramblers along the way as well," Maggie said, puffing her chest out in pride.

"You're nuts. I'm glad though, will I see you tomorrow?" she asked.

Maggie nodded and they hugged. I waved as I climbed onto the tractor and when Maggie was ready, we fired her up and made a seventy-two point turn. Maggie heaved on the steering wheel to the point her brow leaked exertion. I offered to take over, but she was having none of it. Twenty minutes later, and with an audience offering encouragement, we were facing the right way and off back home. I hadn't checked my watch so had no idea if the two hours was up and we'd meet Ronan on the way. We laughed until we pulled into the courtyard. We laughed harder when we saw Joe.

"Erm, Joe had a little run in with some pigs," Ronan said, and I caught the smirk and the twinkle in his eye that told me he'd known all along Joe was going to get covered in shit that day.

"Bloody things. This is why I don't do the country, Lizzie. This is why I live in London and the only pig I see is on my dinner plate," Joe said, waving his arms up down his front.

"Ye need hosing doon." Before anyone could answer Charlie, a blast of ice cold water hit Joe and he screamed. The hose was frozen of course, but Charlie had dunked a bucket in the horse trough after breaking through the ice.

"Oh my Lord," Maggie said and I doubled over holding my stomach.

Joe's mouth was flapping open and closed, he couldn't catch his breath and his eyes were wide.

Ronan slapped him on the back a couple of times until he squealed. "Cold was it? Probably not as cold as crawling through the snow to dig you out, though, huh?" Ronan said, and then gave Joe a wink. Joe at least looked contrite.

"Come on, lad, let's get you in," Charlie said, taking Joe by the arm. I'd never seen Charlie so concerned for someone's welfare before and wondered if he was like that when Ronan was a child.

Joe peeled off his coat and hat and then his gloves and Maggie took them. She held the coat at arm's-length and they escorted Joe inside for a bath and change of clothes, I imagined.

"What on earth happened?" I asked when Ronan and I were left in the courtyard.

"Come and muck out this llama of yours and I'll tell you."

I grabbed my fork and broom and followed him. Ronan headed to the stable next door, which held the pigs until they could move them to the barn. They'd need to relocate the dogs before they did that, he told me.

"I hooked a trailer to the quad and headed over to MacCor-mack's. Joe had mastered his quad so we let him ride alone. Charlie came on the back of mine. There were three sows and eight piglets. Instead of waiting for instructions, Farmer Joe thought he could round them up like sheep."

I had already started to laugh. Sheep wouldn't attack you if you got between mum and baby, but a pig would, they could be real grumpy things.

"The sow didn't want Joe ushering her babies into the trailer in the hope she'd follow so she bowled him over."

"And you didn't think to stop that happening, I take it?" I said, smirking at him and raising my eyebrows.

He shrugged his shoulders. "He needs a little country training, that's all," he said, and laughed.

I mucked out Colleen's stable, scratched her behind her ears while she rested her head on my shoulder, and then cuddled Gerald. He was as grumpy as the pigs and I guessed it was because they couldn't go out. Ronan and Charlie needed to re-fence the parts that Gerald had managed to escape from before they could head out for an hour or two.

"Oi, stop that," I said. Gerald had started to headbutt me, and then he fell over. "And don't try to pull the dying goat on me, either. You've caused enough trouble," I added.

I topped up their water, and hung fresh hay in nets from hooks. I loved the mucking out and grooming part of owning them and I wondered how I'd fare with horse riding. I wouldn't mention that to Ronan just then, though. What with the dogs, the llama, the goat, and the pigs, he had enough animals to worry about, considering he was a landowner and not a farmer.

By the time we went back in, Joe was cleaned up and sitting at the table with his hands wrapped around a mug of hot chocolate.

"Country life's not for you, is it?" I laughed, as I pulled the teapot towards me and opened the lid to look in.

While I refreshed the pot, Joe told me of how the pig had viciously attacked him. He feared for his life because, *pigs eat people, did you know that?* he told me. I guessed Charlie had told him a story or two, although I did actually know that pigs would eat a human, and their own, if hungry enough.

"I don't know how you do it," he said. "Although, seeing the deer was nice." The thought of the deer brightened him up a little.

"Are you missing London? I think the trains are back on today. They've cleared the line this end but you have to change a couple of times, I think."

"Trying to get rid of me?" he asked, and then laughed to show he was joking.

"No, but you do seem out of sorts at the moment. I thought you might be missing Danny," I replied. I wanted to take that moment of us being alone to talk.

"I am. I don't know, Lizzie. I feel a real shit that I let you climb out of the window. I seem...I seem to always just step back and let others step up to the plate nowadays, and I don't know why."

I would question the *nowadays*, Joe had always been happy to let everyone else do the hard work. Not that I would voice that, of course.

"Maybe this relationship with Danny is making you relook at your life," I added, softly.

"Do you think I'm selfish?"

His question threw me and I took a moment before I answered truthfully. "You didn't used to be. But the last couple of years? Maybe. We've all changed, Joe, especially me. It's okay to re-evaluate. You're in a long-term relationship, a lifelong one, I hope. That in itself will change you. What does Danny think?"

"He thinks I can be selfish. I lied to you, Lizzie. We had a blazing row and I told him he couldn't come. I haven't spoken to him since I've been here."

My eyes widened in shock at his confession. "Well, that's petty and childish and you're neither, normally. Ring him now, if you have any battery left. And tell him you're sorry and you're on your way home."

I was surprised that Joe had done that. He wasn't that kind of a person normally. But then, as I'd kept saying to him, he hadn't been in a real relationship before Danny.

"I'm meant to be spending time with you," Joe said, he didn't, however raise his gaze from his mug.

"You're meant to be spending time with *him*. Now go and get yourself sorted and I'll find out the train time. I have a dongle!" I retrieved it from my pocket and waved it around.

"I think Ronan was cross with me, until the pig thing."

"Yes, he was. Ronan's an old-fashioned man in most ways. He didn't like that you let me go out in the cold, which is something he wouldn't have done himself."

He nodded slowly and sighed. "See, I'm selfish."

"If you recognise it, change it. If you don't, don't complain that more people will be cross with you." I knew I sounded like his mother, or a teacher, with my lecture, but it was the kindest way I could tell him he had to change.

The last few conversations that I'd had with him had made me worried because of some of the things he'd said. He was overly critical of people, moaning about things that would have passed over his head before. I truly felt he had been single for such a long time, it would take a period of adjustment and although they didn't live together, I wondered if he was secretly holding back on the proposal because he was scared.

"Why haven't you asked Danny to marry you?" I asked.

Joe shrugged his shoulders. "If I tell you this, you'll think I'm nuts. He has his shit together in his life, his job, and emotionally. I seem to be childish in comparison. I love him to bits, but he seems way more grown-up than me."

"Hold up. The man that had a blow up doll on his bed, a stuffed cat, handcuffs? The man who let me think he'd shagged a hooker? And who commented when I farted? You think he's more grown-up than you?"

He squinted his eyes. It looked like he wanted to frown but Botox had other ideas. "He commented when you farted?"

"Yes, now back to my question."

Joe laughed. "I'm a right misery at the moment, aren't I? He's no more grown-up than I am, but I get scared he's going to leave me."

"He isn't, so don't try to sabotage your relationship by being a jerk. I won't forgive you if you do that."

He smiled and reached over to take my hand. "I've been a jerk to you. I'm sorry. I think the pig thing might have been a little payback from your other half."

I nodded. "I think I agree with you on that one. You did look funny, though!"

After finishing our drinks, Joe went to pack. I was a little relieved for two reasons. Joe was irritating me and I didn't want that, and I honestly believed he needed to be back with Danny. Or I was using their falling out as an excuse. Something had changed between us, I wasn't exactly sure what. I didn't feel as close, like I could tell him anything, and I hadn't felt that way for some time. Perhaps it was because I was settled in a relationship, living a whole new life as well.

"Where's Joe?" Ronan asked when he came in. I was still sitting at the kitchen table.

"Gone to pack. I'm meant to be looking at train times. Can we get him over to Oban?" I asked, forgetting there was a ferry ride to undertake as well.

"I'll find out."

In my haste for Joe to get back home, I'd forgotten the part about getting to the train station in the first place. Ronan made a couple of calls and wrote down some times. When he'd finished his call he told me the only ferry out was in an hour's time and the trains were running, although not directly. He'd have to change before getting his last one back to London. I met Joe on the stairs. He was coming down with his holdall as I was climbing up to meet him.

"Ronan has found out the times, we're going to have to leave now, though."

"How will I get there?"

"I think, after Maggie flattened the whole route with the tractor, we'll be safe in the Land Rover," Ronan said with a laugh.

"Don't come, will you. I think I'll cry, otherwise," Joe said, and his comment surprised me.

"You're only going back home, Joe. I'll be back down in a month or so, and I'm sure you'll be back up here," I said.

He mumbled as we hugged and I didn't catch what he said. He then walked to the front door.

"Joe?"

He raised an arm and waved over his shoulder without turning around.

"Don't be so fucking dramatic!" I scolded. He laughed, turned his head, and gave me a wink. "I'll see you soon," I added.

I shut the front door to keep the cold out and walked back to the kitchen.

"Are you okay?" Maggie asked, concern laced her voice and her brow furrowed.

"Yes…No… I don't know."

"Let me get a cuppa and you can tell me all about it," she said.

When she'd sat I relayed our conversation and that I felt there had been a crack in our friendship. Maggie agreed that she felt Joe was different during his visit but we put it down to his falling out with Danny. Hopefully, in a day or two, the pair would be on the phone being silly and taking the piss, as usual. I thanked her for the chat, took the dongle and headed to the library. I had a website to investigate and emails to check.

———

Later that evening, over dinner, Charlie laughed at Joe's epic fall in the pig shit and I mused some more on my conversation with him. Ronan had confessed that Joe was quiet on the way to the ferry and that, although he gave a friendly goodbye, there was something not right.

"I think he might be seeing how different our lives have become now. I know this sounds terrible but I don't fit in his world anymore, and he doesn't fit in mine."

I surprised myself by saying the words that had been whirling around my mind for a few hours. I really felt he didn't fit and he didn't make much effort to. He loved Ronan, Maggie, and Charlie. He loved the house, but I felt a little like he lorded it up sometimes and was expecting to be waited on. We didn't view Maggie and Charlie as staff, they were family, and I wasn't about to allow him to do that, either.

After we'd headed to bed, Ronan held me in his arms and kissed the top of my head. "You know, if you want for us to be in Kent more, we can," he said.

I looked up at him. "I don't want to, and I think that's where part of the problem is. I think both Joe and I are feeling the separation that's coming. I'm not sure we should even keep the barn anymore."

I wasn't sure of Ronan's thoughts but I got the feeling he preferred Scotland to the south as well.

He smiled at me. "We have plenty of time to make decisions like that. Who knows, once you've cleaned out those pigs a few times, one of which you now own, you might be rushing back to Prada and Harrods, and afternoon tea at The Ritz."

I sat up. "You bought me a pig?"

"I bought you a piglet, but it has rickets and should be slaughtered."

I clapped my hands in delight. "You bought me a pig with rickets? Oh my God, that's so amazing of you. I love you… I love you."

I peppered his face with kisses, having no idea what rickets was and how it was likely to affect my piglet. I wanted to rush outside and hug him, or her, but Ronan wasn't letting go of me anytime soon. I laughed as he suggested ways I should show my appreciation for the piglet, of course, I obliged.

15

The following morning the pigs were moved, leaving one piglet that had already been weaned. He was distressed, though so I sat in his stable and he was absolutely adorable. He collapsed into my lap and allowed me to stroke him. Ronan told me that we needed a very specific diet and he was going to rig up a lamp to give as much fake *natural* light as possible. The piglet was deficient in various vitamins and the rickets was down to a poor diet. I questioned whether the whole lot should go back to the owner. Ronan shrugged his shoulders and told me it wasn't for him to make that decision. I hoped, since the piglet was the only one with rickets, the rest were better treated.

"Charlie, do you think you could take out some of these planks?" I showed him what I wanted removing between the two stables.

"I can, but why?" he asked.

"I think, if the pig can see the llama and goat, he might not be distressed."

Charlie pursed his lips and scratched his chin. "I think I might have a better idea," he said.

He set about to remove the lower half of the internal wall and replaced it with one of the iron railings used to make the dog pens. It took him an hour and I often heard him swearing at the animals, particularly Gerald. It was time to take action on that headbutting goat.

I grabbed the keys and headed up to the loft rooms. There were four in total, originally they would have been for staff but over the years each room had been filled with many unwanted items. Maggie and I had cleared two of the rooms and set one up as her sewing room. The other remained empty. The two I headed for, however, hadn't been touched and were on the list, particularly if the plumbing was upgraded. The engineers would have to get into those rooms.

"Ah ha," I said as I spotted what I was looking for.

I climbed over some old furniture and leaned to grab what I was after. I smiled as I ran one hand over it to brush off the dust, then I carried it downstairs and grabbed a large pair of scissors as I walked through and out of the kitchen.

"What are you doing?" Ronan asked, he'd returned from moving the pigs.

"Watch," I said. I opened the door to the stable and slid in.

Ronan waited outside and looked through the bars. He started to laugh when he realised what I was doing.

I cut two pieces of pipe lagging and rammed them over Gerald's horns. He could headbutt us as much as he liked from then on and it wouldn't hurt. He wasn't impressed, neither was Colleen. She stood still and stared at him for an age. If llamas could squint and frown, she would have done both. When Gerald decided to leap all over the stable either in joy or utter horror that his horns had been wrapped, she snorted at him. The piglet squealed when Charlie moved and he was able to see his neighbours.

"That's a great idea, Charlie," Ronan said. I half expected him to accept the credit.

Charlie nodded my way. "Yer lassie's idea," he said.

I smiled at both. "I thought it might make a great weaning area for any other animals we end up with," I said.

Ronan's eyes grew wide. "These three will be it, trust me. I've seen the licence for a petting zoo. Bloody nightmare, that's going to be," Ronan moaned but I knew he'd continue to investigate the idea. He wrapped an arm around my shoulder. "Are you feeling better knowing Joe and Danny are okay?"

I nodded. I'd taken a call that morning from Joe apologising for his dramatics. He put Danny on the phone, who also apologised for Joe's dramatics, and promised me that it wouldn't happen again. He was going to drag Joe kicking and screaming into his real age and stop him from being so childish, so he said. I laughed at the comment. I was pleased to hear them both.

As we walked back to the house, we saw the lights flicker on and off. It appeared the electricity had been fixed, finally. Ronan left to turn off the generator and save some fuel. It had been powerful enough to ensure we could ignite the boiler but it wasn't up to having the lights on at the same time. I wondered if us going off-grid might be something to look at as well. I'd heard of many grants for solar, wind, and alternative energies and I'd recently watched a television programme about a farmer using all his own muck and waste to generate gas.

"What does the tenant farmer do with all his animal waste?" I asked, when Ronan joined me.

"Spreads most of it," he replied.

"I was wondering about biomass and alternative energies. We can get grants for those, I think."

"I know. To be honest, it was something I thought of when I had to drag that old generator out of the shed in the pissing rain and snow!"

I decided to keep the dongle for any future emergencies since the electricity was back on. Ronan and I put all our devices on to charge and I laughed.

"All this talk about going off-grid and here we are, rushing around to find enough chargers for our phones, laptops, and iPads. Oh, I mustn't forget my Kindle," I said, rushing upstairs to grab the lead.

Since it was still way too cold out, Ronan and I camped in the library to work. He had accounts to go through, payments to make to suppliers, and invoices to send. I smiled to myself, for a man who hadn't thought he'd make a great estate manager; he was doing a grand job. He had given the students some time off, it was their college half-term anyway and there was no point trying to work in the snow.

Once my laptop had sufficient charge I opened my emails. About half were for Bitcoin traders and penile enlargement gadgets and the rest were exciting.

We'd received an email from a film company, they were to record a series about extreme hobbies and someone had nominated Petal. She had sent an email as well. I closed down the film company one and read her's first.

"Ronan, listen to this," I said and I then read. "My lovelies, I've been approached by a company who want to film us old wrinklies doing our art. I've given them your details because they asked where we hold our meetings. I think they just want to see our saggy tits and wobbly bits, or was it limp dicks ha ha ha (I love that, btw). Anyway, I've spoken to the group, and providing you are happy, we're quite excited about showing off our *art*. But who knows, nothing may come of it. I look forward to hearing back from you. Love, Petal aka Saggy Tits."

I was laughing as I'd read, partly in embarrassment, I wasn't aware she'd heard that I'd called her and Eric that before I knew their names. I did mean it with affection and as a term of endearment, but it was awfully rude as well. I was relieved she'd taken it in jest.

"They're happy to be filmed running around the woods, naked, hugging trees, and painting crap?" Ronan said.

"I don't suppose they think they're painting *crap*, that's not nice," I chastised.

Ronan held up his hands in surrender. "I stand corrected. So, they're happy to be filmed running around the woods, naked, hugging—"

"Yes, it appears they are. Now they need your permission, as does the film company. I doubt it's a paying gig, I doubt, but the publicity could be good."

Ronan raised his eyebrows. "Have a think on how we can capitalise on that. Considering we're inviting families to use our camping park, I'm not sure. Of course they can film, but I think we need to keep the venue name out of it."

He had a fair point. We didn't make money from the art retreat; we were hoping to do so from the campers. We didn't want anything to scupper that.

"I'll reply asking for further details, shall I?" I asked and Ronan nodded.

I replied to a couple more emails, one from the location agency who wanted to send a scout to assess us for the pilot of another drama, a *Midsomer Murders* type thing. I was excited about that, as it could run into a series. That was good money. With appointments made, I decided to take a break and logged in to my Facebook account. I hadn't visited it in two years and was surprised to see no messages. It appeared no one was missing me, and I laughed at the thought. I hadn't thought once about any of the old *friends* I'd had, realising long before Ronan, they hadn't been genuine. Something did catch my eye in my notifications, though.

Although old, there was a mention of me from my ex. I clicked on the link and I was taken to one of Joe's many pages. The post was a picture of me, a very unflattering one. My ex had commented that I was *'looking good'* and Joe had 'laughed' at his sarcasm. Not just liked with a thumbs up but used the laugh emoji. I guessed, I'd just taken a shower and perhaps tried one of my many facial scrubs. My skin was red and blotchy, I looked wretched. I couldn't remember when it was taken but I knew I hadn't been crying. I'd have looked way worse. Joe and I had tried a chemical peel one time and I wondered if that was where the image came from. However, it wasn't the image I was worried about, although it was horrid. It was the fact Joe hadn't bothered to correct my ex on what was going on.

I scrolled around that particular page and it appeared to be dedicated to me!

The more I looked the more furious I became. "What's

wrong?" Ronan asked after hearing me huff and, I guessed, seeing the scowl on my face.

"Look at this shit," I said, turning the laptop slightly so he could see.

We looked at unflattering image after unflattering image of me and read some of the stupid and derogatory comments. I was not only blown away by the snippiness of some of Joe's, and my old *friends*, but the fact appeared to be supporting it. Some of my images had hundreds of likes and one or two had shares as well. I wasn't aware of most of the images, but I could most certainly explain a few. There was one where I was bending over with my legs straight. I was practicing my pilates in preparation for my one time of attending. I'd worn black leggings but white knickers. Joe had zoomed in on my bum. My knickers were visible through the threadbare material, but not only that, there was a slight bulge from a Tena Lady. I covered my mouth in shock and my eyes filled with tears.

He'd made a comment about thanking God he wasn't a woman of a certain age with a weak bladder. There were some comments in support and a couple who blasted Joe for posting the photo and questioned his friendship with the owner of the arse.

My fingers flew over the keyboard despite Ronan telling me not to reply.

Why would you do this to me? I typed. I pressed send before I could change my mind. Then to make sure he knew I'd seen the whole series, I put an angry emoji on every one of his posts, his comments, and my ex's comments.

Ronan placed his arm around my shoulder without a word. He leaned over and moved the mouse to the cross in the corner and shut down Facebook.

"Why would he do that?" I verbalised my typed comment.

"Because he's insecure, an arsehole, a jerk, a shit friend," Ronan said quietly.

"I don't get it. We've been friends since primary school. I'd never do anything to purposely embarrass him, ever."

I was truly baffled and actually regretted Ronan shutting the page down. I'd have liked to see what else he said on any of this other accounts. I bet there wasn't anything as awful on his business one.

"I'm going to ring him," I said.

Ronan placed his hand on my arm. "Give it until tomorrow. Think about this and how you want to respond. This could make or break your friendship," he said, sensibly.

I sat back. "I'm gobsmacked, Ronan." I wanted to sob. Joe was my best friend and the level of betrayal I felt was like a kick to the chest. I wanted to place my hand over the pain and rub it better. "That was a whole account dedicated to embarrassing me."

I didn't think I'd be as upset if he'd added some joint

pictures or goofy ones of himself, but it was all me. I frowned some more trying to get my head around why he'd do that. Why wouldn't he defend me when my ex commented, even? I started to think. He'd been all over my ex when he and Saucy Sally had bought their million and whatnot pound house from him. He'd been more all over them when he attended their moving in party, for the sake of *business*, he'd told me. He was still in their *circle* because he was buttering up the neighbours to sell their houses for them.

How quickly one can be deserted by a best friend when big money came into play. I shook my head with sadness, and closed the laptop lid. I'd gone from laughter about Petal, excitement about the house being a feature on the television again, to utter sadness and loneliness. Yes, it was loneliness that crept over me. It felt like the crack in our relationship had just widened as much as the Grand Canyon. In that moment, it further cemented my reluctance to return to Kent.

Ronan was correct, of course. I needed to sleep on it before I confronted him and I also knew I'd do that over the phone. I didn't want to be face-to-face, simply because he could often win me round with silly faces and empty promises or lame excuses. Yes, he could *hide* on the phone but so could I. I wasn't sure I wanted to see him.

"How about a walk to the pub for a break and some lunch?" Ronan asked.

I did fancy the distraction. "Will they have food in?" I asked, as I rose to layer up.

"Of course," he replied with a laugh. I guessed nothing put the locals off their pint and a pie in the evenings, not even a ton of snow.

———

It was nice walking with Ronan. The air was cold and crisp and the brightness of the weak sun reflecting off the snow ensured we shielded our eyes. We should have thought to wear sunglasses or ski goggles. I hadn't told Ronan of how that pang of loneliness had lingered, I didn't want him to think he wasn't enough, because he was. I had, however, a lifetime of history with Joe and, should our friendship be irrevocably broken, that would take another lifetime to replace. I began to get angry. As irrational as it was, my only thought was I'd wasted all those years with my ex, and I'd also wasted all those years with a best friend who had betrayed me. For the first time ever, I wasn't going to let him get away with it. I wasn't going to let him just do the doe eyes and say he was sorry. My level of hurt went beyond that. I wanted an explanation, a satisfactory one, before I could even consider forgiving him.

We pushed through the door into the pub, stomped the snow from our boots, and removed our coats, gloves, hats, and scarves in the door well and hung them up.

"Afternoon. How was the journey?" Patrick called out from behind the bar.

"Cold," Ronan replied with a laugh. "You got your power back on then?" he asked.

"No, not yet. We're still on the genny and running out of fuel," Patrick replied.

"We have spare, I'll run some cans down later for you, just in case. Our power came back on an hour ago."

"I think they're concentrating on the houses before the businesses," he said, and I detected, rightly so, annoyance. Patrick lived at the pub; it wasn't just a business. It was also important to the local community who, like the café, could visit for warmth and sustenance.

I wriggled onto a bar stool and grabbed a specials menu from the rack. There wasn't the full menu on, of course, but anything that didn't necessarily need cooking was there. I opted for a ham and mustard sandwich, accompanied by crisps and a salad. Ronan chose the beef. He chatted with Patrick about the weather and I sipped on a glass of cold white wine. I enjoyed listening to them. When Ronan conversed with anyone outside the house, his accent became stronger. He wasn't aware of it, I guessed, because he was always surprised when I mentioned it. Even though Ronan was deep in conversation he kept his hand on my thigh, squeezing every now and again to let me know he hadn't forgotten I was there. I appreciated him for that.

Eventually, Patrick apologised for monopolising Ronan and

left us to settle in one of the sofas in front of the fire. He'd taken our order and headed back to the kitchen. Although the estate owned the pub, it was leased to Patrick who also had the accommodation above. Before, Ronan had installed a manager but it made more sense to just lease it out. It was income without the hassle and it certainly had stopped Ronan's ex from bugging him. I was loathed to think about her, or even mention her name for fear of conjuring her up. She had disappeared of late and we were both thankful for that.

"I love this place," I said, settling back into the old and cracked leather. The smell of burning logs, the crackle and spit of sap could have lulled me to sleep if I'd let it.

"Tired still?" Ronan asked.

"It's this bloody menopause," I replied straightening up so I wouldn't doze off. "The things it does are way beyond what I thought."

Like most women pre-menopause I thought I'd get night sweats, perhaps a little hairy in places I didn't want it, a little dryness, and that was an easy fix, and maybe some weight gain. I hadn't banked on the tiredness, the memory loss, trying to find the right words for things (which was rather frightening in the beginning), in addition to the hot sweats, the cold sweats, the peeing a lot, and the tossing and turning in bed.

"Well, I've been doing some research. Green tea is good,

ginseng, and some essential oils. I've ordered some from Amazon."

I laughed at him. "You're not like many men, Ronan. Most would be running in the opposite direction with talk of menopause and whatnot."

"Your menopause is important; it affects you *and* me, so why would I not get involved?" He genuinely seemed baffled that I thought it odd.

Maybe I was wrong. "Well, I appreciate it and I happen to love green tea. Which reminds me, one thing I miss is a decent Chinese restaurant."

"We haven't had a proper date night in a long time, have we? I'll have to organise something." He scratched his chin and his brow furrowed as if he was immediately planning.

"Make sure you give me plenty of notice. I don't even know where my posh clothes are now."

Ronan and I had taken over one of the smaller bedrooms to use as a dressing room. I didn't want to clutter our bedroom with tons of furniture and, between us, we seemed to have a lot of clothes. Mine, however, were more spread between the two locations and most of my posh frocks and high heels were back down south.

"I could ask…No, I can't. I'll make do," I said, then giving him a broad smile. I was going to say that I could ask Joe to package some items and send them to me, but I wouldn't.

"I'm sure you'd find some new shoes in town," he said.

"Yeah, if flat backs or Wellington boots were what I wanted." I laughed at the lack of Louboutins on offer.

"Do you miss all that?" he asked. I frowned at him, not sure, initially, what he meant. He clarified, "The London life, the parties and theatre, restaurants."

"No, not really. It's nice to go out for a meal that isn't the pub, of course, but I'm not craving it," I replied.

"I just wondered. Still, you can have a hen party or whatever they're called now back in Kent," he said, laughing and winking at me.

"Oh, no need to worry about any of that for a while," I replied, totally sure he was joking...*hoping* he was joking.

He'd mentioned marriage a couple of times...well, not marriage as such, but things relating to marriage. He'd talked about getting that marriage licence so we could set up an area around one side of the loch as I'd suggested.

He fell silent and looked into the fire. I hoped he didn't think I wouldn't marry him; I was simply worried about the whole event. As awful as it sounded, I wasn't sure I wanted all the hoopla of a wedding. My parents would be a nightmare, I'd have to invite Joe and Danny, I didn't have anyone else, so my side of the venue would be empty... There were a ton of reasons I didn't want a wedding, but that didn't mean I never wanted to get married. I should've voiced my concerns, but I still wasn't sure if Ronan was serious or not.

"Although, we can always run away to Gretna Green and not tell anyone," I offered in appeasement. Ronan smiled at that.

The more I'd thought about it, the more I'd be happy with a quick private ceremony, maybe just with Maggie and Charlie, and the go for a meal somewhere. As tacky as Gretna Green was, once I'd said it, it had actually started to appeal.

16

Of course, I woke early hours of the morning to pee, but not only that, Joe's Facebook page had been on my mind. I climbed out of bed gently, so as not to disturb Ronan, wrapped my robe around myself, and left the bedroom. I avoided all the creaking treads on the staircase and headed to the kitchen to make myself a cup of tea. As I passed the library, I nipped in and grabbed my laptop. I did what I shouldn't have done and that was to open that blasted page again.

Anger flowed over me, more than before, when I saw that one of my *supporters* had commented under my comment and chastised Joe some more. He had replied to her! I didn't know this supporter but the fact he had seen what I'd posted, had taken the time to comment to his friend but not made any attempt to contact me, made me furious. I unfriended him, blocked him, and then, as a final insult, I posted on my page how life was treating me wonderfully and I'd soon be sharing details of my new life in Scotland. When I thought about it, it wasn't a bad idea. My parents lived on Facebook as well. It could be a nice way to share my life with them instead of photographs over Whatsapp. I played around until I found the family only button, effectively cutting everyone outside of my parents from my life. It hadn't occurred to me, then, Joe wouldn't see my nice new life post.

"Bollocks to you," I said.

Before I closed the lid something caught my eye. A tab had been left open and I knew what the words meant but also that I hadn't looked it up. I opened it to see the words, *Marrying at Gretna Green.*

"Oh, gawd," I said. Ronan was the only other one who used my laptop when he couldn't be bothered to retrieve his own. He'd hinted at marriage, I'd backed off and I wasn't sure why. He hadn't mentioned it again.

I was super surprised by what I saw, though. I expected getting married at Gretna would be a quick in and out of a registry office in your work clothes. How wrong I had been! It was a beautiful blacksmith's with a choice of three 'rooms.' In addition, there was a hotel.

If Ronan surprised me with a wedding, of course I'd marry him. I just didn't want a *public* wedding. Eloping would be my choice, so I didn't need to worry. Perhaps he was thinking about my idea of getting a wedding licence and making a beautiful area by the loch. I really liked that idea.

With positive thoughts in my mind, I drank my tea and headed back to bed. I snuggled into his back, spooning, and breathed in his scent. He clasped one of my hands and held it to his heart. I kissed the back of his neck and then settled back into sleep.

————

The more the day wore on, the more despondent I grew, Joe'd had plenty of time to contact me and he hadn't. Ronan was upset for me after I'd told him I'd visited the page again and Joe had seen my comment.

"Maybe get in touch with Danny?" he offered.

I shook my head decisively. "No, if Joe can't do this without being told, I don't want to hear from him." I was adamant, I was cross, and there was a part of me so terribly disappointed still.

I sat with Maggie and told her what I'd discovered. She was as baffled as I'd been. We explored every explanation we could think of and dismissed them all. He wasn't jealous of me, income wise we were about the same I imagined. He couldn't be missing me because some of the images were prior to meeting Ronan. We started to lean towards Charlie's diagnosis that he was just a *spoilt wee brat that's had it tae easy and doesnae consider anyone else's feelings.*

I had blossomed at Charlie's comment. It made me feel like his daughter; like he really cared for me. I had a loving, if somewhat odd, father but we hadn't been in the same country for decades. Charlie's comment made me realise I'd missed that bond and I was grateful to him and Maggie. When Charlie and Ronan had left to catch up with some estate work, I filled Maggie in with what I had discovered about Gretna plans.

"Do you think he actually wants to get married?" I asked.

"I think so, he's mentioned it before."

"But was he serious? I'm not sure."

Maggie folded her arms over her chest. "I'll test the waters, and I promise not to give away that you've seen the page," she said. I wasn't entirely sure she could keep that promise, of course.

"It would be lovely, wouldn't it?" she said, and then rested back in the kitchen chair. It creaked and I worried she might end up on her backside. For a few days, I'd been asking Ronan or Charlie to look at the chairs. "We'd love you as a daughter-in-law. As would have Verity," she added with tears brimming in her eyes.

I gave her a hug and headed to the library to get some work done. I'd promised Ronan I would investigate an online accountancy package that was simple to use and would save both time and money. I hadn't realised just how confusing that was likely to be! Still, it whiled away a couple of hours where I didn't have to think about Joe. Once I'd done that, I started on government grants for alternative energies. That was a minefield and it became quite obvious to me how disproportionately government money was distributed around the UK. Scotland had the perfect environment for solar or wind, yet I couldn't find any help towards those costs. I could find a lot of dos and don'ts and plenty of ways the local council would interfere, but not many offers of help, considering the whole community could benefit if we could put electricity back into the grid. I was on a mission though, an ecological mission. It also started me thinking about how wasteful I was.

I grabbed my *ideas* pad and wrote – second-hand clothes fashion show.

I thought that more appropriate than my first idea. The whole community could be involved, and we could donate money to charity. In addition, we could invite local producers to showcase their wares. It could be a mini country fair.

Oh, kilts! I thought. I hadn't the opportunity to see Ronan in his kilt. I'd seen it, the tartan was very impressive as was his sporran and I was surprised by the weight of it. He'd wear it with a smart dress shirt and jacket.

"Unless I'm going *grunge*, then it would be work boots and a torn T-shirt," he said at the time. My heart and hooha fluttered at the thought.

Yes, a mini country fair where Ronan could show me his

grunge look for sure. It might also attract campers at the same time. I doubted I'd have time for that year, but it could certainly go in the calendar for the next.

———

A week had passed and I hadn't heard from Joe. I became angrier but I wouldn't give in. I wasn't going to make the first move and I could only hope his silence was because he was embarrassed and not because he just didn't care.

The snow had melted to a muddy slush and storms were predicted to follow on. Maggie and I drove into town to drop off cakes for the bakery, and do a little shopping for ourselves. Ronan had told me we had a date night looming and I was excited. I wasn't to know what it was, but I'd need an overnight bag and a posh frock.

I was loathed to buy online, I was an awkward shape and a size between two others so it didn't exist. I had spotted a little clothes shop and although some of the items looked very dated and very *mother of the bride*, I hoped I might find a sexy little black number somewhere on their racks. I was pleasantly surprised when I walked through the door. I was welcomed, offered a cup of tea and any assistance. I said I wanted a frock for a surprise night out, so couldn't offer any further details, and low and behold, I was directed to a nice collection of… *My Big Fat Gypsy Wedding* came to mind. There were acres of tulle and fluff and sequins and not one little black slinky number. I pretended to search through and feigned interest, until Maggie joined me.

"She's not a bloody drag queen in the pantomime, Shelly," she scolded, and I had to cross my legs to stop pee leaking.

"Well, what does she want then?" came the response, as if I wasn't standing there.

"Something our Ronan would want to rip off with his teeth," Maggie replied, and she even mimicked the action. She bared her teeth and shook her head side to side.

"You look like one of the dogs with a bone," I said, mortified at her statement.

"Well, why didn't she say that?" Shelly replied, ignoring me. "I've got just the thing."

I dreaded to know what *just the thing* was. Shelly rushed off to the back of the store and I heard her call me to the makeshift dressing room. It was two clothes rails on either side and a curtain draped over the front. It would be fine until someone parted the dresses on the rail, of course.

However, hanging there was slinky black number. It wasn't sequined but had a shimmer to it. I guessed the cotton had been threaded with some sort of silk thread. I quickly tried it on. It was a little loose around the boobs but Maggie assured me she'd take it in. It slid off the shoulders because it was misshaped, but I actually liked that. It accidently formed a cowl neck. With a nip in at the waist and hips as well, it would do the job. I checked the price tag. If Shelly thought I was paying slinky black, rip it off with your teeth prices for that garment she was in for a surprise.

"I like it, but I'm not paying that. I'm sorry, Shelly, I'm sure someone else would but I've got to get it altered and it's just too expensive," I said, showing her the hundred pound price tag.

"Huh?" she replied. She grabbed the tag and then removed her glasses. She waved them across my face. "Put these on and look again," she said, snottily.

"Ah, okay, I misread," I said, when I did as she offered and saw the bargain price of ten pounds.

I laughed. I didn't think I'd ever bought a dress for a tenner. It was a bargain, even if it needed some alteration. With a nice silk scarf and silver jewellery, it would be fine. How the dress would look with my flats, boots, wellies, or Converse, I wasn't sure. I highly doubted I'd get some shoes in the high street.

"She did write one hundred pounds on that. Thought she could have you over, she did," Maggie said as we left the shop.

"I thought it had but then there was a dot."

"But not enough zero's for ten pounds. She's a cheeky mare, that one. I'll keep my eye on her from now on. Now, it's a crappy dress but we can do something with it," she added, bolstering my lack of desire to actually wear the bloody dress!

Not knowing what Ronan had planned was a nuisance. I had a pair of court heels that would do but I'd rather have had some strappy sandals. But then, as far as I knew, we could be out in a field somewhere. He was going to have to give me a clue.

"Anything from Joe?" Maggie asked as we drove back to the house.

"No, and I'm not giving in, Mags. I don't believe that he didn't see my comment, and for whatever reason he can't bring himself to ring me. That's on him. I'm not giving him an easy route out of that one. I've done that a lot, I can see that now," I confessed.

It had taken a few long drawn-out conversations with Ronan for me to see that I had often given Joe an easy get out when he had offended me, for fear of upsetting him or rocking our relationship. I remembered back to his constant 'cougar' comments when I was single and even after telling him I was upset, he'd continued.

We arrived back at the house at the same time as a soaking wet Ronan arrived in the courtyard on a quad.

"What happened?" I asked.

"Bloody stag got stuck in the banks of the loch. I had to wade in and push him out," he said.

"Could've towed him," Charlie said, joining us.

"Then we would have damaged him," Ronan said, grumpily. Charlie rolled his eyes so dramatically I thought they might fall out. I wanted to laugh but I wasn't sure Ronan thought it funny.

"Was he okay?" I asked.

"Yeah, we'll check on him tomorrow but I want to know why he was there. The herd wasn't anywhere near," he said in a worried voice. He climbed off the bike. "What do you have there?"

"A cheap crappy dress, according to Mags. You might have to give me a hint on where we're going," I said, waving the blue plastic bag around. "Do I need a posh dress?" I asked.

He took a deep breath in and then exhaled slowly. He squinted his eyes and pursed his lips.

"Don't piss around," I said, and he laughed.

"I think you'd like to wear something nice for one evening, for sure. I'll be wearing a suit and tie. I'll pack the rest of your things." He smiled and then left.

"He'll pack your things," Maggie repeated as if I hadn't heard. She sighed as if it was the most romantic thing in the world.

"I'm going to make sure I lay stuff out on the bed otherwise he's bound to forget my makeup and hair brushes," I said, rushing off to get that done before he finished his shower.

I had laid out all my makeup and brushes, underwear, toiletries, when Ronan came out of the bathroom with a towel around his waist.

"You won't need that, or those," he said, throwing my toiletries to the other side of the bed.

"I need to wash," I said, laughing.

"You need to trust me," he replied.

He threw the towel over the chair the corner and while I admired his naked form, he pulled clothes from the wardrobe. I studied each piece as if it would give me a clue to where we were going. The problem was, the collection was too mixed. There was a pair of jeans, a woollen jumper, and fluffy socks. Then there were a couple of smart shirts and a pair of trousers. Ronan kept a shirt and the trousers slightly to one side. It was a smart casual outfit.

"For travelling," he said, following my gaze to the outfit.

"For travelling?" I enquired. It seemed rather too smart just for a car journey.

"Yes. Now, will you sod off so I can get this done?"

"No. I'm rather enjoying the view, if that's okay."

"That's perfectly okay, but you're distracting me."

"Mmm, good, I like distracting." I climbed on the bed amid the clothes and laid back.

He swiped my clothes over the floor and climbed on the bed beside me.

"Okay, you win," he said, with a laugh.

It was an hour later that he managed to pack my overnight bag.

17

"Are you kidding me?" I squealed. I wanted to run towards the helicopter that was parked on the front lawn but knew to wait until instructed to approach. "This is our date?" I asked.

"This is how we get to our date," Ronan replied. He held our overnight bags and I wore the smart shirt and trousers.

The pilot stood beside and waved us over. He held my hand as I climbed aboard the small helicopter and was strapped in. He told me to place the earphones on my head and I'd be able to speak to him and Ronan, who was buckling up beside me.

"I've always wanted to do this," I said, into the mouth-piece. I jumped as Ronan replied.

"I remember you said one time." He turned to smile at me.

"I can hear you," I shouted and then laughed.

"You don't need to shout," he replied, also laughing.

The pilot gave us some vague details of what we were going to fly over, too vague for me to know where we were heading, of course. Then we were off. I expected the helicopter to simply lift straight off the ground in a vertical take off. It didn't. It was as if the back end rose, the nose stayed down, and we travelled forwards for a little while before eventually gaining height. I wanted to scream with delight. I grabbed hold of Ronan's hand and held on while I watched the landscape. We headed inland and across the country so I guessed we were staying in Scotland.

It wasn't long before the most glorious house came into view. It was surrounded by a golf course, woodland, and small buildings. I thought I recognised the house, a stately home, I thought. As we lowered to land, the pilot welcomed us to Gleneagles.

I strained my neck looking around Ronan and the most amazing building to our side. Impressive wasn't a good enough word. Ronan patted my knee to gain my attention. He had removed his earphones and I did the same. Once the rota blades had stopped, the pilot opened the door for us. He reached behind our seats to gather our bags and we followed him to an entrance. He handed our bags over to a porter and bid us a good stay. We were encouraged through to reception. All I could do was stare. I'd been in some super hotels in my time, but there wasn't anything in

London, in my opinion, that compared and I told the receptionist so.

"We hope that you enjoy your stay, Mr. and Mrs. Carter-Windford," she said, handing over a key card.

"It's not…" Ronan started.

"Thank you, that's very kind of you," I interrupted and took the key. I smiled at Ronan.

Had he wanted to correct her for my sake, or his? I wasn't sure but the minute she'd said those words, I liked the sound of them. Maybe it was time to stop being a twit about marriage and embrace the thought.

The room was wonderful. Not a full suite, I'd have had a heart attack to know Ronan had paid the prices I imagined those cost, but a lovely room overlooking the park. There was a large double bed and separate seating area with two sofas facing each other in the bay of a large window. The porter left our bags on the bed and we stood looking out the window.

"This is amazing, thank you so much," I said, taking his hand in mine.

"You're worth it, as the advert says. Now, we have a spa day starting in a minute and I'm fucking terrified of that!" He laughed.

"A spa day? How fantastic. I haven't done anything like this in years. Why are you scared?" I asked.

"Because, unlike you, I've *never* done this. The closest I've come to a massage is the osteo cracking my spine one time. I thought you might like a little of that luxury you've given up," he said, gently.

"Whatever I've given up, Ronan, I've gained far more with you, the house, Maggie and Charlie, and Scotland. I don't *need* fancy hairdressers and nail salons. I don't *need* Louboutin shoes. I'm happy with a pair of woollen socks and my boots, dirty nails from helping you on the estate, and a hat on my head."

He pulled me into a hug and I could feel his heart beating rapidly. He kissed the top of my head as I wrapped my arms around his waist.

"I love you, and I love all there is about you. I willingly give up London and all that false crap for your honesty any day of the week," I whispered.

His arms tightened around me. "Well, we can't stay like this. I doubt they want to massage me with a raging hard-on," he said, pulling me away.

"Do we have time for...?" I enquired, he checked his watch.

"For what they're charging, I'm sure they can wait half an hour." He gave me a wink as he reached out to undo the buttons of my shirt.

—————

"If you would like to make yourself comfortable, I'll bring some tea and your therapists will be with you shortly," we were told and shown to a sumptuous seating area. Within a few minutes, a ceramic white pot of the green tea we'd ordered was placed on the coffee table with dainty cups.

"Oh, this is nice," I said. I ran my hand over the velvet I was sitting upon. "I guess this mood lighting is to make us look good," I added with a chuckle.

The blue and green subtle lights weren't actually doing me any favours as I squinted to see. I had my reading glasses but wondered if I needed *seeing* glasses as well.

"You look good to me in any light," Ronan replied.

"Such a charmer," I laughed at him. "Honestly, though, if you think I'm missing all this, I'm not. But I really appreciate what you've done, especially since you're a spa virgin."

With that, two therapists walked over. They sat with us and I learned we were to have a couples day that involved a back, face and scalp treatment, a pro facial, and eye treatment (I wondered if there was a difference between a pro and non pro facial), a personalised massage; we could choose Balinese, hot stone, or aromatherapy, we chose aromatherapy. We then had lunch in the spa café and use of their pool, heat and thermal facilities (whatever they were). Once we'd completed our forms we were encouraged to follow to the changing facilities. We had our own *couples* changing room as well. I giggled as we undressed and Ronan waved around the *shorts* he was to wear.

"What if we make out in here?" he whispered. "Is it as prestigious as the Mile High Club, do you reckon?"

"I bet we'd get a certificate," I replied, with a laugh. "I'd at least want a free massage because I'm sure we'd both get a dodgy back doing the naughty in here."

When we had the correct spa attire on, we left our changing room and were greeted by the smiling therapists. It was only then that we could hear the whispered conversation of the couple in the next room and realised, we'd probably been overheard.

One of the therapists leaned forward and whispered, "It's a ban, I believe, which is a shame." She winked and we laughed, embarrassingly so.

For our first treatment they had us lying on beds side by side on our backs. Ronan reached over and held my hand. I wondered if that was because he was rigid as hell at the thought someone was going to massage him. I wanted to laugh but squeezed his hand instead.

"You can relax now, Mr. Carter-Windford," he was told. To which he replied, "Mmmm."

"He's a spa virgin," I answered for him.

"Ah, okay, well, I'll be sure to go gently and I bet you'll love it," she replied.

The room was warm, and soon the smell of essential oils wafted around. I could hear Ronan sniffing and then he sneezed.

"What's that smell?" he asked.

I laughed out loud. I didn't think the therapists were going to have an easy day with him.

Soon enough, we'd shut our eyes and enjoyed the treatment. I loved a scalp massage, and if I was honest, it was one thing I missed from my old hairdressers, even knowing it was a con to earn an extra twenty quid.

"Would you like to turn over now?" a voice said, rousing me from my doze.

"Sir?" I also heard. Ronan had fallen asleep, totally. He lay on his back with his mouth open, not quite snoring, but more snuffling. I wished I'd thought to take my phone in with us. That would have been a lovely photograph. He looked so relaxed, way more than normal.

"I guess he enjoyed that," I said, giving him a prod.

He snorted, "What?"

"Time to turn over."

"Have I been asleep? Did I miss it all?" he asked, and then laughed. "It must have been riveting." He gave the therapist a wink.

"The biggest compliment you can give is to fall asleep," she replied, clearly enjoying his cheekiness.

For the next hour and a half we were pummelled, we winced, *ouched* on regular occasions, and I rather embarrassingly farted. Ronan moaned. It was wonderful and we loved every minute of our aromatherapy massage that was somewhat close to a beating. I hadn't realised just how tight my muscles were but when knuckles were run over my calves, I wanted to leap from the bed.

"I thought this was meant to be nice," Ronan said, wincing as the knots in his shoulders were teased out. "You pay for this normally?" he hissed out. His moaning spurred her on and she winked at me. I gave her a nod and chuckled.

We finished the morning with a facial and a chance to relax after the massage.

"I think this is all too poncy for me," Ronan said, as cream was slathered over his face.

"But aren't you loving it? Now stop moaning," I replied.

I knew he wasn't moaning for real, it was clearly something he'd never experienced before, and probably wouldn't again, but the skin crinkling beside his eyes showed his contained mirth. He bloody loved it but being the *man* he was, would never admit to it.

We robed up and with our complimentary slippers, headed for lunch.

"I need a pint after that," Ronan said, and to his dismay, he found a café perfectly suited to a spa and wellness centre. "Wine it is then," he said. He did, however, order us a bottle of champagne to compensate for the *power pulses* that masqueraded as food.

Ronan and I laughed way more and way louder than anyone else in the café and it made me smile more to see the staff laughing with us. I doubted they had anyone like Ronan on a regular basis. He was analysing every second and why this wasn't a *bloke's thing*.

"Can you imagine if I had to go and shoot something now? I'm all sticky and *slidey*," he said. I nearly spat my champagne over the table.

"*Slidey?*"

He held up his hands and his calloused palms glistened. "Yes, I wouldn't be able to hold a gun, look!"

"You can wash your hands, you know. You don't have to leave that on. Wipe them on your robe," I explained. As much as I loved a good spa, I also hated to sit oiled up for any length of time.

We ate, we drank, and then we showered and changed into swimwear. We spent an hour in their pool and then lounged beside it.

"I honestly don't know how to thank you for today," I said, resting back with my eyes closed and enjoying the warmth.

"No thanks needed. Although I'm sure I can think of some things if you insist," he replied.

I opened one eye to see him smirking. "Make a list, Mr.

Carter-Windford, and I'll check it over," I mumbled. "You know, if we did get married I might add my surname to yours and we'd be Carter-Windford-Richie." I laughed but he didn't. "I'm kidding," I said and he smiled.

"About the getting married, or about adding your surname?" he asked, quietly.

I guessed we'd got to *that conversation* and although I'd have rather we did it in private, we were alone.

"If you asked me to marry you, of course I'd accept. I'll be honest with what bothers me; you'd have family and friends, and I'd have just my odd parents. I'm not ashamed of them in the least, but it just highlights how isolated my life has been and how fake and crappy my *friends* were. I literally have no one I'd want to invite, and it would make me sad and you'd be worried, and then it wouldn't be the day we wanted and…"

"Lizzie, take a breath, please. When, and not if, *when* we get married, we'll shoot to the registry office in our jeans and boots and sign the papers. Drag a couple of people in from the street as witnesses if we have to. You might have made up with Joe by then…don't shake your head, you don't know what will happen there. Anyway, Lizzie, marry me?"

I had been too busy shaking my head at the *Joe* part; I hadn't listened to the rest of what he'd said.

Ronan climbed from his lounger, with his white robe opened to expose a pair of board shorts and rather nice muscled stomach, he knelt on one knee. The white fluffy slippers with Gleneagles sewn in silver were not so romantic but I overlooked those.

"Lizzie, I love you more than anything or anyone. Will you marry me, in any type of ceremony you want, whenever you want?"

I stared at him, he held my hand.

"Is everything okay?" a therapist asked as she walked past.

"Can you give her a prod? I'm asking her to marry me and I fear she's gone mute. I'll blame your facility if she says no, because I'm sure that facial has suddenly stopped her mouth working."

The therapist looked aghast. Her gaze flipped between us, and she was as frozen as I had been. I started to laugh and nodded my answer. Ronan wrapped his arms around me and, finally, the therapist woke from her trance.

"Oh my God, you had me going there. Did you really ask her to marry you?" she asked.

"Yes, he did, and I've said yes." I laughed through my statement.

She scuttled off only to return with a bottle of champagne and two glasses. "I can't say it's on the house because I'd get fired, but I'll work something out," she said.

"I want to get married at the Blacksmith's in Gretna Green. Just us, my parents, Maggie and Charlie, and maybe a few others." I remembered that I thought he'd checked out that venue.

I'd gone from ignoring Ronan's hints, being paralysed with fear he'd ask me, not wanting to think about it, to demanding we organise Gretna Green.

He laughed. "Slow down. I haven't given you a ring yet. And I do have one, I wasn't expecting to do this right now so I didn't bring it."

Tears pricked at my eyes. "You have a ring?" I asked.

"I have a ring that's precious to me. It was my mother's and my grandmother's before her. I've never found the person I'd want to wear that piece, until you," he said.

I cried. Big fat tears fell from my eyes and plopped into my champagne glass. Snot formed in my nostrils and Ronan had to fuss around to find me a tissue.

"Jesus, Lizzie, this is supposed to be romantic." He laughed, as I loudly blew my nose. The sound echoed around the cavernous space.

"I can't believe this," I said, screwing the tissue into a ball and placing it in the robe pocket.

"Well, it's not quite as I planned it."

"What did you plan?" I asked.

"I haven't. Every time I hinted you ran for the hills, so I was biding my time."

"I saw you'd looked at Gretna Green on my laptop," I said, smiling at him.

"Ah, you spotted my cunning plan. The more ideas I left around, the more it might have softened you," he said, and then he added a terrible attempt to replicate a villain's laugh.

"I only saw that one," I said.

He raised his eyebrows at me. "Damn, that's why it didn't work then. I was way too subtle when I left that bridal magazine around," he said.

"No, you left a magazine about horse tack. Bridles, not bridal."

I knew he was messing with me and the one thing I loved the most with him was the banter.

One side of his mouth raised in a wicked smile. "Maybe I'd like to see you in a little leather."

"No chance. I went to pilates, remember?"

What pilates and leather bridles had in common stumped even me but, like most things, I seemed to spurt random words.

"You went once, Lizzie, once. And you told me you had to leave because you needed to fart," he reminded me.

"I needed to pee," I tried to correct him, even though I was sure I needed to pass wind as well.

We fell silent for a little while. "You won't change your mind, will you?" Ronan asked, and I heard a slight hitch as he spoke. He was worried I might.

"No. We're now officially engaged. In fact…" I reached for the bottle of champagne and peeled off the gold wrapping from the cork. I fashioned it into a ring and handed it to him. "Ask me properly now," I said, and then stood.

Ronan laughed and slid off the lounger. "If I have to keep kneeling, I won't get up so this is the last time, deal?"

I tilted my head and raised my eyebrows in mock thoughtfulness. "Deal," I replied.

"Lizzie Richie, would you do me the honour of becoming my wife?"

For the second time someone walked past, a pool attendant that time, and he was carrying a small tub of chemicals.

"Aw, gosh, I'm sorry I've interrupted. What did she say?" he asked.

"We haven't got to that bit yet, hang around," Ronan replied.

I held out my hand and he slid the gold wrapper onto my finger, I caught the pool attendant looking puzzled.

"He forgot the ring," I said, answering what I believed had made him frown. "Yes, Ronan. Yes, I would be delighted to marry you, again."

"Again?" the pool attendant asked.

"Long story," Ronan replied. We accepted his congratulations and he left. We collapsed onto the loungers in fits of laughter.

"I need to pee now," I said, crossing my legs. "I think that has to be the best proposal in the history of proposals!"

"I think I'm fucking exhausted with all the proposals and I won't be doing it again," he said, laughing.

I kept that wrapper on my finger all the way through a fabulous dinner in the restaurant that evening. I loved the feel of something there, and I looked at it as often and as lovingly as someone stared at a diamond engagement ring.

"I can't wait to show off my ring," I teased, and I took a photograph of it.

I had half a mind to post it to Facebook but declined. It was petty and I didn't need any comments about not having a ring to defend. We did send the pic to Maggie, though, who phoned back immediately. I handed the phone to Ronan as her squeals of delight were hurting my ears.

Ronan and I skipped dessert; we had other plans of how to celebrate our engagement and after three bottles of champagne we were getting a little too giggly for the other diners at the restaurant.

We woke the following morning with sore heads, bed sheets in a tangle, and my golden wrapper ring squashed into my side after I'd laid on it all night.

While I took a shower, Ronan opened the door to allow for our breakfast to be wheeled in. The contents of the trolley were laid on the coffee table in the bay window and Ronan shouted for me.

"Breakfast," he said, waving his arm over the rather obvious meal.

"Coffee is what I need. How much did we drink?" I asked.

"Not enough. Now today you need those clothes." He pointed to the bed where he'd laid jeans, boots, a shirt, and a woollen jumper.

"Oh, intriguing. I guess this is an outdoors activity. And then do we leave?"

"Sadly, yes. And also sadly, not by helicopter. Instead, we travel back by train."

"I don't mind. We can't spoil ourselves too much with all this luxury," I said, with a laugh. Ronan handed me a coffee and I settled on the couch to eat.

"I ordered these because it reminded me of when we drove to London that morning," he said, also handing me a plate with a smoked salmon and cream cheese bagel.

I bit into one. "Not as nice as your salmon..."

"Ours. *Our* salmon," he corrected me and it pulled me up.

"I guess we might need to sort some kind of paperwork out, do we?" I asked.

"For what?"

"The estate and all that if something should happen to us." I wanted him to know if he wanted a prenuptial it would be okay. It was a historic house that needed to stay in his family.

"Bollocks to all that. I'm the last of the line, Lizzie. There are no more to leave that property to, so it becomes yours when I die, which I hope isn't for a while. And then, maybe we need to think about Scottish Heritage taking it over."

"There's Rich," I said.

"He's nothing to do with the estate. I bought his share so it's up to us what we do with it. No prenup, if that's what you're thinking, but we'll have to decide its future for when we're gone."

"Do I become the *laird's wife*?" I asked, joking.

"A *lairdette*, I think they're called," he replied with a chuckle.

We finished eating and, once dressed, headed down to reception. I was presented with a new wax jacket, a Barbour, and a gift from Ronan that had been kept at the hotel with a matching trilby hat in blue. He donned his old one that stunk of dogs and we were taken out in a Land Rover to learn falconry.

I'd never wanted to learn falconry but I knew Ronan was interested as a possible means of pest control. He often called in a local man to scare off the many pigeons and the magpies that decimated the smaller bird population. He chatted to the centre manager about the prospect of introducing more wild birds of prey on the estate. It seemed, over the years, their numbers had dwindled for various reasons, and Ronan was keen to get them back up.

We met falcons, harriers, and kestrels, but the ultimate was a golden eagle. I was kitted out with a large leather glove and the weight of some of the birds was astonishing compared to their size. Ronan, however, got the pleasure of not only holding the birds, but also allowing them to fly and land back on his wrist. He was in his element, stroking and cooing to the animals. He was a natural falconer and I wondered if I could incorporate his desire to increase that population on the estate with a wedding gift. Obviously, I knew I couldn't just pop out to buy a few birds, but I was sure there might something I could investigate.

We spent a pleasant hour before we were ushered off for some shooting. Ronan, again, obviously, came into his element. He hit every clay no matter if it was in the air or skimming the ground. He was an expert shot. I, however, missed most and it was discovered I couldn't keep one eye closed to be able to line up my sight. My eyelid just didn't hold still. I managed to keep myself on my feet and not, as I'd done before, land on my arse from the recoil. I also managed, much to Ronan's delight, not to scream each time I heard a bang. I only apologised once for my nervousness, explaining I was from London as a reason for my unease.

The instructor laughed. "More guns down there than up

here, so I hear," he said in a gruff voice but with no discernible accent.

"Knives, sadly, are the weapon of choice right now," I corrected.

I was handed a pair of safety glasses with one lens blacked out. "This might help," I was told. Ronan laughed, and I imagined I looked silly. It did, however, help and I managed to smash three clays on the trot. I ignored the fact that Ronan stood directly behind and held the gun with me, took aim, and tracked across the sky just in front of the clay. When he shouted for me to fire, I jumped and my finger automatically pulled the trigger. To me, I'd mastered shooting and I was sticking to that.

"Can we get me my own gun?" I asked, as we packed up to head back to the hotel.

"Of course, I'm sure we have some that will be a fit," he replied.

"I want a smart black one, like that one in the cupboard back there," I said.

We'd seen an array of shotguns and there was one that looked more suited to Jason Statham and one of his shoot 'em up movies.

"Unless you're planning on the odd bank job, we'll get a nice side by side for you."

I had no idea what he meant but would, of course, take whatever he suggested.

A vintage Rolls Royce was standing on the drive when we left the hotel. I was looking for a taxi to take us to the station when Ronan started to walk towards it.

"What are you doing?" I asked.

"Gonna see if he'll give us a lift." He spoke to the suited driver standing by the open rear door. "He says, if you give him a hug he'll drive us home."

The suited driver laughed but his cheeks also coloured. I walked over and slapped Ronan on the chest.

"Your ride home, Ma'am," the driver said and I laughed.

"So no train?" I asked.

"No train," Ronan said as he slid across the stiff leather back seat. "That would take about ten hours," he added with a laugh. "This way you get to see the scenery."

I settled into the back and took hold of his hand, then leaned over to kiss his cheek. "I love you," I said.

The journey back to Oban took a little over two hours. It was slightly quicker as the roads had been cleared of snow but people were still avoiding the smaller roads for fear of getting stuck. I was actually disappointed to see Charlie and the Land Rover waiting for us by the ferry. I thanked the driver and we took our bags. There was no handing them to Charlie to place tenderly on the back seat, he hadn't gotten out the driver's one. I laughed as I climbed in.

"So, he did it, did he?" Charlie asked.

I waved the repaired gold wrapper. "He did, and I accepted."

Charlie laughed, well, did his usual cackle and gave Ronan a good old handshake once he'd climbed into the passenger side. He smiled at us, me in the rear-view mirror and over to Ronan, all the way home despite me telling him many time to keep his eyes on the road. Maggie was waiting at the front door and I wondered if she knew exactly, to the minute, how long the journey would be. She embraced us both and announced she had a special dinner planned for us. I told her I didn't want a fuss but she was having none of it.

"It's just for us," she said, as she led the way back into the house. "Now, tell me all about this spa," she added.

We laughed over dinner as I recalled Ronan's experience for him. Of course, I exaggerated at every opportunity and he took it all in good grace. Maggie was laughing and Charlie was backing Ronan and telling us, "That kind of thing isn't good for a man." Maggie and I found that hysterical and without realising I was doing it, I told them of Joe's beauty regime and that it was quite normal for men to have waxing and manicures, facials and massages now.

It had been almost three weeks since I'd seen Joe and my heart ached, especially when we raised our glasses of wine to toast our engagement.

Later that evening we Skyped my parents, who appeared to be naked, but I was thankful the camera wasn't a wide angle and we could only see down to the start of my mother's breasts. My father was so pleased, and my mother was bouncing on her chair at the thought of another wedding. It took all my sturdy resolve to tell them it was a tiny weeny wedding, no guests, just parents. And, no, Aunty Rose, someone I'd never met and who lived in Canada, could not be invited this time. I wasn't even sure when my father had last met his sister. I knew they spoke but that was it.

"Just parents, nothing more," I reiterated, many times. "And clothes, you'll need clothes. Scotland is cold," I said, nodding as I spoke.

My mother sighed. "We'd hardly turn up naked. Now, darling, is there anything you want us to do? Can we send you money?"

My parents didn't have a ton of money, they had their pensions but that was it. I declined their offer of both help and money, not because I didn't want it, although I didn't want the money, but because I didn't need it. My mother actually breathed a sigh of relief. She was a great mother but organisation wasn't her strongest suit. I often reminded her of the many events at school I'd missed because she'd forgotten it was book day or some other rubbish.

"Once we get things booked, we'll send the dates so you can arrange your flights," Ronan said. He had often invited them to come and stay and they hadn't managed to fit it into their busy naturist swinger's schedule.

I'd never known oldies to be so busy and there was a part

of me that envied their *don't give a shit* attitude. They lived in a community of like-minded people, did no harm, volunteered for lots of charities, and lived their best life. When we said our goodbyes and I closed down the screen, I took in a deep breath.

"What's that for?" Ronan asked.

"I don't know, I guess I don't spend enough time with them and they're getting on now."

"They look healthier than we do," he replied, laughing. He was correct, of course. My parents were tanned and fit from all their naked walking up and down mountains.

After Maggie and Charlie had left us, Ronan and I sat with a nice red wine in the living room. The fire was blazing and the lights were low.

"Wait here," he said, suddenly springing up.

"I wasn't going anywhere, but okay," I laughed in reply.

A couple of minutes later, he was back. Sitting in his palm was a black velvet box and I felt tears spring to my eyes again. He opened it slowly, and nestled on the cushion was a clear and sparkling, square cut, single diamond. To either side were two smaller ones and then a band of white.

"The Mountford Diamond, so my grandmother used to call it; Mountford was her maiden name. One of her ancestors smuggled some diamonds on the Titanic to give to a cousin, it's the cousin my gran was related to. Dorothy Mountford survived the sinking, obviously, and so did some of the diamonds she'd stolen from her father. There's a real story to this ring and it's all documented, she wrote a book about it, I believe. This diamond is half of the original one."

I was gobsmacked when, from behind his back, he produced another black velvet box. He placed the ring box on the sofa and opened the other. The other half of the diamond was set in a white gold frame and hung from a delicate necklace, above were two earrings that matched.

"I can't take that," I said, and felt my cheeks heating because I was assuming he was giving them to me.

"You can. This is your engagement ring." He took the ring from the cushion and placed it on my finger. It was too large, which I was surprised at, I would've thought from the paintings, his gran was a slight woman. "We'll get it resized."

He then closed the second box and I was confused. "This," he said, holding onto it. "Will be my wedding gift to you to wear on the day."

"I don't know what to say," I told him, and I genuinely didn't.

The pieces were family heirlooms with an astonishing history. I'd be terrified to lose one of the items and made a mental note to discuss having a replica ring made to wear everyday. Ronan hadn't given them to his first wife, but then his mother had been alive. Somehow, I believed his mother wouldn't have wanted them to go to Carol and I looked up at one of Verity's paintings above the fire. I smiled and silently thanked her.

Ronan and I curled back into the sofa and I snuggled into his side with gentle tears rolling down my cheeks. I stared at the ring, felt it, over and over.

If an object could tell a story, then what a magnificent story that ring would tell.

18

Getting a precious ring resized wasn't something that could be done anywhere on Mull. It took a trip to Edinburgh, a place I'd visited once, many years prior. Ronan and I had made an appointment with a jeweller that only dealt with high-end and bespoke pieces.

He was overly excited to have the Mountford Diamond in his store. "I've heard about this diamond but I've never seen it," he said, donning white gloves to handle it. The enormity of the piece started to sink in then.

"Do you think you'd be able to make the replica?" I asked.

Ronan had been hesitant at first but accepted that I would keep the ring, I'd wear it on special occasions, but I was too scared to wear it every day. I would be the first person I knew to have two engagement rings. The replica, however, wouldn't be identical and we'd opted for a much cheaper diamond, obviously. To ensure that I'd be able to tell the difference, the inside would be engraved. Ronan had wanted the original to be engraved, but I'd talked him out of that. One day, who knew, I might die before him. Without children, or nieces, I'd want the ring to go back to him. When I'd argued that he might give it to another woman, he really got very annoyed with me.

A compromise was found. Well, I'd gotten him to agree that it was the right thing to leave the original as was, and he decided he would make all the decisions on the replica.

My finger was measured with aplomb and fanfare. The jeweller reminded me of Dave, the art gallery owner. All pomp and ceremony for something that should be so simple. I rolled my eyes and Ronan chuckled. Eventually, we were shown a design for the replica. It was very similar but instead of two smaller diamonds each side, there was just one. I tried to get Ronan to discuss money but he was having none of that. I didn't want him to spend too much, considering he had already given me the family heirloom.

"I can afford it, and I want to buy it. So, give it a rest. Go shopping and I'll meet you in that coffee bar," he said, laughing.

"No, I'm worried," I replied.

"I don't think I've ever met a bride-to-be who tried to talk her fiancé out of spending too much," the jeweller said.

Ronan took hold of my shoulders, he turned me around,

and marched me to the entrance. I laughed as he pretended to kick my backside. "Go shopping," he said.

I'd told him I'd wanted to buy some new face cream and, bearing in mind my age and the menopause, I wanted a decent one. I'd noticed my skin getting dryer over the past few months. I was still laughing when I entered Harvey Nichols. The London store had been a second home and I thought I'd get a sense of nostalgia when I pushed through the doors. The opposite happened. The bright lights and smells of artificially perfumed air pumped around, designed to give a sense of opulence, irritated me. I made my way to the makeup hall and then straight to my favourite face cream stand. I quickly purchased the item I needed. There had been a time I'd have bought everything, been convinced by all the sales pitches. That was before Scotland. My skin hadn't been in better condition. Love, fresh air, lack of pollution, I had no idea what it was and if I could have bottled it and saved the near one hundred pounds, I would have. But I couldn't, and after doing some research, Elemis was the most recommended for what I wanted.

I took my cream and placed it into my bag. Thoughts of browsing clothes and shows evaporated. Instead, I headed to the underwear section and picked up some socks and sensible knickers. I also grabbed some skimpy lacy white ones and a garter—just in case I decided on a wedding dress.

I wanted something for Ronan but he was the most difficult

person I knew to buy for. His birthday had been awful and I'd ended up buying him silly and funny gifts, with only an engraved leather gun case as his main, and sensible present. I deliberated on a nice watch. He had one but he wasn't a *brand* man. He wouldn't wear jewellery because of his job, and most certainly not a ring. After his episode at the spa, I highly doubted he would be a necklace or bracelet wearer, either. I chuckled to myself as I walked around. I was killing time, really. I'd have to do some research to find a suitable wedding gift for him.

I was on my second coffee when Ronan entered the shop. He strode over to me and it made me smile when I saw a table of women gaze after him. I smiled as he leaned down to kiss my cheek before he took his chair.

"Those women were eyeing you up," I said, shuffling my chair so he had space for his long legs.

"Were they? Luckily, I'm owned by you," he said, laughing. "Now, go grab me a coffee and I can wallow in their desire for a minute or two."

I laughed as I left the table to go and order his drink. While I waited, I watched him. He checked his phone for most of the time I was away. His facial expressions told me of every email he went through. The snort was for junk mail. The quickly raised eyebrows and pursed lips were for something that had surprised him. The frown and frantic typing was probably work. He still had building projects on the go back in Kent and London. He had told me they were the last; he hadn't taken any new work on in months. There was still too much to do on the estate.

That reminded me of something. "How is the decorating in your cottage going?" I asked as I returned with his coffee.

"All done. Funnily enough, I just got an email about it. I just have to decide whether to sell or rent it out."

"I've been thinking about it." I hadn't but something had just come to me. "Why don't we sell the barn and keep the cottage?"

"Why would you want to do that? I thought you loved the barn?" he replied.

"I do but let's be practical here. The cottage is much easier than the barn to lock up for periods of time. We don't need the two properties, do we? It would be easier just to manage one."

"What about all your things?"

"What I want can come up. It's not like we don't have enough empty rooms that could do with some modern furniture."

"I don't know, Lizzie. That was a big deal for you, remember?"

"It was. So was moving here. So was accepting your proposal. I've moved on, *we've* moved on. I honestly think we have to make a decision on where to actually *live* now.

We're not getting any younger and I can't keep travelling back and forth for my doctors' appointments."

Ronan laughed. "You're assuming we even *have* a doctors, aren't you?"

"Well, yes, but even so. The cottage makes more sense."

Ronan had moved into the barn with me when our relationship had gotten serious. Something always niggled me, though. He had bought that cottage, despite being able to afford something ten times the size, because he wanted small and cosy. He wanted something that wasn't the vast and sprawling estate he had. The cottage was his respite. He'd been willing to give that up. I'd gone from a large London home to a flat. I'd craved the space the barn offered when I'd first moved in. I desired the outdoor space. I didn't need that anymore, but he still needed the cosy.

"Think of this as my wedding gift," I said, with a laugh.

"Whoa, hold up. I'm expecting a Bentley or something similar as my wedding gift."

"You'd like a Bentley?" I asked.

The skin around his eyes crinkled as he smiled. "No, of course not. Can you imagine a Bentley around those lanes? Can you imagine a Bentley on the same lanes as Maggie?"

There was no need to answer but I raised my empty coffee cup to him, anyway. He had downed his coffee and we were ready to leave.

We drove home and chatted more about the barn. It was decided we'd both travel back down, pack it up, and move what we wanted to the cottage. Ronan admitted the majority of his furniture had come from other property renovations, so we'd refurnish from mine. I'd miss Pam and Del, the pub, and other neighbours, obviously, but I hadn't been there long enough to form relationships that would be heartbreaking to leave behind. Ronan suggested we had a six-monthly reunion in Scotland for the neighbours we wanted to keep in contact with.

"While we're there you might want to meet up with..." he started.

"No, Ronan. It's been weeks now. I'm absolutely *not* making that first move and the longer it goes on, the harder it will be to reconcile." I knew he'd be talking about meeting up with Joe while we were in Kent.

I'd spoken to Danny a couple of times, but he wasn't completely aware of why we'd fallen out and it wasn't for me to tell him. He'd pushed Joe, so he said, to phone me but he believed he felt so embarrassed for *whatever he's done wrong*. I hoped he was correct, although I would've expected the length of our friendship should've been stronger.

I knew that Ronan was concerned for me, but he hadn't experienced my stubborn streak before. "Well, we can worry about that another time."

"Maybe Maggie and Charlie might want to come with us?" I offered.

"We can't really lock up the estate. Someone has to feed the animals and the students aren't back for another week," he said.

"We're getting busy, aren't we?" I said, with a level of excitement that he caught.

"We are, and most of it's down to you. I love it though. My mum would be over the moon to see what we've done. My gran would be turning in her grave." He laughed.

We arrived home still laughing and happy without realising that was all about to change.

———

Ronan and I were sitting in the library working when Maggie walked in.

"There's a phone call for you," she said. It was an unusual statement because she'd normally find out who was calling and announce them by name. "It's long distance," she added.

He looked up from his laptop and frowned at her. "Long distance?"

"It's not your father but an American man," she said, then shrugged her shoulders. She had kept the handset to her breast so the caller couldn't hear.

Ronan reached out and she handed it to him. "Ronan Carter-Windford," he said, introducing himself to the caller.

He listened for a moment and his frown deepened. He took a deep breath in, allowing it to seep out slowly before he spoke. "Right. Well, I'm sorry for your loss. I'm not really sure it's something I'd be interested in but…well, this has come as a surprise, to be honest."

I could only imagine what the call was about. I stood from my desk and walked to sit beside him on the sofa. He held my hand and squeezed it. Maggie held her hand over her mouth.

"Yes, I'll take all your details. I don't have a pen to hand. Why don't you email me and when I've had some time to process this, I'll call or email back?" Ronan then slowly gave his email address. "I appreciate the call, I think," he added.

He said goodbye and switched off the phone. For a moment he just sat looking at the handset. "My father died. Apparently, he had wanted to see me before he did. He'd asked for me and he'd written a letter that never got sent. I don't know why he couldn't just pick up the phone himself. Anyway, that was my half-brother who has just learned of my existence."

"Wow. I bet that was a shock," I said, gasping.

"I imagine so. I guess I ought to tell Rich. He'll be devastated, even though he hasn't bothered with Dad for years himself."

"What can I do?" I asked.

"I don't know, to be honest. I'm a little shocked by that call. What a way to discover I had siblings!" Bitterness laced his voice and I watched his jaw work from side to side with tension. Ronan had said, in the past, he wasn't interested in his father, but his death certainly seemed to have affected him. He had to be harbouring unresolved emotions.

"If you don't mind, I think I'd like to call Rich on my own?" Ronan said.

"Of course. I'll go and make some tea with Maggie," I said.

He squeezed my hand as I rose and went to walk away. "Thank you," he whispered.

"Blimey, that might cause some problems," Maggie said, as we headed to the kitchen.

"In what way?" I asked.

"Well, I wonder if Rich might want some kind of memorial for his dad?"

"Well, he can do that himself, can't he? That doesn't have to be here, does it?" I said.

"I have no idea. Such a shame that dick kept Ronan and Rich a secret," Maggie voice rose in anger and her lips pursed. All she needed was to add her hands to her hips and we'd have the complete picture.

"How long ago did he leave?"

She huffed air through her puffed cheeks. "Oh Lord. Years ago. He left a couple of times and came back. I think the first time was when the boys were very young. The last time, they were men and he and Ronan fought. I remember it. Ronan's last meeting with his father was when he punched him, sending him flying across the room. Verity screamed at Ronan even though Felix was beating on her." Maggie's eyes filled with tears.

The thought gave me a pain in my heart. I couldn't imagine having such a toxic relationship with my parents. I also thought his last memory—a physical fight with his father, if only to protect his mother—must be hard to accept. I wanted to hug him. I wanted to wrap my arms around him so tightly. I made his tea and headed back to the library. I'd just leave it for him.

When I arrived outside, I heard him shout, "You can do what you bloody well want, but don't for one minute think I'm going to fund or organise it. Go, fly out there and meet them. Me, I'm just going to raise a glass that the fucker is dead."

I didn't believe for one minute Ronan felt that way, but whatever Rich had said had annoyed him enough to that point. I gently pushed open the door.

"Anyway, let's end this with some good news. Lizzie and I are getting married soon. I'll let you know the details when we have them." There didn't appear to be any congratulations from Rich. "Yeah, goodbye to you, as well. Let me know what you decide." Ronan put the phone down and took the tea from my outstretched hand. "Just what I expected," he said.

"Which was?"

"Oh, he wants to have a bloody memorial for him, and he wanted it here!" His voice rose as he spat the words. His eyebrows were raised in utter surprise at the request, at the absurdity of it.

He didn't need me to verbally agree with him. It wasn't my place to, but I did anyway.

I sat beside him. "What did you say?"

"No, obviously. Sorry, I don't mean to snap." He sighed as he spoke. "I told him to do whatever he wants and to do it where he wants, but I wasn't going to be part of it. I think he's going to fly out there for the funeral. I don't agree with that, either. We weren't part of that family. We don't know how he treated that wife, what life those kids had growing up. It could've been magical and then we walk in. It could've been hell and then we walk in. Either way, they've just heard of us. Why the fuck would I want to attend a funeral of a man who didn't want to know me?"

It was a rhetorical question, of course. He fell silent and I just sat with him. Other than being with him, there was nothing I could offer. I rested my head on his shoulder.

"I don't know what to do for the best," he whispered.

"The best is whatever makes you happy, Ronan. Don't do anything for anyone else, least of all, Rich. Promise me that."

The last thing I wanted was for him to be guilt-tripped into doing what Rich wanted. Felix didn't deserve either of his sons, especially Ronan, but if Rich wanted to mourn him, I wasn't going to let him drag Ronan into something he didn't want to do.

Charlie and Maggie came and sat with us. "Yous do what's best for yous, lad, ken?" Charlie said and he placed his arm around Ronan shoulders. I wanted to sob when he kissed him on the temple.

Ronan simply nodded in reply. "His name is Jack Carter," he said, randomly. "He sounded pleasant enough, sad, obviously, and rather embarrassed that we hadn't known each other. I wanted to say that was his father's fault, but didn't think it the right time."

I noticed the *his father* and not *our*. Ronan rarely talked about his father and when he did, he didn't refer to him as such.

"Anyway, he's going to email something over. I'm not going to his funeral, and I guess I'll need to tell him why. Rich will go to see if there's any inheritance, I imagine," he added.

Maggie huffed. "Well, you have plenty of time to think things over. We'll all agree with whatever decision you make, and you're allowed to change your mind when this has sunk in, if you want to," she said, sensibly.

"Yeah, I think I might head to bed now," he replied.

"Okay, I'll clear up then join you," I offered. Ronan smiled at me and left.

"Well, that was a turn up for the books," Maggie said, as we carried the glasses back to the kitchen.

"I know. I wonder how Jack got our telephone number. Aren't we ex-directory?" I asked. Surely everyone was ex-directory nowadays?

"I have no idea, to be honest. We hardly use the landline. It's there for the *wify*." I smiled at her pronunciation of Wi-Fi.

"I guess we should check. The number will still be able to be found once we have our website up and running."

I wasn't sure why I was rattling on about a website and whether the phone number was private or not. I guessed, as I hadn't been in that situation before, I was struggling to know what to do.

I did as all good Brits do in a crisis; I made us a cup of tea and took one up to Ronan.

He was lying fully clothed on the bed; his hands were behind his head and his feet crossed at the ankles. I placed the mug of tea on the bedside table and sat next to him. I didn't say anything, I just wanted to be with him. He'd talk when he wanted to. Boy, did he want to.

"I don't know how I should feel?" he started. "I hate him, Lizzie, and that feels wrong because, no matter what he did to her, *she* didn't hate him. And then I dislike her for that, as well. I don't want to do that. So, it's a big old circle because that initial hate doubles. Does that make sense?"

"Yes, and I think it's perfectly natural. But you don't have to like a relative, just because that's what they are. I don't go for all that, *forgive because he's your dad* stuff. You forgive because you want to, *if* you want to."

"I don't think it's even about forgiveness. I don't feel anything. I don't care about him one way or another. Jack sounded really sad, I thought he might cry at one point. I can't summon up that level of emotion."

"Then don't, Ronan. Don't force something that isn't there, that would be unnatural."

He reached out to take my hand without looking, and I quickly shuffled my mug into the other.

"Rich's argument was that this was his home so this is where the memorial should be."

"It's not his home now. We don't get to go back to somewhere we lived in the past to hold a party, now, do we?"

He chuckled at that. "I should have told Rich, this was also the place he made our mother's life awful and where he stored all the whores that voluntarily wanted to live in his wife's house. That's the kind of man he wants to mourn. I don't get him. He hasn't been in contact with him for as many years as he hasn't been in contact with me. I think."

"Maybe he had. Maybe Rich had kept up dialogue with his father. And maybe Rich needs to know that his father had deemed neither of you important enough to tell his new family about." Even I heard the bitterness in my voice, and I wondered if I'd gone too far. I was never that nasty about anyone, but my man was hurting and that made me angry.

He turned on his side to look at me. "You've always got my back. No matter how many times I've fucked up, you're there for me."

"The past is the past and I choose to leave it there. Yes, I'll have your back even in times when I don't agree with you."

"Do you agree with me now?" he asked, and perhaps I shouldn't have said what I did.

"Absolutely. This isn't the place for Rich to come and go, and do what he pleases. This is *your* house, and it's *your* rules. It's not even about what your mum would've done anymore."

"You know, I was just thinking that. In her latter years, despite her depression, she didn't speak about him at all. I always knew she would take her life one day, and I think it was right that she did, isn't that terrible? She was in so much pain, mentally, and there was no curing that. She couldn't live anymore, and why should we have made her?"

The switch from his father to his mother surprised me. I didn't answer his question, I wasn't sure how to. I'd been low, been down, but I hadn't suffered with depression or had any mental health issues. I hadn't witnessed it, either, so I didn't feel qualified to answer him. He'd lived with it, and it clearly had affected him whether he'd admit to that or not.

I reached over and ran my hands down his cheek. "You need a haircut," I said, gently, as I brushed his fringe from his eye.

He smiled, but it was a sad one. "Probably," he answered.

I placed my mug on the nightstand and slid down the bed. I wrapped him in my arms and held him until I felt his breathing deepen and slow. We stayed that way until I fell asleep, too.

19

Ronan was sat at his desk in the library when I walked in with some crumpets for him. I placed them and a pot of jam on the side, next to the tea he had. He slid back slightly and patted his knee.

"Come and read this," he said.

He'd opened up an email from Jack Carter.

Ronan, thank you for taking my call and I'm sure I, and the news, was a huge shock for you. I can only apologise on behalf of Felix that we weren't aware of each other. Although, I don't expect you want that apology and I wouldn't blame you.

Felix died after a long drawn out battle with cancer. We first heard your name when he was moved to a hospice. We thought he was delirious, that he was confusing my broth-

er's name, Ronny. Mispronouncing it, perhaps. He then started to talk about a letter. My mom found the letter and handed it to me. She knew about Verity, she knew about you and your brother and right now, I'm so very angry with her but I have to support her decision to stay quiet, and her, at this time. I don't think your father divorced your mother, that's the impression I have. He was a bigamist and my mother was aware.

"Is that true?" I asked, pointing at the bigamist line.

"I don't now. I always thought they divorced, that's what my mum always said," Ronan answered.

I want to invite you and Richard to his funeral, but fully understand if you don't wish to attend. I'm not sure what I would do if I were in your situation. I'll add the details as an attachment. More importantly, Ronan, I wondered if we could meet. If we could find a way to build a relationship. I don't expect us to be brothers, of course, but...I don't know. It just feels like it would be the right thing, for me, to do. I'm sure you have as many stories about Felix as I do. I'm rambling, apologies for that.

I'd like to hear back from you, there are three of us, my brother, Ronny, and a younger sister, Serenity. I'll also understand if you'd prefer not to.

Kind regards, Jack.

Something came to my mind as I read the email for a second time. "It's very...British, don't you think?"

"I thought exactly that. He spoke with an American accent, although, the more I think about it, it was pretty much a mix of British and American. As if he's English but lived out there a while. I wonder if his mum was one of those down at the gatehouse. He might have shipped her back with him when he left."

"What are you going to do?" I asked.

"I'll reply that I don't wish to attend the funeral, however, my brother may but that will be for him to organise, and I'll tell him I'll pass the details to Rich. Then I'll have to have a think. Did you notice that he didn't call him Dad at all?"

"Yes, I wonder if perhaps his life wasn't nice, either."

Ronan shrugged his shoulders. "He said he has stories about him. You know, I'm curious to know what they are, but I don't know if that means I want to get to know the family. I certainly don't want to meet his mum," Ronan said.

I stood and moved behind him. "I don't blame you for that." I wrapped my arms around his neck and kissed the top of his head. "Pass those details onto Rich and then just take some time to think about it. We have a lot coming up that will keep your mind occupied."

We'd had notification that the artwork had been paid for and needed shipping to Bahrain. That would take some researching and I wondered if we ought just pay the auction house to do it. We had also been selected as the location for the murder mystery. The filming company wanted the house to make the pilot show and then, if it proved successful, a further six episodes in the first season. Reasons for selling the barn were piling up and I thought, perhaps, a trip back south to organise that might be just the tonic for Ronan.

Later that day I mentioned the trip to Kent and Ronan readily agreed. I think he was of the same mind as me, then. We just couldn't keep going back and forth and it made no sense to keep paying bills for two properties we weren't going to use much at all that year.

———

It was a few days later that we packed the car for the trip. Maggie insisted on not only packing a picnic for us, but for Max as well. Ronan had wanted to leave him behind but, as I informed him, the barn had been Max's first real home with me so he might want to say goodbye to it as well.

"He has precious bones buried in secret places in the garden. He might want to bring them," I said, patting the dog's head as he shoved it between the two front seats.

"Mmm, he'll get in the way, and if he runs off, that's down to you. Now, Maggie, stop piling all the food in the car, we need to get going."

She huffed and slammed the rear door shut. I blew her a kiss as we drove off down the drive.

"We need peacocks," I said, looking at the expanse of lawn in front of the house. I could imagine the brightly coloured birds wandering around in the summer.

"Shit all over the cars, they do," Ronan grumbled.

"So do regular birds, but we have them. And the cars are parked in the courtyard," I reminded him. I was pleased to hear him laugh, albeit not as raucous as he would normally.

"I heard from Rich earlier. He's been in contact with Jack and has decided to go. Jack offered to put him up but I think he'll book a hotel. I had a thought during the night; as much as I said Rich was probably on the hunt for any inheritance, I hope Jack doesn't think there's anything here for them."

"This was all your mother's though, wasn't it?"

"Yes, and never his. But I don't know if they think there might be something. I'm still thinking on this bigamist thing. I'm going to give John a call over the next day or so," he replied.

John was the family solicitor and one I'd met because of the filming contracts. He was an all round decent man, someone I'd taken to straight away. An old-fashioned solicitor who had a big old oak desk with green leather on the top. That desk had been in his family, as had the company, for years, so he'd told me as he'd stroked it.

I agreed with Ronan. "I think that's a great idea. From what

I know, the second marriage would be annulled but you just don't know what actually happened at the moment. John might have been involved in their divorce."

"That's what I need to find out. I can't find any paperwork pertaining to a divorce in her private papers."

Ronan had spent hours sitting in the one room we had kept Verity's things in, including the remaining paintings. He hadn't decided what to do with all her paperwork, and although I'd filed it into a nice wooden cabinet, he'd left the room in a state after his rummaging. I hadn't necessarily read what I was filing away but I had glanced over it, and I hadn't come across anything to do with a divorce either. The more I thought, something else came to mind.

"Were they really married?" I asked. I hadn't seen anything with the double-barrelled surname, either.

Ronan looked at me and frowned. He shrugged his shoulders. "I assumed so, but knowing my mother, it could have been a wedding in the garden with a local earther doing the ceremony." He really did laugh then. "I don't know, Lizzie. I think things are better just left. What's the point of knowing it all? I'll speak to John just to cover ourselves, but then I'm going to ignore that it ever happened."

I dozed part of the way until we stopped at a drive-through Costa and then parked up to let Max pee while we sipped our drinks for a break. It was dark when we pulled onto the driveway. I hadn't notified Pam that I was coming back; I didn't want to disturb her because I knew she was packing for her holidays. The house was in darkness and that day's junk mail was strewn over the stone floor. It was chilly when we entered.

"Did you leave the heating on low?" Ronan asked.

"I normally do. I can't feel any heat, can you?"

I slipped off my shoes and felt no warmth from the under floor heating through my socks.

"I'll check the boiler," Ronan offered. In the meantime, I emptied the rest of the picnic and food essentials Maggie had packed, grateful for the milk.

"I'll have to call someone out tomorrow," Ronan said when he returned. It appeared the boiler was out and wasn't about to restart. "I'll get the fire going."

"Why don't we just have an early night and watch TV in bed?" I asked. It seemed silly to light a fire and then have to let it burn itself out so quickly.

With that decision made, we climbed the stairs.

Ronan tossed and turned most of the night, disturbing me. I lay awake for hours listening to a roaring wind outside and worrying about Ronan. It had been a long drive for him and what with the worry sitting on his shoulders. I'd hoped he could have a restful night.

At some point early hours of the morning I got up. I crept

downstairs, shivering with the chill and headed for the kitchen. A cup of tea would warm me up, I decided. I was sitting at the table with just some cabinet under lights on when I heard Ronan moving around above me. I heard the loo flush and then it went quiet. I wondered if he even realised I wasn't there. I was sure he could sleep pee if needed. The floor was still cold and I grabbed a wrap to put around my shoulders. I'd acquired the same habit as Maggie but for different reasons. My dining room chairs were a little tatty and I'd taken to placing shawls and wraps over them, bringing colour to the room and covering the chairs at the same time. I headed to a drawer and pulled out a pad and pen. I sat and started to think about all the pieces of furniture in the barn and placed a tick beside the ones I'd like to keep. All I had to decide was whether it came to Scotland or the cottage.

Before I realised, light started to creep over the garden. Although too early for the sun to peep over the horizon, it wasn't far. I looked at my watch, it was approaching seven and I'd been up for three hours. Annoyingly, I yawned and my eyes felt itchy with tiredness. There was no point in returning to bed, Max was sitting by the back door, having woken when I did, but then had the advantage of dozing. I let him out for a pee.

I looked out over the slightly overgrown garden. I'd need to get it tidied up. I'd enjoyed living in the barn, it was perfect for me when I needed it and it would be perfect for someone else. I had no idea of its current value but didn't believe it to be too much more than what I'd paid. I hadn't owned it for that long. I could've rented it out but I didn't want the aggravation, considering I'd be too far away to deal with any problems. I could've left it with an agent but somewhere in my heart I knew it was time to make that move.

"Hey, you've been up a while," Ronan said, and I smiled as he kissed the side of my neck and then called Max. "It's bloody freezing in here."

"How about a cup of tea in bed?" I said.

"You go up and I'll do it."

I smiled and closed the back door. Ronan poured some dried food into Max's bowl and I left the wrap in the kitchen. I was snuggled in bed, on the cold side, obviously, when Ronan came in with two cups of tea.

"What had you up so early?" he asked, settling next to me.

"I don't know. I'm not sleeping well and that's the menopause, I believe. I got to thinking about the barn. I've made a list of what I think we should keep and what can go."

"How do you feel about that?" he asked.

"Fine. There are some pieces I'd like driven to Scotland and I think there are some nice things for the cottage."

"We can organise a removal company to come in. What else do you want to get done while we're here?"

"I think that's it, really."

"No trips to London?" he asked, gently.

"No, no trips to London. There's no need since I discovered the same shops in Edinburgh," I said, knowing full well what he meant.

"It's been a while now," he said.

"That's all on him, Ronan. He could've called. He needed to call and apologise and he hasn't."

"I spoke to Danny…"

"Not about me, I hope," I said. I turned to face him, unsure how I felt about that.

"It wasn't about you, initially. Danny knows about the Facebook page, he says that Joe is distraught, paralysed with embarrassment. He wanted to know if there was any possible way you would meet with him."

I frowned. "Danny?"

"Yes, Danny." Ronan offered a small smile to soften the conversation, I thought.

I folded my arms over my chest. "I'll meet with Danny, no problem. I'm not going out of my way to meet Joe. When he's ready to explain, he knows where I'll be."

It was the best I was going to offer. I was still hurt by his betrayal and further angered by his silence. I did, however, miss Danny.

"I'm sure he'll look forward to meeting up," Ronan said.

"We'll meet him for dinner."

"Are you annoyed with me?" he asked.

"Yes, I'd rather you not try to engineer a meeting. I'd hate that even more than I hate his silence. If I thought he was forced to meet me, I'd be devastated. Please, I know you mean well, but…"

"I don't like seeing you hurt. I don't care if you sort things with Joe or not. I know what I'd choose, but it's not me, or my decision. I just don't want that hurt to continue to dull your eyes, Lizzie."

I hadn't noticed the sadness that he said he saw. I hadn't noticed the additional wrinkles that aged me.

After my shower, I stood in front of the bathroom mirror with tears in my eyes. I wasn't sure what I was tearful about, but my menopause became a convenient excuse. I brushed them away. I missed Joe, bitterly, and sometimes I hated my stubborn streak. Maybe I should have contacted him, bawled him out, screamed and shouted at him, and then listened to his reasons before deciding on our future relationship. I splashed cold water on my face; I wasn't going there. I wasn't going to have a moment of doubt or remorse.

I pinched my cheeks to add some colour and brushed my hair. With a smile, I walked back into the bedroom and dressed. Ronan strode, naked, around the bedroom, making the bed and then dressing. As he pulled up his shorts, he caught me looking at him.

"Checking out the goods, are we?" he asked, his eyes twinkled with mischief.

"Of course, I'm allowed now," I said, waggling my ringless finger as if one adorned it.

He laughed. "You've always been allowed. Now, plans for today?"

"Call some estate agents. Call the removal company for quotes. Maybe start to pack up some things? I still have boxes in the shed from when I moved in."

"Okay, I'll make the calls while we're waiting for Derek to repair the boiler, and you pack the boxes with what you want for Scotland. Maybe get some coloured stickers for the furniture."

"Well, that's very organisational of you," I teased. I was a huge fan of Post-it notes, and colour-coded everything with them. Ronan often mocked me for it.

Once we were back downstairs, I found two coloured pads in a kitchen drawer. "How about yellow for Scotland, Pink for Kent?" He nodded as he opened a laptop and scoured for local estate agents.

I was utterly convinced Ronan wouldn't remember which colour was for which house so I also wrote on them. I walked around the barn sticking Post-its everywhere. I left them off items I thought probably needed to go to the charity shop. I was surprised to see I didn't actually have a great deal of furniture. Each bedroom had built in cupboards so it was three beds that would go to Scotland, two televisions, and three bedside cabinets. There were some lamps, mirrors, and my wooden Buddha plaques. There were plenty of unfurnished rooms at the castle.

Ronan called up that he'd got the boxes and some packing tape from the shed, and I headed downstairs to grab them. He was in the utility room chatting to a man who had the boiler in pieces but assured me it would be up and running in no time.

For the rest of the morning, we packed up the two spare bedrooms. There wasn't much outside of furniture to box up; we wrapped mirrors and pictures, but there was one cabinet that held my childhood items. We spent ages sitting on the floor going through old school reports, a love letter from someone I couldn't place, a few Valentine's cards, and I'd laughed because I knew they were from Joe. I remember crying one year that all my friends had received a card and I hadn't. From then on, he anonymously sent a card to my house every year; except, he was dyslexic and the only person to misspell my name so I knew they were from him. I'd never thank him for the cards; he wanted to keep the mystique that I didn't know who they were from. We'd discuss all the boys in our class to see if we could identify who.

I sighed, how wonderful of him to do that when he was having his own troubles back then. He was persecuted for being gay, yet he'd taken the time to make sure I had a Valentine's card each February for years.

"How can someone who does that, also do what he did?" I asked, not expecting an answer.

"You need to ask him," Ronan replied. I didn't answer.

We laughed at some of my notebooks. They were covered in scribbles and hearts. My initials were intertwined with whatever pop star was popular at the time. We made two piles. One was for the bin, and one to be packed up and stored, its contents, albeit worthless, too precious to let go.

I picked up the panda that had sat on my bed since I had been one year old. He wore a red bow tie but had lost the black bands around his eyes and his nose. He was grubby, but I loved him. I laughed at the childishness of that. Still, he would be wrapped gently and taken to Scotland.

We had packed up both spare bedrooms before my stomach started to grumble.

"How about lunch at the pub?" I offered.

Ronan stood and placed both hands on his lower back. "I'm all for that." He rubbed and stretched.

"Are you aching?" I asked.

"A little. All this retirement lark isn't actually good for the bones." He laughed as he spoke.

"What do you mean?"

"I haven't built, demolished, smashed, or painted anything for a year. I'm getting fat," he said, rubbing his stomach.

"I'd love to be as fat as you," I said, rolling my eyes at him.

"You're perfect to me," he said, holding out his hand to help me to my feet.

I hadn't realised just how dusty the floor was, I patted my jeans to clean my hands and then grabbed my purse, keys, and Max. "Come on, let's fatten you up a little," I said.

We walked to the pub and an unfamiliar face greeted us from behind the bar. She introduced herself as the new manager. I was taken aback at first.

"Lizzie, Ronan," came a voice behind us. We turned to see Jake, the pub owner, come in through the door holding the lead of a little black dog. He came straight over and hugged me, shook Ronan's hand. "It's good to see you, how long are you down for?" he asked, taking the stool next to us.

Max was super interested in the little dog and I had to put him on the lead. Max hadn't been 'done' as of then. Ronan hadn't wanted it just in case there was a chance of putting him to stud. He wasn't worth anything as a working dog because of his leg, but he might be worth a lot as a stud dog. The little black dog was quite happy to show him her backside.

"Not for long. I have some news," I said. "We're going to sell the barn and just use the cottage," I said.

"I thought it silly you keeping two properties going. How's Scotland?"

Ronan told him all about the activities at the estate and I ordered us some drinks.

"On the house, Shelly," Jake said, as she handed over the drinks.

"You don't need to do that," I said.

"I do, you're friends. Now, what do you think of Maisy here? I thought she'd be good company for me, and she gets me out walking. I had a little heart problem a while back—"

"He had a whopping heart attack because he eats too much, drinks too much, and doesn't exercise," a familiar voice said. I laughed, immediately recognising it as Pam.

I turned to hug her. "Why didn't you tell me?" I asked. We had a WhatsApp chat thingy that we communicated in.

"We didn't want to worry you. Anyway, he lived, so all is okay. We persuaded him to get a manager so he could take a step back and live a few more years."

Her dry humour had made us laugh at something that was quite a serious issue. We all sat and caught up and it was like we hadn't been apart. Pam asked me to hold fire on the estate agents, her sister was looking to move into the area and might love the barn. She told us she could afford it if we dropped the price to take into account there would be no agency fees. She gave me a wink, always bartering for a better deal, that one.

"Okay, have a chat with her and let us know. We're only here for a few days but you have keys, so show her around if she's interested," I said.

We ordered a round of sandwiches and Pam caught us up on the local gossip. The charity calendar we'd organised had all sold out and even though I wouldn't live in the village, I was more than happy to take part in the next. Ronan's cottage was technically one village over, but The Ship was his local as well.

We spent a pleasant couple of hours and, once we left, I felt a pang of sadness knowing I'd miss them.

"We'll be back down as frequently as we are now," Ronan said, picking up on my mood.

"I know, I'm being silly. Menopause," I said, defaulting to my go-to excuse.

He placed his arm around my shoulder and we walked back. We spent the afternoon packing up the second spare bedroom. I tried to remember how many boxes came into the barn, but was then reminded, I only brought half the contents of my old home and I hadn't really bought anything to add.

By the time we called out for Chinese to be delivered, we had a stack of boxes with coloured stickers and a pile for the charity shop.

"It would be handy if Pam's sister was interested, wouldn't it?" I asked.

Instead of sitting at the kitchen table, we'd opted to eat from our laps on the sofa. The fire was blazing and we were watching a nature programme on the television. Max was snoring on his bed and I swore I could smell his hair singeing considering how close he was. Twice, Ronan had slid his bed, with him on it, out of the way, and twice he had jumped off the bed and dragged it back in front of the log burner.

Ronan's phone vibrated in his pocket and he pulled it out to look. He sighed. "Rich wants to visit before he flies to America," he said.

"Okay." I was surprised. Despite being invited, Rich had never visited us in Kent. He'd never been back to Scotland all the time I'd been there, either. "Did he say when?"

"Now, it appears. He's about twenty minutes away."

My eyes grew wide. "Now?" I checked my watch; it was coming up to nine o'clock in the evening. At least his twenty minutes gave us time to finish our meal.

"I'm going to tell him it's too late," Ronan said.

"No, don't do that. You don't know what he wants to tell you. It could be really important. We have time to finish this," I said, waving my arm over our plates.

While we ate, Ronan mused over the surprise visit.

We had eaten and I'd stacked the dishwasher before we saw a sweep of headlights as a car drove onto the driveway. Both Ronan and I walked to the front door. I hadn't seen Rich since that first time I'd met Ronan and I was surprised. He had been very dapper, very groomed at that time. Walking towards us was a man who had not only aged tremendously, but also looked as if he'd been dragged through a hedge and then done ten rounds with the heavyweight champion of the world.

"What on earth...?" Ronan started. Rich held up his hand and limped into the hallway.

"I had an accident, nothing to worry about," he said. He looked over to me and smiled.

"Looks like someone helped with that accident," I said. "Do you want a coffee?" He nodded.

I thought if I took some time to make the coffee, Rich might open up to Ronan about who had very clearly done a number on him. Although cleaned, those grazes to his face were clearly fight marks. I even wondered if security would let him through at the airports. He looked, and smelled, like a homeless person. While I made coffee, I sent a quick text to Ronan.

Offer him a shower and some clean clothes. He can't travel like that.

I could hear Ronan speak the words as I poured hot water into a coffee jug. It seemed, however, that Rich had declined the offer. I walked through to the lounge with a tray. Rich stopped speaking as soon as I did. I placed the tray on the coffee table and started to pour.

"Do you think I can speak to my brother alone?" Rich asked and I stood, taken aback by his statement.

"You do realise, that not only is she about to become my wife, so deserves a little more respect than that from you, but that this is her house. You're in *her* house, sitting on *her* sofa, about to drink from *her* crockery?" Ronan's voice belied the tension he clearly felt and his jaw pulsed with anger.

I smiled at Ronan. "It's okay. I was about to head to bed anyway." I turned to Rich. "It was a pleasure to see you again," I said, not that I believed that, of course. I didn't like Rich, never had, and wasn't begging to be in his company.

Half an hour later, Ronan walked into the bedroom. I was under the covers reading a book when he did.

"What a prick," he said, taking the words from my mouth. "He's in trouble, obviously, owes some money for drugs. That's why he's fucking off to America, he needs to hide!" Ronan paced the bedroom.

"Surely he has the money to cover his drug tab, or whatever it's called?" I asked.

"I don't know. Maybe not. Perhaps he's spent the fucking lot doing dumb stuff. I told him I don't want any part of it. I'm not supporting him at all in this."

"Is he still grieving?" I asked.

Ronan snorted and then laughed. "Grieving? I doubt it. He didn't have contact with my mum for months before she died. He treated her worse than a dog sometimes, Lizzie. No, that's just Rich being Rich." The anger that laced his words was evidence of his distaste as he spat them out.

He sat on the edge of the bed and I kneeled up behind him. I placed my hands on his shoulders and massaged. He was so tense; his muscles were rigid with anger.

"Take a breath, let it out slowly," I said, remembering some of what we went through in our couple's spa day.

"I think it'll take more than a breath to get this out of my system. I asked him if those he owed money to knew he was off to America. He said he didn't think so, but if they came calling, could I say he was in Australia!"

"Jesus, what did you say?"

"I said I'd give them the exact fucking address of where he was going. If anyone turns up at our place, those bruises he has now will be nothing in comparison."

I wrapped my arms around his neck and rested my chin on his shoulder. "I hope that's just anger talking." I hated the thought of him fighting with anyone, let alone his brother, despite how much he might deserve it.

Ronan turned his head to catch a kiss. "Let me have a shower," he said, gently unwrapping my arms. He stood and held out for one of my hands. He kissed my knuckles. "I'm sorry he was so rude to you," he said, gently.

"Don't ever apologise on behalf of someone else, just because you know them. We don't do that crap," I said.

I watched him walk away, before he entered the en-suite he turned. "Oh, and he said that he believes he's entitled to half what we earned on the paintings since they should have formed part of Mum's estate!"

My eyes were wide. "He hated them, he hated the thought of them," I said, incredulous that Rich could even suggest such a thing. He had stated he wanted no part of them, I believed.

Ronan shrugged his shoulders and carried on into the shower room. I slid back under the covers and waited for him. He was dripping with water, carrying a towel, when he emerged back in the bedroom. He ran the towel roughly over his skin and then through his hair until it stood up on end.

"I can't believe it, Lizzie," he said, as he climbed under the duvet still slightly damp.

"Does he have a point?" I'd been thinking. He was paid his half of the estate but what did that break down to? Maybe Ronan needed to look at that.

"Our lawyers worked the figure out. I didn't just come up with a figure, so I'm guessing he was paid half of the property and land, and a sum to cover half the value of the contents I would imagine. I don't know, now. I'll have to have words with them tomorrow. If he wants some of the paintings, he can bloody well have them and organise a sale himself." Ronan was determined. His tone of voice didn't give any room for argument.

He placed his hands under his head and stared up at the ceiling. I turned on my side and rested one hand on his chest. Every now and again he'd take in a huge deep breath and let it out with a snort. His chest rose and fell.

"My mum was devastated by his dismissal of her. Whether he realises or not, that added to her depression. She reached out to him many times and he shoved her away, every time. I used to get angry because I'd be there to pull her through one of her *episodes* and it would all be about him. No thanks to me, just sadness about him."

Ronan shook his head as he spoke and I began to realise, his feelings towards his brother went a lot deeper than just annoyance at his inability to be a grown-up.

"I don't suppose, in that situation, your mum meant any harm to you. She can't have been thinking straight," I said, gently.

"I know that, but it always hurt at the time. He doesn't care about her art, it's just about the money. I don't know what he does with it, he can't be broke already, Lizzie."

I didn't know what amount Ronan had given his brother; I did know there was hundreds of thousands of pounds owed in inheritance tax before any part of the estate could be settled. I assumed that Rich's half would have also included half the debt.

While Ronan slept, I stayed awake seething on his behalf. It had been clear from the beginning that Ronan was the one who *did it all* and Rich just took. A few things Maggie had let slip over the year had confirmed that. I was glad he was off to America and for whatever reason it was, I hoped he extended his stay.

"Holy shit, Lizzie," Ronan said, covering his racing heart with his hand.

He had been asleep but something had come to me in the middle of the night and I'd spent most of the night sitting up, watching him. I must have dozed at some point but woken again before he had. I was staring at him and I guessed he could sense that. It had startled him.

"I had a thought," I said.

"Does it have to come out now?" He stretched and I spotted a rather outstanding tenting to the sheet.

"Well, I guess it can wait for half an hour, but I don't want to forget what it was," I said, reaching down to check out the tent.

———

It was later that day, while an estate agent was walking around the house to give us a valuation, that I remembered what had kept me awake.

"Oh shit, I just remembered something," I said, startling the estate agent. I bounced from foot to foot, wishing she could hurry up. "Sorry, please carry on," I said.

We were sitting at the kitchen table and the estate agent was going through all the reasons why we should choose her company. I just wanted to know a valuation. My sudden outburst seemed to spur her on and when she gave me the valuation, I stared open-mouthed at Ronan.

"Thank you. If you can leave your brochure with us, we have other agents coming, obviously, but we'll get back to you as soon as possible," I said, ushering her to the door rather rudely.

She did the *I'm sure I have clients just waiting for this property* as we walked to the front door.

"If you do, then you'd be willing to look at your fee, I imagine," I said, knowing a little about estate agents' tricks from Joe. "I mean, there would be less work for you, wouldn't there?" I asked.

She spluttered and no more was said. I closed the door long before she'd left the drive.

"What was that all about?" Ronan asked when I returned to the kitchen.

"Sorry, I forgot what had kept me awake, and then I remembered. Hold on..."

I grabbed a laptop and brought up Facebook. I'd have to

confess to not sticking to my promise to stay off social media, but I had been *keeping an eye* on Joe's page.

"Lizzie!" Ronan said, as I brought his page up.

"I know, but look." I pointed to a photograph posted yesterday. I'd seen it on my phone while we'd been packing one of the bedrooms.

There was a picture of Joe with Rich and a caption from Joe wishing Rich all the best on his upcoming trip to the States. I circled Rich's face. There wasn't a mark on it.

"Now, unless something happened to him between 6:00 and 9:00 p.m., are we actually sure what he said was true?"

It was possible he had been attacked in that time, of course, but what wasn't was the fact that he'd decided to run to America because of it. I didn't believe for one minute in that short space of time, he'd managed to pack, get a ticket, and then decide to visit us on the way to the airport.

"Something doesn't add up, Ronan. What exactly was he here for? All he did was complain about the paintings but he didn't need to visit to say that."

Ronan recounted the conversation as much as he could remember it. It seemed more of a casual catch-up but at the wrong time of the day.

"I need to speak to Joe," he said to me. I nodded. It would be the sensible thing to do, as Joe would likely know Rich's state of mind at that time.

"Call him now, I'll leave you to it," I said. Max needed a walk and I wanted to be out of the house when he spoke to him. I didn't want to be coerced into speaking.

Max and I took a walk to the village green. We sat on the bench outside the cricket pavilion. I'd certainly miss the laughs I'd had in that pavilion when we'd organised the first charity calendar. Male villagers posed naked for our Limp Dicks and Saggy Tits calendar to raise money for testicular and breast cancers. Of course, my mind went to Joe. I wondered what they were talking about. Whether Joe asked about me or not. Or even, if he'd answered the call. Perhaps he ignored it. I didn't imagine he would but there was always that possibility. Max and I circled the green, the pub was closed and I thought I should have called Jake to see if he wanted to join us on a walk. Then I remembered that Max was quite taken with his new dog. The last thing we needed was to be doggy grandparents.

After twenty minutes and with the chill getting to me, I decided to walk back, slowly. I wasn't sure how long Ronan's conversation would take, but I hoped it would be over. If I heard him on the phone when I walked in, I'd take myself off for a fake pee.

It was quiet when Max and I entered. I let the dog off his lead and he galloped, wonkily, ahead to the kitchen. I heard Ronan welcome him home as I slipped off my shoes.

"Hey," he called out.

"Just getting my coat off. It's cold out today," I said,

leaving it hanging over the bannister. "How did you get on?" I asked when I joined him at the table.

"You might be right. Joe said, among a lot of other things about you, but I'll tell you later, Rich showed no signs of being worried about anything, didn't mention there were any problems. He also said that he'd never known Rich to take drugs and was surprised by what I'd said. He'll do some asking around. They run in the same circles, if there was anything to find out he was sure he could." He stood to make a hot drink. I was itching to ask what else Joe had said, and I wondered if he was waiting for me to do so.

He sat with two mugs of coffee and looked at me. "He misses you, badly. He said he emailed you because he was just too embarrassed to call…" He held up his hand to stop my protest before I'd even started to offer one. "I called him out on that bullshit, of course. I told him you're forever on your emails for work so you would've seen it. He was sheepish and confessed that he just didn't know what to say. He believes he's lost your friendship and he's not only devastated by that, but he also just doesn't know what to do to recover it."

"What did you say?" I asked, saddened to hear that.

"I told him that an apology immediately and an explanation as to why, would have been good and he was a fucking coward for letting it get to this stage." He paused to sip his coffee and I wondered if he expected some backlash. "I told him how deeply hurt you were, how angry I was—still am —that he could do that to you and, although I understand the friendship should be strong enough to overcome this, I wouldn't blame you if it didn't. He wanted to know what I meant by that. I explained. His selfishness didn't take into account that the man he was joking with was the man who had broken your heart, had betrayed you with his lies for so many years, and the man who had wasted your chance of being a mother. That was the most significant thing, for me, that he'd cosied up with your ex. I'm as open-minded as they come, Lizzie, but not where deceit of the level you were subjected to is concerned. And most certainly not when one of the two men you should be able to count on also betrays you."

He sat back and folded his arms as if to say, *there, I'd said it.*

"What do you think I should do?" His last sentence had thrown me. I wasn't sure if my relationship with Joe was repairable but if it was, how did that leave Joe and Ronan?

"I can't answer that for you, Lizzie. Whatever you choose you have my full support, regardless of how I feel about Joe. I'd never make it awkward for you, you know that."

I nodded. I did know that and I smiled at him before I sighed. "How did you leave it with him?"

"He'll call me back about Rich in a couple of days. He asked if I'd speak with you and persuade you to call him. I said no, I wouldn't do that; it was for him to make the approach. I suspect he will, soon."

I nodded again. "Okay, I guess I'll just wait and see what

happens. In the meantime, is there anything you need to do about Rich?"

"I'm going to call the lawyers next and see what they say. Maybe make an appointment for when we're home. Why don't we head over to the cottage with some of those boxes?" Ronan said. I got the impression he didn't want me sitting around wondering and worrying about Joe.

20

We packed up the Range Rover with as many boxes and pieces of small furniture as we could, grabbed Max, and headed off.

The front of the cottage had been repainted a light cream and I was pleased to see the foliage that grew over the small porch roof was still there. It would be wonderful in spring to see it in flower. The window had been repaired, and I chuckled at the memory of the *burglar* on my last visit.

Inside, the cottage had been transformed. I walked from bare room to bare room. Each one had been repainted, floors had been re-sanded and varnished. Beams that were originally painted dark colours had also been sanded down and brickwork had been cleaned.

"Blimey, Ronan, it looks like a different cottage," I said, placing a box on the floor of the living room.

"I thought you'd be pleased." He smiled as he passed me to grab some bits from the car.

It didn't take long to bring in the boxes and some small pieces of furniture. Ronan had kept his bed, and I was glad as it was super comfortable. I was sad to see the sofa in the kitchen diner had gone, though. I thought that was lovely and told him so.

"It was here when I bought this cottage," he said, laughing. I enjoyed hearing him laugh again. "We'll buy a new one. I quite like the idea of furniture shopping together."

I hadn't thought about that. We hadn't done any of those *newly living together* things because we both had existing homes. Somehow, however, I didn't see Ronan as the furniture shopping type.

We spent the rest of day unpacking the boxes, Ronan hung pictures and mirrors and I cleaned up. As much as the builder had done a wonderful job of redecorating, he hadn't done such a wonderful job of cleaning up after himself. It was nice to be busy and to keep my mind occupied on scrubbing the toilet rather than worrying about speaking to Joe. I asked Ronan to measure for blinds and he told me he'd make some shutters, something I'd always wanted. I hugged him.

"There's something so sexy about a man who builds his love a home," I said.

"I'm not exactly building a home, just something to cover the windows." He laughed, hugging me back. "And I'm not doing them today. Now, let's go and order a sofa. I'm sure those places are open all hours."

We drove to a retail park and found a sofa company. Again, the bright strip lighting and music pumping around the store made me want to cringe. I would need to ask someone if the menopause affected shopping as well.

"This one's nice," I said, coming across a light brown brushed leather four seater. At that point, we were ambushed.

"This is a lovely sofa; people can't get enough of this one." Two, not one, but *two* salesmen were rushing towards us, bustling each other to get to us first.

"Then we won't want it if it's that popular," Ronan said, giving me a wink. He started to rattle the back and the arms. "Just checking how sturdy this is. It's gotta sustain a lot of action, if you know what I mean," he added, and then winked to the salesmen who stopped their advance rather abruptly.

I didn't fully understand what he'd said until he asked me to lie down on it.

"Huh?"

"Gotta see if we fit. You lay down on it, I'll lay on top, and then we'll know if it's suitable."

My jaw clicked open and I stared open-mouthed at him. Ronan just waved his hand between the sofa and me. I pretended to take off my shoes.

"We'll give you some time and be over there if you need us," one of the salesman said, and they both bustled off as quickly as they'd bustled in.

"You bastard," I said, putting my shoe back on and laughing.

"I can't stand being hassled the minute I walk into a store," he said. "Now, sit and let's see how comfortable this is."

We sat for five minutes and chatted about the sofa. Ronan moved to the matching chair and put his feet up on the footstool. He rested his head back.

"What do you think?" I asked.

"Honestly? I could have made this and I don't do furniture. It's cheap with a hefty price tag," he said, looking at the tags hanging from the arm.

"I know what you mean. What do you want to do?"

"Why don't we check out some smaller stores and see if we can't find something better made?"

I agreed wholeheartedly. As we walked past the salesman, Ronan shook his head. "Sorry, mate, but I don't think that one will do the job." He didn't receive a reply and we continued to laugh all the way to the car.

We collected Max and headed back to the barn. As we pulled onto the driveway we parked alongside a red mini.

"Did you know he was coming here?" I asked, angry that I might have been hoodwinked in some way.

"On your life, no, I didn't. He said he'd get back to me, that was all. I'll tell him it's not convenient right now," Ronan said, and he started to get out of the car.

Joe was looking at me through his car door window. The anguish on his face was blindingly obvious. His brow was furrowed way more than his botoxed skin should have allowed and his eyes held unshed tears. He bit on his lower lip, something he used to do when nervous.

"No, it's okay. Might as well get this over with."

I opened my car door and waited. Slowly, Joe wound down his window. "Can I come in?" he asked.

"Of course." I didn't smile, but I wasn't going to have a conversation with him in the front drive.

Max, ever the traitor, ran to him and bounced with happiness when Joe got out of the car. I called him away as I opened the front door. Ronan gave me a sly smirk. When I turned, Joe was standing outside holding a vase filled with lilies.

I sighed. "I'm allergic to them, Joe. I thought you might know that," I said, dryly.

"I know, that's why they are silk. You said once, years ago, that you were sad you were allergic because these always reminded you of your gran."

I blinked a couple of times. I remember saying that. I remember holding onto Joe's arm at my nan's funeral and wishing they'd chosen a different arrangement of flowers for her coffin. They had been her favourite flower and I'd rather remember them in her living room than on the oak casket that held her. It never stopped me from remembering her with such fondness, however, whenever I saw white lilies.

"Come in, you're letting all the heat out," I said, trying to keep a level of crossness going.

We stood in the hall, facing each other. Ronan had disappeared. Joe held his arms out, offering me the flowers and I stepped forward, took them, and smiled gently.

"Thank you, they're beautiful and I'd never believe they were fake," I said. I placed them on the floor since the unit that generally stood by the door had gone to Ronan's.

"Lizzie, there aren't enough words to tell you how sorry I am and I'm not going to insult you with crap excuses. The truth is, I'm heartbroken that I've upset you so much. I put money over our friendship and I'm fucking selfish. I know that. And I hate that about myself. Until now, I'd taken our friendship for granted. No matter how shitty I've been, you've always been there and this past couple of weeks has been just awful."

Ronan came out of the kitchen. "If you want to sit down,

there's coffee on the table," he said. I nodded and we moved to that room. I took Ronan's hand and encouraged him to come with me.

"That page started as a place just to share our photos. I don't know if you scrolled back, but they were of us both being goofy and doing silly things. People liked them, enjoyed seeing us together. I don't think I changed it deliberately, it just seemed that there weren't many of us together but I still kept posting ones of you. I didn't think, and that's about the worst thing I could've done to you. I didn't think."

I hadn't said a word until that point. In the silence that ensued, I poured us all coffee. "You didn't think, you're correct there. However, it wasn't the images that hurt the most," I started.

"I know. And that's where the money over you came in. I started to pick up a lot of work from..." Joe was reluctant to mention his name so I did it for him.

"Harry. You started to pick up a lot of work from Harry. What kind of work?"

"He had colleagues and clients who wanted to invest their money in property instead of stocks and shares, and he put them my way. I got caught up in that. My greed overtook me, as Danny says, and he's right, of course. When he'd comment, I liked or laughed because I felt I had to. One thing this time has taught me is how weak I've become. I don't like myself, and I'm not trying to turn this into a *woe-is-me* type thing at all."

"I was about to say that," I replied. I had initially meant the comment as a joke because Joe was the king of *woe-is-me*. "This isn't about you and your shortcomings, it's about what you did to me."

Ronan squeezed my hand and although I didn't look at him, I was grateful for his support.

"I've deleted the whole page and I've told Harry I won't be working with him," he said.

"I appreciate you removing the page but you didn't need to cut ties with...*him*," I answered.

"Yes, I did. He betrayed your faith in him, and then I did the same. I haven't come here for your forgiveness," he said, taking a deep breath in. "I don't think I deserve that, I wanted to apologise and I wanted to explain, even if that wasn't exactly what you wanted to hear. I miss you so much, yet I fully appreciate the enormity of what I've done and I don't expect anything from you in return," he said.

I wondered if he'd rehearsed that. He sounded sincere but it wasn't Joe. Not the Joe I knew...or thought I knew.

"I don't know what more to say," he said, he picked up his mug and raised it to his lips. I watched a tear track down his cheek.

"Ronan and I got engaged, so you bloody well better get your act together for my wedding," I said.

It wasn't what I'd planned to say. The whole time Joe was speaking I had a reply building up in my mind. I had cusses and snarks all lined up for him. But then I remembered, Joe had suffered when growing up; he had been persecuted as a teenager and still saw homophobia on a regular basis. Those weren't excuses for forgiving him, of course, and I wasn't sure I had. But they were considerations in how long I took to get over what he'd done. More importantly, I didn't want to be a vengeful person, someone who held a grudge because, ultimately, it was only me affected by that.

Joe's eyes widened and his smile was slow to form, but form it did. He reached over to take my hand. "I'm sorry, Lizzie," he said, softly. I nodded. "I'm going to leave now, but I'm calling you tomorrow and you can tell me all about this engagement!" The level of excitement in his voice made me laugh.

"It's quite a funny story really," I said.

"I hope it was romantic," he said.

"Not initially," Ronan replied. Joe smiled at him. "Joe, one more thing. If you ever hurt Lizzie the way you did, I'll make sure you feel that by putting you on your arse, okay?"

Both Joe and I turned to face him. He raised his eyebrows as if in challenge and was waiting for a reply.

Joe's face paled and he slowly nodded. "Absolutely okay," Joe replied, he then held out his hand to shake Ronan's. "Oh, I almost forgot. Rich isn't into drugs other than a little coke at parties. No one knows of a drug dealer after his money that I've spoken to, and according to Zack, the bloke who runs the bar, the accounts are very healthy, Rich would have ransacked those if he was desperate."

Ronan nodded his thanks and we walked Joe to the front door. He stopped and turned to face me. I didn't move, but he came and hugged me. I hugged him back.

"Thank you," he whispered.

"For what?"

"For letting me come here with my pathetic reasons for being, again, a shitty friend," he said. I smiled at him.

"Drive carefully," I said.

Ronan and I watched Joe reverse from the drive and then panic because someone beeped at him. He waved as he roared off and I closed the door.

"What did you think of that?" Ronan asked.

"I thought Rich might be pulling a fast one," I replied.

"Not that. What did you think of Joe's apology?"

I took a deep breath and let it out slowly. "I think he was honest. It was pathetic in one way, and although I don't *forgive* him, I guess I've just parked it all to one side."

"Don't do that because you think you won't have people at our wedding," Ronan cautioned, and I remembered that had been something I'd been fearful of.

"It's not that. I've known him most of my life. I'm way more grown-up than he is sometimes, I guess it's time to just move on."

"I'm surprised, considering how strongly you felt," he replied.

"I still feel strongly about what he did. I'm still annoyed and embarrassed. I don't know, when he sat there, it just didn't seem to matter as much anymore. I think we have such amazing things coming up, he didn't seem as important. I don't think our friendship will get back to where it was for a while, though."

"Well, I'm proud of you. I half-expected a brawl," he said and then laughed.

"So what's the plan now?" I asked.

"You need to get that valuation over to Pam. We have another estate agent coming in the morning, and we need to look at removal companies."

"Can we talk about Rich now?" I asked.

Ronan rolled his eyes. "Do we have to?"

I laughed. "Not if you don't want to."

"I've got a meeting with the lawyers next week, but I think he's a fucking knob and I'll happily tell him that when I see him next. Which, hopefully, won't be for a while. I'm only going to contact him through the lawyers from now on. Even if he's right. Even if there are druggies on his tail, we don't want any part of that. He made his bed, he lies in it."

By the end of that week we had cleared out the barn, met Pam's sister—who was over the moon with it but not sure she could raise the funds—had furniture winging its way to Scotland thanks to a cancellation, according to the company, and we settled in two lovely arm chairs in the cottage that I'd spotted in a charity shop.

"I wished there had been a little sofa to match these chairs," I said, running my hand over the arms.

The chairs were patchwork and multi-coloured. Ronan hated them, I loved them. He had grumbled as he'd made two trips to bring them back home but once we sat in front of a roaring fire, we were hooked on them. They were so comfortable.

"What about all your work tools and things," I said. I was looking out the back window and to the large shed-come-workshop at the bottom of the garden.

"I'm going to take them all back. We could do with some of the things back home."

"How are we going to get them there? We should have asked the removal company to take them."

"I have a van, Lizzie. I'll pack that up and you can drive the car," he said.

Beside the house, on the drive, was a large grey van. It hadn't been there before and Ronan had told me that he'd let one of his contractors use it. It seemed that all his projects were complete and now he was going to sell the business on. He had maintenance contracts for a couple of stately homes that one of the lads would take over, he'd said.

"What about the other cottage?" I asked, reminding him of the one I had looked at that he'd bought to do up.

"Selling that. It was always a turnaround property. It's half-done, someone just needs to come in and put in their kitchen, decorate, and furnish."

"We really are making that move, aren't we?" I said, reaching out for his hand.

"We are, as long as you're still sure about it."

I was. I was excited to sell the barn and hopefully to Pam's sister. I'd liked her and it would be nice for the two of them to live near each other. It was lovely to combine our things in the cottage. It wasn't a case of his or her house anymore. Although Ronan had bought it, obviously, I was surrounded by familiar things making it feel even more homely.

———

The second estate agent came in at around a similar price and I actually liked that one. He was a young lad and really enthusiastic about the house. He could've been telling me a load of lies, of course, but he reminisced about his grand-parents' barn and how he'd loved being there.

"You're a salesman's dream," Ronan said, as he closed the door behind the agent.

"I liked him, didn't you?" I asked.

"He's an *estate agent*, I don't know him enough to form an opinion," he said, laughing.

"Well, if Pam's sister doesn't want it, I think we should list with him."

"Whatever you want is fine by me."

It felt strange to walk around a near empty property. It had been furnished when I'd viewed it and only empty until the removal men unloaded a ton of boxes. The beams weren't hidden by furniture and I stood in the hallway and just looked up to the vaulted ceiling.

"There's bird crap up there," I said, pointing to a splodge.

"Oh yeah, it will stay up there as well," Ronan said, not taking me seriously at all.

"How did it get there?"

"Well, I imagine, see that beam?" He stood behind me and pointed, I nodded. "A bird sat on that and shit."

I tutted. "That wasn't what I meant," I said.

"I know. How the fuck would I know how it got in here? Probably through an open window or door. Or down the flue one day. There's not much we can do about it now, I'm not climbing up there to clean it off and I doubt anyone will notice."

I bet Pam would have. She was a stickler for detail and noticed even the tiniest of things. She was also a germo-phobe. She'd want a couple of thousand off the asking price, I imagined with a giggle.

We left the barn to pack Ronan's tools and ready ourselves to travel back to Scotland. I was sad when I locked the door, although I knew that Pam would still check on the property each day until it was sold. I was also excited about the next stage in our lives.

Packing Ronan's workshop was way harder than the barn.

"For fuck's sake, Ronan, it's just a screwdriver. Put it in any old box and we can sort them when we get back," I said, frustrated.

Ronan's tool were in a very specific order but I'd found a rogue screwdriver, a little one that tested for electricity, so I was told. Therefore, that little screwdriver needed to be placed in the box marked *electrical* and just so happened to be at the bottom of the pile at the back of the van. I wasn't about to unload the van just to pop that screwdriver away, so I shoved it in my pocket instead.

"There, all gone," I said, waving my hands in the air.

"You sit wrong and that will stab right though your hooha." He smirked as he spoke.

"Then you won't be going there for a while, will you? Now, can we please just go and get something to eat?"

Ronan and I worked wonderfully together back at the estate; but we fought every ten minutes in that bloody workshop. It was all over his precious tools. I was holding them wrong, by the wrong end, upside down, or not being gentle enough. Twice, I'd told him to clear the room his bloody self. He had wanted to leave some basic tools because, obviously, we were still keeping the cottage and he needed to make my shutters, fix things, but he had more power tools than the large chain DIY stores. I held up the fifth drill.

"You know what they say about men and their power tools?" I said.

Ronan sighed as if he'd heard the line a million times. "No, Lizzie, what do *they* say about men and their power tools?"

"They're a substitute for…" I waved the drill towards his crotch.

Ronan caught the drill as it began to slip from my hand. "How about I show you that substitute, huh?"

He grabbed my hand and dragged me from the workroom. I laughed all the way back to the house, and then up the stairs. Before I could do anything, Ronan had picked me up and thrown me over his shoulder. I grabbed on to the waistband of his jeans and he walked me to the bed where he let me fall. I bounced, still laughing. As he rushed to get his jeans off, I did the same. I only managed to clear one leg before he was tugging on my knickers.

"Oy, these are expensive," I said, trying to grab them back from him.

"I'll buy you another pair," he said, growling at the fact they wouldn't tear.

"Not like the fucking movies, is it?" he said, and dragged them down my legs. I managed to get the one leg out before he showed me just how wonderful a substitute he had.

There were many things I loved about Ronan, but the best was his ability to laugh while we had sex. He could be loving and romantic. He could be forceful and demanding. He could also be so playful that we laughed as well as climaxed.

"Should we get back to packing your tools?" I asked, as we lay on a very messy bed.

"Didn't I just do that?" he asked, then smirked at me.

"You're always so very sure of yourself, aren't you? I wish I was more like you," I said, rolling to my side to face him.

"Are you kidding me? You're way more empathic than me, way kinder. I'd take those qualities rather than a large ego any day of the week." He reached over to run his fingers down the side of my face. "Although, you are older, so maybe I'll grow into those things."

I thumped him on the chest, rather hard, and he winced and laughed at the same time.

"Watch it with the age thing, buster," I said, then sat to clean up and dress.

"Does that bother you?" he asked.

"No. It did in the beginning but you're mature for your age, I'm not so much, so we meet in the middle," I laughed.

We were back down in the tool shed, loading the last of the boxes, and the sun started to dip.

We decided on a night out. It was nice to get dressed up, to wear heels that immediately made my feet protest, to put on a full face of makeup, and style my hair. We were taking his neighbour, Mrs. Sharpe, with us. She had missed us, although she had a couple of Ronan's lads' details as contacts should she need anything in an emergency. She'd never eaten in a seafood restaurant, so she told us, so that's where we headed. There was a nice one in Sevenoaks that I hadn't been to before but Ronan recommended.

I let Mrs. Sharpe sit up front and she chatted all the way. She was thinking of adopting an elderly cat for company, and Ronan promised to take her to the rescue centre the following day. He also said he'd make sure she had enough logs split and kindling made to see her over the next month or so. Watching Ronan wield an axe had been a highlight of mine back in Scotland, I was looking forward to seeing it again. I was yet to convince him to do it in his kilt with work boots and no top, but I hoped to wear him down enough…or wait for the summer months when he'd be more up for the idea.

"Lizzie?" I heard.

Not even the blast of cold air and Ronan opening the rear door for me had brought me out of my thoughts. "Sorry, I was thinking of you in a kilt again." I smiled sweetly as I climbed from the car.

Mrs. Sharpe took my arm. "This is so kind of you both," she said, as I steered her to the restaurant door. Like Ronan, I was concerned. She was becoming frailer and more reliant on someone helping her each time we saw her.

Ronan detailed the menu for her. Much of which she had eaten on her many world travels, to our surprise. We chose our meals before Ronan announced our engagement to her. She was thrilled for us, wanting to purchase a bottle of *something nice* to celebrate. Of course, Ronan wasn't having any of it. We had wine and we toasted with that.

"If we send someone to pick you up, you'd come to the wedding, wouldn't you?" I asked. I hadn't discussed guests with Ronan other than to say I wanted it to be a small function, but she was important to him.

"Oh dear, if I can still walk, I'll be there," she said. Something in the look on her face, in the tears that welled in her eyes suggested otherwise. She didn't look at Ronan but nodded very subtly. I took her hand and squeezed it. She wouldn't make our wedding; I'd understood her silent message.

"Tell me all about your plans, though," she said.

While we dined, I regaled her with stories of a wonderful wedding. I detailed my dress to her, down the every last bead and button. Ronan constantly frowned at me, until Mrs. Sharpe needed the ladies'.

"I don't think she'll be coming, Ronan. I'm giving her our wedding now," I said. He didn't reply but he blinked a few times and swallowed hard. A sure sign he was upset with the news.

He nodded. "Let me tell you about the reception," he said. He took over the wedding, telling her all about the party on the lawn with the peacocks, her favourite bird, and the cake. She placed her knife and fork down and leaned back. She closed her eyes and smiled. She nodded occasionally as she pictured the story she was being told. Whether she knew we were winging it or not, I had no idea, but when she dabbed her eyes with her napkin and announced it would be the best wedding ever, I was pleased we'd done that.

———

We had been back in Scotland a week when the news came in that Mrs. Sharpe had died in her sleep. We were invited to the funeral, of course, but Ronan had decided he'd rather remember that meal in Sevenoaks as our last meeting, and not one at a crematorium. It seemed that Mrs. Sharpe had left a will and Ronan was mentioned. He hadn't expected that at all. She had relatives, not that any visited her, of course, and he wasn't aware of a will. Thankfully, she'd lodged that with a solicitor and it was he who had contacted Ronan. It was arranged that information would be shared with the family solicitor and Ronan would find out what she'd left him.

It turned out to be her cottage.

So started a round of arguments, of bitter emails and letters from Mrs. Sharpe's family accusing Ronan of manipulating her. Her will was legally binding and, in the beginning, Ronan was happy to have the house transferred back to them. That was until he'd found out they'd ransacked it for whatever possessions they could with absolutely no care or thought of its previous occupant. They'd trashed one room, turning out drawers as if looking for something. Ronan had contacted the police but it was hard to prove for sure who had undertaken to do something so awful. He decided to sell the house and to give the money to charity instead. Ronan had to travel back to Kent to clean up, remove what possessions were still there, and secure the property. I had offered to accompany him, but he hadn't wanted me there in case anyone returned. I also wondered, since he was so sad by her passing, if it was something he wanted to do by himself.

"You know what? We'll have peacocks when we get married," Ronan said. He'd phoned me from Mrs. Sharpe's house to tell me he missed me and he was returning the following day.

"Okay, what brought that on?" I asked.

"She has loads. Not live ones, of course, but pictures and ornaments. I'm boxing them all for the charity shop at the moment, but there's one I want to keep."

He took a photo to send me. Mrs. Sharpe had a small silver peacock that was so intricately carved. It looked like, many years ago it had colour, I could see some in creases in the metal and wondered on its age. Maybe we could have it restored, I'd mentioned.

"Drive carefully, won't you?" I said.

"I will. I'll call when I'm leaving in the morning."

"Is he okay?" Maggie said. She and I were in the kitchen baking pies for the bakery.

"He's sad, obviously, but I think so."

"When are you going to book this wedding?" she asked.

"Not yet. I think we have too much going on. Let's get the properties sold and then deal with Rich before we think about that."

We hadn't heard from either Rich or the newly discovered half-brother, Jack. Ronan wasn't bothered; I was by the silence. A conversation with the lawyer confirmed that Rich wasn't entitled to any more money or any of the paintings. The contract he'd signed was for half the estate and the estate comprised of all assets, including the paintings. We doubted Rich would be happy about that but a letter was prepared and sent to his home. We had no idea when he'd get it.

"It's been a funny few months, hasn't it?" Maggie said. We had moved from the kitchen and were walking Colleen from her stable to her paddock. Gerald bounced around free running, as Ronan called it, with his pipe lagging on his horns to protect us and the piglet trotted, or rather, stumbled on rickety legs, behind us. They made a fine group of friends.

"You could say that," I said, and then laughed.

"I'm glad you made up with Joe, though."

"So am I, although we're not talking as much as we used to. I think it will take us some time to get back to how we were, if we ever do."

"It would be nice, dear, if you could. I thought I might cook Italian tonight," she replied, somewhat randomly.

"Okay, what did you have in mind?"

"Spaghetti bolognaise," she said, and I had to stop and cross my legs at her attempt at an Italian accent.

"Don't, I'm going to pee," I said, as she started saying garlic bread and olives also in Italian.

Colleen took that moment to fuck off. She pulled away, the lead rope ran through my gloved hands and off she trotted. Luckily, to her paddock where she leapt the fence like a

Grand Prix horse at The Horse of the Year Show in Olympia. Gerald just headbutted the gate until it opened.

"Do you think he has some kind of brain injury and that's why he behaves that way?" Maggie asked.

I locked up the paddock with a padlock, knowing it might keep the pig and Gerald in, but Colleen would take herself off for a wander and we'd get a call from someone to say she was in their garden. She was like Max. I could whistle and she'd come back so it was quite nice for her to have her freedom. Ronan disagreed, of course. It seemed the locals didn't necessarily appreciate her shitting in their gardens, eating their plants, or attempting to break into their houses. She had become partial to sitting on one of the dog beds in the boot room.

"No, Mags, he's just an arsehole," I said, scratching the skin between his horns as he tried to ram my hand onto the fence post. Then he keeled over and played dead as if I'd done something terrible to him.

Maggie and I laughed; we weren't fooled by him anymore. We linked arms and started the walk back to the house.

"What about some chickens?" I said. "Be nice to have our own hens and fresh eggs."

"They stink, but yes, maybe a couple of little ladies. No cocks, though, there's been way too many on this estate over the years for my liking."

I'm sure our laughter could be heard for miles. I know we scared some birds that had been sitting on a bare branch.

We rounded the corner and the house came into view. I smiled as I always did. The Saltire was flying and just under it, a St George's flag in honour of me, so Ronan had told me.

"I'm going to get married right here, Mags," I said. Forget Gretna and it's wonderful blacksmith, nothing would top getting married on the terrace or the front lawn of the magnificent house that stood in front of me.

"We need to get rid of the scaffolding," she said. We stood still and looked up.

"We do."

She turned to smile at me. "It will be the best thing this house has seen. It's been years of misery and doom. Because of you, there's life in this old place, and a wedding…well, that will just top the lot," she said. She grabbed my hand and we walked into the kitchen.

The following morning, I ran down the stairs and opened the front door. Ronan had told me he was returning the following day but he must have driven through the night. He looked dishevelled but gorgeous. I flung myself into his arms.

"Whoa, what's this for?" he said, stumbling as he caught me.

"I've missed you. And, we're getting married here, on that

lawn, we're having peacocks and chickens but not cocks, Maggie doesn't want more cock, and I…"

"Lizzie! Breathe!" Ronan said, and I laughed.

"I missed you, that's all," I said.

"Good. Now, yes to marriage here, no to chickens. And I mean *no* to chickens, they stink."

I smiled at him and he rolled his eyes. I was sure that, in a few days, I'd see a lovely chicken coop waiting to find a home somewhere near the paddock.

"I can't refuse you anything, can I?" he whispered.

"I love you, Ronan. Way more than I did yesterday."

"Way more, huh?"

"Yes, way more."

"Want to show me how much *way more* is?"

There was a twinkle in his eyes, the skin around them crinkled with mischief. He smiled that lopsided grin, and his fringe flopped over his forehead. He picked me up and I wrapped my arms around his neck, my legs around his waist.

Still laughing, he carried me up to the bedroom and deposited me on the bed. He slowly stripped naked and I admired every single inch of his body.

"Soon, that will be all mine," I joked, as he stalked towards me.

"I'm all yours now, Lizzie. Nothing could change that, ever." He held my head in his hands. "I love you way more today than I did yesterday," he said, repeating my words. I wanted to cry at the depth of feeling I had for him. "Oh, I have something."

He slid from the bed and kneeled. He pulled a blue box from his pocket and he opened it.

"For the third, and last time, Lizzie Richie, will you marry me?"

He placed the replica ring on my finger as tears rolled down my cheeks. "For the third and last time, yes," I replied.

The End

You can catch up with more from Ronan and Lizzie later in the year with Posh Frocks & Peacocks. Here is a handy link:

mybook.to/PoshFrocksPeacocks

ACKNOWLEDGMENTS

Thank you to Francessca Wingfield from Francessca Wingfield PR & Design for yet another wonderful cover.

I'd also like to give a huge thank you to my editors, Lisa Hobman and Karen Hrdlicka, and proofreader, Joanne Thompson.

A big hug goes to the ladies in my team. These ladies give up their time to support and promote my books. Alison 'Awesome' Parkins, Karen Atkinson-Lingham, Ann Batty, Elaine Turner, Kerry-Ann Bell, Lou Dixon, and Louise White – otherwise known as the Twisted Angels.

My amazing PA, Alison Parkins keeps me on the straight and narrow, she's the boss! So amazing, I call her Awesome Alison. You can contact her on AlisonParkinsPA@gmail.com

To all the wonderful bloggers that have been involved in promoting my books and joining tours, thank you and I appreciate your support. There are too many to name individually – you know who you are.

ABOUT THE AUTHOR

About the Author

Tracie Podger currently lives in Kent, UK with her husband and a rather obnoxious cat called George. She's a Padi Scuba Diving Instructor with a passion for writing. Tracie has been fortunate to have dived some of the wonderful oceans of the world where she can indulge in another hobby, underwater photography. She likes getting up close and personal with sharks.

Tracie likes to write in different genres. Her Fallen Angel series and its accompanying books are mafia romance and full of suspense. A Virtual Affair, Letters to Lincoln and Jackson are angsty, contemporary romance, and Gabriel, A Deadly Sin and Harlot are thriller/suspense. The Facilitator books are erotic romance. Just for a change, Tracie also decided to write a couple of romcoms and a paranormal suspense! All can be found at:

author.to/TraciePodger

facebook.com/TraciePodgerAuthor
instagram.com/traciepodger